LIES COME TRUE

THE AVERY HART TRILOGY
BOOK ONE

EMERALD
O'BRIEN

For my grandparents.

Betty and Jim, you've always been there for me, and through my writing journey, your support has been paramount. Your kind words, encouragement, and love have contributed to every part of my life. Your love for each other is unlike any I've ever seen. I've learned so much from both of you about life and how I want to live it. I couldn't be more thankful to have you both in mine.

Grandmother and Granddad, I am blessed to have had you in my life for as long as I did. You taught me about the importance of family, and you were so proud to be the head of ours. You were both pillars of strength and warmth. You always believed in me and I like to think you're watching all of us now. You are truly missed by all your loved ones, and we think of you often.

Chapter 1

THE WHISTLING WOKE HER UP. It was a quick, unfamiliar tune that sounded joyful.

Pain shot through her leg, and forced her to roll over on her side. The path felt cold beneath arm and leg.

"Help." She whimpered out into the park.

Blood poured from where the bullet had ripped through the side of her calve. She cupped her hand over her wound and felt the warm blood coat her fingers. When she applied pressure, her hand jumped off of the wound, and she yelped in pain.

She wiped her hand on her shorts and strained her neck to look back down the path, toward the whistling.

She took a deep breath and yelled. "Help, I'm over here."

Trees surrounded her, and as the sunset cast their shadows across the path, she could make out a dark figure.

She scrambled to stand, and her leg burned as she eased pressure onto it. When she turned back, the whistling stopped, and the figure ran toward her.

Everything in her told her to run.

Her foot hit the ground for the first time, held all her weight for a moment, and in that moment, the pain was worse than anything she had ever felt.

She saw the dark figure from the corner of her eye, still shrouded by the shadows as it approached, and something swayed behind it.

She turned back up the trail, and pushed herself to go forward. The next few strides hurt less than the first. She picked up her pace, and squinted into the last of the sunlight, as her heart pounded in her chest.

She took deep breaths as she pushed herself harder, confident that she was gaining ground, and when she reached a clearing by the lake, she looked back.

It was a man, or what looked like one, but his face was white. And red.

He lunged past the place she laid bleeding only seconds before with a rifle over his shoulder.

She turned before anything else registered, back toward the street she parked on just behind the bushes at the end of the path. She heard the footsteps behind her slap against the path, and when she looked back she saw the figure clearly.

He wore a mask and wild strands of dirty hair flew behind it in the wind. The eye holes were dark, but the face looked wrinkled, pale, and bloody.

She forced herself forward, closer to the road behind the bush. She watched a car drive by, and if she wasn't mistaken, it slowed before disappearing behind the tree line.

Someone pulled into the parking lot. Someone's coming to help me.

Her leg felt numb underneath her, and she focused on reaching the car.

A repetitive animalistic grunt was added to the sound of the feet pounding the pavement behind her and the sound of a car door slammed in the parking lot.

The rhythm her legs kept fell out of sync, and each stride was more painful than the last. She looked over her shoulder as she started to limp, and in that time, she saw enough to make her scream.

She jerked away and tripped over her tangled feet.

She heard barking as her body hit the ground, and howls mixed with her screams, which eventually drowned out everything else.

Fiona fought to keep her eyes open, but they closed as the last of the sun dipped below the horizon.

Chapter 2

AVERY CRACKED INTO HER fortune cookie over the table as the credits of her favourite TV show started to roll. A muffled cry from the baby next door rang through the wall behind her and she turned the volume up to drown out the wails. She pulled the tiny piece of paper from the cookie bits, and the news came on as she unfolded her fortune.

"...at Birch Falls Park on Glenn, and Fourth Street, in Birch Falls, Ontario, less than three hours north of Toronto..." The reporter droned on, but Avery focused on reading the paper.

You will soon gain something you have always wanted.

Avery read it twice, set it down beside the broken cookie, and folded up the small box of left over veggie noodles.

"Peace and quiet?" She grumbled as she gathered the boxes, and took them to the kitchen fridge. "I doubt the Donovans are moving anytime soon."

As she made her way back to the living room, the baby cried again, as if to taunt her. She'd thought about tapping on the wall, writing them a letter, and even paying the Donovans a visit, but the simple fact was, babies cried.

At all hours.

She tried to sympathize with the parents, but when it came time for her early morning classes, she cursed them.

She grabbed the napkins from the table, and threw them in the garbage, before she settled in on her soft couch again. When she looked at the TV, she did a double take.

Her mouth hung agape as she focused on the picture beside the reporter.

"This man is considered armed and dangerous. Please contact the Crown River Regional Police with any information you may..." The segment was ending, and the picture disappeared from the screen, as a phone number crawled along the bottom.

That has to be wrong.

She stared at the screen, stunned, as they began to broadcast a different story.

She thought about calling the news station, but they wouldn't have any more information, and she had already seen the sketch. That was the part that mattered.

For a moment she thought about calling the number on the business card in her purse.

The only one she carried.

Instead, she sat still on the couch, and twisted her blonde hair around her finger.

What if she was wrong? What if she only imagined the picture was familiar? That's what Inspector Jacoby would tell her. She wondered why she hadn't torn up that business card after he gave it to her. She thought about calling her parents, but they'd say the same thing as Jacoby. Sadie might listen, might even believe her.

The feeling that glued her to the couch turned into something she recognized.

She couldn't be sure what she saw. That's what they told her after all and that's what finally stuck after years of therapy.

Avery took a deep breath, turned off the TV, and tossed the remote across the couch. She went to the sliding glass door and took in the view of the town's landscape from above. Lights twinkled down the main roads, trees on hilltops blew in the breeze, and the sky was a deep blue. She tugged on the door handle, and pressed the lock up tight against the resistance she felt. After pulling the curtains closed, she hurried to the front door of the apartment, and ran her fingers over each lock. One, three, four, and five.

Everything in its place.

Once she was ready for bed, she pulled on the latch of her bedroom window, and when she was satisfied with its resistance, she hopped into bed.

Even in her shorts and tank top, the room felt hot, and she kicked her blanket off. Her mind raced and she couldn't get her mind off the police sketch.

If it was real, she thought, she had to tell someone. She thought about all the calls the police would receive, and how silly hers would sound among them. Even if she was sure of what she saw, who would believe her?

She snuggled her face against the cool pillow, and closed her eyes as she worked to clear her thoughts.

It's just your imagination Avery. It was a long time ago. Let it go.

She fought to push the image away, and when the goose bumps covered her arms and legs, she covered her body with the blanket again. After several deep breaths, she drifted off.

It was chasing her, but this time, Avery knew she was dreaming. The tall figure was reaching out for her, and her screams echoed through the woods. Avery tried to look ahead, but her dream-self slowed down, looking back.

She saw the figure coming for her; it's pale, motionless face coming closer and closer.

Turn around, she yelled at herself, but dream Avery was repeating the events of that day.

The figure was only a few paces behind, reaching its arms out for her. The face was white and wrinkly, and she locked eyes with the black holes, just as she seemed to lose her footing.

That's what she thought she did. She thought she tripped, and the thing was going to grab her, but instead, she was falling.

The day of the attack, she realized she ran off the ledge only moments before she hit the water, but in her dream, she knew where she was the whole time.

Avery woke up just before she sunk into the Crown River, and gasped for breath.

It was a dream she had many times in the past, but the face of her attacker had never been so vivid.

She threw the covers off of her body, and realized she had been sweating when the cool air hit her skin. She scrambled out of bed, down the hall, towards the front door where she kept her purse on the table. She grabbed her wallet and yanked out the card.

There was no mistaking the face in her dream with the sketched face on the TV.

To her, it was the same one.

The reporter called it a mask, the same thing everyone had told her when she woke up in the hospital ten years prior.

She knew it had to be true, but in her memory, her attacker was a monster.

She grabbed her cell phone and began to punch in the numbers from the card. If she could help to lock this guy up, to finally catch him, this would be worth it. To stop this monster from hurting anyone else, so that no one had to feel what she felt that day, and what lingered in the darkest corners of her mind ever since.

Regardless of what Jacoby told her, she had to make the call.

Then it would be his problem, but as the phone rang, she knew that was just something she said to make herself feel better.

It was her problem, and it always would be.

Chapter 3

INSPECTOR JACOBY'S NUMBER DIRECTED her to the voice mail of Inspector Noah Cotter. Not expecting the change, Avery hung up. She decided to wait until morning, and although she hadn't slept much, she was thankful she had some time to compose herself.

She could remember the nightmare, although the scenes had begun to fade from her mind, her memory of the night before was clear. The police sketch was of the same mask her attacker had worn. If it was just a coincidence, or the masks were mass produced, she'd feel better knowing she tried.

The truth was that she hoped it *was* him.

She called Jacoby's number at nine that morning, and this time, she got an answer.

"Inspector Noah Cotter here. How can I help you?"

"Hello. I'm sorry. I was hoping to be put in touch with Inspector Jacoby, but his number redirects me to yours."

Avery opened her curtains and beams of sunlight filled the living room.

"Ah, yes, Inspector Jacoby retired not long ago. May I ask what the call is regarding?" His voice was gruff and smoky.

"I... he was an Inspector on my case ten years ago. It's probably silly that I expected him to have the same number. I'll just call the hotline. Thank you Inspector..."

"Cotter."

There was silence on the line for a moment and she wasn't sure she could do it at all. When she thought of the girls she saw taking short cuts through the woods at school, she sat down on the couch, and spat the words out.

"I might have some information regarding a police sketch I saw on the news last night."

"Well, I can direct your call to the appropriate person, but since I've been assigned all of Inspector Jacoby's old cases, may I ask what this has to do with you?"

"The mask. I was attacked by someone wearing the same mask I saw on the news last night."

"Ms...?"

"Hart. Avery Hart."

"Would you have time to come in today and make a statement? I could take it directly to the Inspector on the case."

"Sure," Avery hesitated, "I can come right now."

When Avery arrived at the department, she checked in at the front desk, and was shown to Inspector Cotter's office. It was small, with no windows, and smelt like something sweet. The desk had no picture frames, but Avery noticed a painting on the wall. Seagulls flying over the open water. A pair of glasses sat by the computer, near a mug of coffee that had a picture of golf clubs on the side.

She waited for a few minutes, until she heard the familiar voice behind her.

"Ms. Hart? I'm Inspector Cotter." He strode in beside her and stopped at the side of his desk.

When she looked up, she saw a young man, with short brown hair. He was well dressed, and his honey brown eyes smiled down at her. He looked younger than his voice suggested, but she loved the way her name sounded when he spoke.

"Nice to meet you. Thank you for seeing me." Avery stood, and tilted her head back slightly to maintain eye contact.

She shook his hand and when he smiled at her, she sat back down again. A hint of cologne was left behind as he took a seat behind his desk and the scent made her feel nostalgic for something she couldn't put her finger on.

"No problem." He opened his desk drawer, grabbed a pen, and she looked down at a brown paper bag on the desk.

"Sorry, it's a bit of a mess in here." He grabbed the bag and threw it into the garbage. "Probably shouldn't be having cinnamon buns for breakfast anyway."

He smiled at her, and she gave him a tight lipped smile back. He leaned his broad shoulders forward.

"Okay," He pulled his laptop closer, and slipped his glasses on. "Start wherever you think necessary."

Avery stared at him. She was expecting to be drilled with questions, as she was on the day of her attack, but she hadn't been prepared to be in control of her story.

"Well, I don't know if you've had time to read my case." She fiddled with the rings on her fingers. "I'm sorry, I haven't."

"Well, it happened a little over ten years ago. I was fourteen, and had just started high school. I was on my way home, and I'd never walked home from school before. We'd just moved here, and I hadn't paid attention when my mom drove me there in the morning. I thought I was taking a short cut by going through a forest on the other side of my subdivision. I should have realized it wasn't a shortcut because I was the only one going through there, or so I thought."

"Here in Crown River?"

Avery nodded, and he typed something.

"Crown River runs right through the forest. It was September, so it got dark a little earlier. I went to go back the way I came, and that's when I saw it."

14

Inspector Cotter looked up from his screen at her. "The mask?"

"Someone in a mask, yes. They were running towards me. I turned around and ran the other way. I got a good look at the face, and it looked a lot like the one on TV last night." She stopped for a moment as he typed. "What happened? What did he do?"

He shrugged. "I can't tell you any more than what was on the news."

"I didn't hear the news really. I just saw the sketch."

He brushed his fingers through his hair and pushed his chair back from the desk.

"A young woman was attacked on a trail in Birch Falls Park."

"What happened?"

"Well, she was shot, and then the person who shot her came after her, but a man who had just arrived to walk his dogs interrupted him. The man never got a good look, but the victim was able to give details as to what the perp looked like."

"Is she okay?"

He cleared his throat. "She's stable."

Avery looked around the room and fought back her tears. "Do you think it could be the same person, Inspector Cotter?"

He pulled his chair back up to the desk. "Why don't you tell me the rest?"

"Where was I? I... I was running, and he kept coming. I didn't look where I was going, and I fell off a ledge, into the Crown River."

He stared at her with a straight face, and when she wiped the tears from her eyes, he looked back down at the screen.

"I'm sorry that happened to you."

Avery shook her head and looked at the ceiling. "I was knocked unconscious, and I broke my arm, but other than that I was lucky. The current was light, and the place I fell was deep enough. A man who was fishing saw me fall. Pulled me out and got me help. Joshua Hopkins."

He made another note, and looked back to Avery. "All of this has been recorded?"

"Too many times to count." Avery fidgeted with her rings again. "They never found out who it was. Josh didn't see anything, except me falling."

"Do you remember how far away from the attacker you were when you saw them at the clearest?"

"No further than ten feet." She remembered the number, having told Inspector Jacoby repeatedly. "I know it couldn't have been further than that."

As he typed, she studied the picture with the seagulls. The water below them looked calm, and she tried to concentrate on that feeling.

"And the mask was exactly how you remember it?"

Avery hesitated and folded her hands on the desk. "I think so. The picture was only on the screen for a bit, but...I think so."

He looked down at her hands and smiled. "Okay, I've got all they'll need for now. If they require anything further from you, they will have your contact information. Do I have the best number to reach you at?"

"The one we spoke on, yes, I only have a cell phone."

"A work number?"

She gave him the number for the school, and he repeated it back to her as he typed.

"Okay." He pushed his chair back. "Thank you for your statement Ms. Hart."

"That's it?" Avery grabbed her purse, and felt her shoulders drop.

"I'll pull your file from Jacoby's records to include with this interview. That's all they'll need."

"Okay." They both stood, and he led her to the door. "Inspector Cotter, could you let me know, one way or the other?"

He stopped before they reached the door and looked back at her.

"I don't..."

"It's just, if what I've given doesn't help in any way, I'd rather know. I've waited ten years, wondering where the person who attacked me was."

He looked past her to the door, and pressed his lips together. She knew he was thinking, and he looked even more studious with his glasses.

"Sure."

Avery smiled and held out her hand.

"Thank you Inspector Cotter." He slipped his hand into hers; she shook it once, and left his office.

She felt lighter as she walked down the hall toward the exit and smiled at an officer who passed her by. She could still smell Inspector Cotter's cologne when she breathed in, and she tried to figure out where she knew it from, and why it drew her to him.

Chapter 4

NOAH WATCHED AVERY HART walk down the hall, and couldn't help but take in the view from behind. Her hips swayed as she strode off and hypnotized him for a moment. He shook his head at himself before he slipped back into his office, and closed the door behind him.

When he sat down at his desk, he picked up the phone and dialed Jacoby's cell.

"Cotter! Calling from the office huh? Got an issue? Grab a tissue," Jacoby rattled off the old line he used many times before when Cotter had started in his position and had a question about an ongoing investigation. Cotter heard a few hearty chuckles in the background. "I'm on the course. This had better be important."

"Shouldn't have your cell on in the first place old man." Noah smiled as he spoke. "You losing it already?"

He could tell Jacoby was smiling as he barked at him.

"I'm surprised you remember the rules. You haven't been out in a while."

"Yeah, well, we'll set up a date soon, but this isn't a personal call. A young woman named Avery Hart called this morning asking for you."

"Hart? Oh wow," He could hear the smile fade from his face. "What did *she* want?"

Noah raised his brows. "You've heard about the girl who escaped her attacker in Birch Falls Park last week? The one who provided us the sketch of the mask."

"Sure."

"Well, Ms. Hart believes..."

"Listen here, that girl doesn't even know what she believes. She thought a monster attacked her. A monster, Cotter. I get kids and their overactive imaginations, but for this girl, it was more than that. She was wacko. Don't know if she was like that before the incident, but after, they damn near committed her."

"Who did?"

"Alright, I'm exaggerating, but she was in therapy, probably still is, all over some prank."

"It was all a prank?"

"Sure, probably. Listen, coulda been anyone. Point is, chasing someone isn't a crime Cotter. All the injuries she sustained, she did that to herself. Ran right off a damn cliff."

"Well, she thinks the mask is the same one this killer uses. She saw it on the news, and ..."

"Listen Cotter, this is a waste of your time, and definitely a waste of mine. I gotta get back to the game."

"Alright, thanks Bart. Good luck. If your swing's anything like the last time we were out, you'll need it."

Jacoby chuckled. "Later kid."

That should have settled it, but Noah wasn't convinced. The difference between their stories was too great. Still, as soon as he made a copy of the files, he could hand it over to Ethan, and let him make the call.

He grabbed his mug, and when he got to the archival room with a new cup of coffee, he found the case file. He skimmed over each page as he began to make copies.

His mind drifted to Avery, and how bothered she seemed by it all, even after so many years. Jacoby brushed it off as a prank on a kid with an overactive imagination, but Avery Hart wasn't a kid any more. Far from it, he smiled, as he remembered their visit. She was a young woman who knew what she wanted. He wouldn't have agreed to contact her with an update if it wasn't the only way he would see her again.

Her big bright eyes looked so innocent and lit up the room at the same time.

When she cried, she seemed so vulnerable, and he wished he knew the right thing to say to her in the moment.

He shook it off and focused on the last page of her file, and noticed a name he recognized.

Officer Owen Minicozzi.

Chapter 5

AVERY GOT HOME FROM work just as it started to rain, and she flipped the light on to check the clock in her kitchen as she stepped in the door. It was later than she thought; the natural light cast a gray tone through her apartment, and her stomach growled.

She slipped her portfolio case in the closet and stared at it.

She used her own photos as examples to show her class what she wanted for their black and white assignment. Although she had gotten an A on each of them when she took the class, she always wondered if her students judged her photos, or if they judged her in general. She was younger than half her class and she hoped they wouldn't resent someone they might view as less experienced teaching them.

She wondered if her students around her age felt the same way when they spoke to her as she did with Inspector Cotter.

Intimidated.

She closed the closet door, and ran her fingers over the locks on the front door before she sauntered to the kitchen.

One, three, four, and five.

She wondered if Inspector Cotter meant it when he said he'd be in touch. He seemed to listen to her story, but it wasn't her first rodeo, and she knew if she told him everything, she'd sound crazy.

That's what they all thought she was, including her own parents, until she started telling the story the way they told it to her. Some kid was playing a prank on her. Chasing her. Just fooling around. She should have watched where she was going, but she got carried away with her imagination, and got herself hurt. Almost killed.

It was her fault.

Once she admitted all that, her parents stopped taking her to therapy, and once she graduated high school, they stopped worrying so much about her. After she moved out of their house, into her apartment, she even went months without hearing from them at all.

She said those lies they all fed her so many times, she'd started to believe them, except for the nights when she would let her mind wander.

Avery changed out of her dress clothes and into jeans and her favourite blue tank top. She hurried back to the kitchen and grabbed a pan from under the cupboard. She set it on the stove as her stomach growled, took cheese out of the fridge, and as she began to grate it, the baby next-door started to cry. She tried to ignore it, but the cries turned into wails, and she stormed into the living room and turned on the music channel.

She returned to the stove, and before she laid out the tortillas, she grabbed her cell phone from the counter and checked again.

No calls.

The loud music made her heart beat faster, and she went back into the living room, and turned the TV off altogether. The moment she did, she heard a tap on the glass door of the balcony. She turned her head toward the noise and listened.

The curtains were open, but it was too dark to see anything--even the rain she heard patter on the glass. She felt exposed, and turned off the lights in the living room. She looked out onto the empty balcony, and finally took a breath.

The baby stopped crying, and she turned on the balcony lights.

Nothing.

A thump came from the wall by the front door and she turned away from the balcony toward it.

She stood still and waited for another noise.

Maybe someone bumped into the wall.

She checked on the balcony once more and returned to the kitchen. Just as she got the quesadillas onto the frying pan, a knock on the door made her jump. She stepped softly over to the door to look out the peep hole.

Nothing.

If someone was playing a trick, they didn't realize this was the worst night to try it. Just as Avery turned from the door, there was another knock, louder than the last. She turned back to the peep hole and saw Josh looking at his feet.

She unlocked four of the six locks and opened the door.

"Hey Avery, how's it goin'?" Josh had a dark lab puppy in his arms and a big smile on his face. "Look who came to dinner."

"How long were you in the hall for?"

"Huh?" He slid by her, and kicked off his hiking boots. "We just got here."

"You didn't knock on the wall?"

He laughed, "No, why? Is everything okay?"

"If you're trying to trick me, this is not the..."

"What's burning?" Josh sniffed the air and made a face.

Avery ran for the stove.

"They're ruined." She called, as she flipped the quesadilla, burnt side up.

"Let me order pizza."

"I had take-out last night. Chinese."

"You have to eat something, and it shouldn't be this." Josh poked at the quesadilla.

Avery huffed, and pushed him to the side to get a better view of the puppy.

"And who is this?"

"This is Louie. We've been calling him Lou though." He smiled and held the puppy out to her. "I wanted to surprise you with our newest addition."

"Sorry Josh, but another sweetheart at the shelter doesn't exactly brighten my day." She took Louie in her arms and kissed the top of his head.

"The surprise is that he already has a foster home." Josh shrugged off his brown jacket and hung it over a stool on the other side of the counter.

"Oh." Avery held Louie up and cooed at him. "How old is he?"

Josh rubbed at his scruffy beard. "Little over three months old."

"What a sweetheart. Was he the runt?"

"Not sure. Someone dropped him off anonymously."

"How can people do that?" She looked into Louie's eyes, "who could give a cute thing like this up? Cold, that's what it is. People are cold."

"Bad day?" Josh asked, and walked over to the couch.

She nodded, and when he patted the cushion beside him, she took a seat and cradled Louie in her arms.

"I don't know how to tell you this." She mumbled and he turned to face her. She saw his mood shift by the look on his face. "It's not about the shelter."

"Okay." He leaned back. "Spit it out."

"Did you see the news last night?"

"No."

"Okay, well, I saw something that I think might be related to what happened to me in the forest that day."

Josh stared at her. "In the news?"

"Yeah, a girl from Birch Falls was attacked by some guy wearing a mask. They showed the sketch on TV, and it looked exactly like the person who chased me."

"Avery, are you sure?"

"Well, they said if you might have information to call it in, so I did."

"You called the police about it?"

"Yeah, well, I didn't right away, but the more I thought about it..."

"What did they say?"

"They're looking into it. Listen, I don't have high expectations on this, I'm just happy they heard me out."

"That's good. You seem to be mellowing out."

"I think it's this little guy, calming me down." Avery pet Louie's head as he yawned. "He's *so* soft."

"You alright?"

Avery nodded. "Let's just order pizza. I'll call okay?

"As long as you let me pay."

"Josh, you gotta stop doing that. I know you're a good guy, and you like to take care of me, but it's me that owes you."

"Stop." Josh took Louie from her lap, and set him on his chest. "You don't owe me anything."

Avery thought about the first time she saw him, running toward her along the edge of the Crown River, Jack barking behind him. If he hadn't pulled her from the water, she didn't know what would have happened, and she didn't often let herself wonder about it either.

"You want a drink?"

"Sure. Got any beer?"

"When do I ever have beer?" She grinned.

"Thought you might pick some up some time, you know, cause you know I love it."

Avery rolled her eyes. "Cola?"

"Sure," Josh scratched behind Louie's ears. "Listen, if you keep thinking about it, you'll make yourself sick. It's probably just a coincidence."

As she went to grab their drinks, she knew he was probably right, and she felt disappointed.

"Want to watch a movie or just TV?"

"Whatever."

"Is Asher coming over too? How are you guys doing?"

"Good." He grinned and his cheeks flushed, "It's going well. He's staying home with Jack. I came straight from the shelter. Veronica wondered if you could come in this weekend for an extra shift."

"Yeah, sure. Too bad I won't get to see Louie though."

Josh cocked his head to the side.

"You know what I mean. You know I hope I'll never see him again."

Josh looked at the tiny puppy on his chest. "Me too."

Chapter 6

"INSPECTOR ASCOTT?" Noah knocked on his open door.

"Ethan." He nodded. "You're Cotter, right?"

He stood and met Noah halfway. They shook hands and Noah looked down at the man.

"I had a young woman come in today with something pertaining to your case. At least she thinks it might."

"Huh, why did she come to you?"

"She didn't mean to. It was one of Jacoby's old cases. She was trying to reach him."

"Did you want to sit down?"

Noah looked at the chair and back to Ethan. "No, that's fine, I don't want to waste your time."

"Oh, I'll be here all night. Bastard's gunna do it again. I know he will."

"Mind if I ask you something?" Ethan shook his head. "How did you link the first murder in Crown River with the attack at Birch Falls Park?

"Tamara Sweeten, our first vic, had been shot and carved up like a God damned turkey. Surprised we even found the entryway for the bullet. It matched with the one that hit Fiona's leg. Found it on the path where she was shot. Fiona--that's our girl who got away. We're not one hundred percent, but we're working with it. It's all we've got to link them so far."

"I heard the bullet went right through Fiona?"

"It did. You've got me curious here Noah. What've you got for me?" He stared down at the folder in Noah's hand and rested his hands on his hips.

"She thinks she recognized the mask from the sketch on the news last night."

"Oh," Ethan frowned and reached out for the file.

Noah watched him flip through the pages. "I don't mean to bother you though. Everything you'd need is in there."

"You're not bothering me." He didn't look up from the file, but the frown left his face.

"I wouldn't have brought it to you if I didn't think it was worth looking into."

Ethan looked up at Noah, shut the file, and tossed it on his desk. His expression was hard to read, but he wasn't sure he took the file any more seriously than Jacoby.

"Appreciate it." He went back behind his desk and sat down.

"Alright," Noah began to back away, "Take care."

"Thanks."

Before he left, he turned to see Ethan looking at his computer screen, already checked out of their conversation.

The file on the table was all wrong. The victim was found drowned in the Crown River by a jogger the same morning he died. Another Inspector had begun the case, but in his absence, it was given to Noah.

As he flipped through the case notes, he knew he should have been grateful for his first fresh case, but he eyed his brief case on the floor beside him.

The drowning case came in just before he was about to head home and right after he handed Ethan Avery Hart's statement, along with the copies he made of her case file.

In his new file, the victim, Grant Hornby, was a high school teacher, and had been reported missing hours before he was found. When Noah received the case, he couldn't help but think of Avery, and her fall into the Crown River. A fisherman had watched her fall and rescued her. The victim from his new case hadn't been so lucky.

After a few hours of sleep, Noah knew he should focus on his new case, but he glanced at his brief case once more before he pushed his new case files aside, and grabbed it.

He hadn't intended on making two copies originally, but when he saw Owen Minicozzi's name in her file, he knew there was one more thing he had to do before he could let the case go in good faith, so he gave one copy to Ethan, and kept the other.

Owen was the officer who accompanied Jacoby when he questioned Avery ten years ago. He was also a friend of Noah's.

Noah pulled out the police sketch from Avery's file, and compared it with the police sketch of Fiona Wolfe's description of the masked man.

There were undeniable similarities.

Both masks had a wrinkly white base, and the circles around the eye holes were dark. The differences were also clear. Avery's sketch did not have blood marks smeared across the mask as Fiona had described just days ago. The only way Noah could think to describe it was in Fiona's sketch, the man was wearing the mask. In Avery Hart's, the mask and the figure was one in the same.

He grabbed his cell phone and hit the fifth number on speed dial.

"Noah, what's up man? Everything okay?"

"Hey Owen, I know it's late."

"Actually, it's early. Almost four AM."

"Shit, I'm sorry." Noah looked at his watch, "Did I wake Missy?"

"Naw, she's used to it. What's up?"

"I know this is going to sound out of left field, but a girl from one of Jacoby's old cases called in the other day. She said she wanted to speak to him about the mask from the case you're on now, and how it might be related to a case of hers you were on ten years ago."

"You've got my attention."

"Avery Hart. Ring a bell?"

"You're taking me back, man."

"She was attacked by someone wearing a mask. Fell over a ledge into Crown River."

"Yeah, I remember."

"She thinks the mask is the same one that was used to attack her."

There was silence for a moment.

"Really?"

"Yeah, so I took a statement from her, and I passed it on to Ethan, but I saw your name on the file. I wanted to just run something by you."

"Shoot."

"Now that I've told you what I'm calling about, and I know it was a long time ago, could there be something to this theory?"

"You're asking if I think there are similarities."

"Just what are your thoughts in general?"

"Well, I remember she was traumatized. What kid wouldn't be? I don't remember all the details of what she described, but I remember the mask. I hadn't linked it to our perp though. I'd have to see the sketches."

"I called Jacoby, and he told me the girl is crazy, told me not to waste my time."

"But here you are calling me at four in the morning, asking me general questions."

"I'm sorry; I just thought you might..."

"I'd have to see the sketches, and I'd have to see the girl again. It's been ten years Noah, did you really expect me to remember..."

"You're right. I'm sorry I'm wasting your time now." Noah rubbed the back of his neck. "It was a bad idea."

"I'll see her."

"You will?"

"Yeah. Listen, I'm swamped with backed up paperwork, but I think there's a reason you're not giving up, even when old man Jacoby told you to drop it." He chuckled, "If you want to pick my brain, just set up an interview with her, and let me know. If you decide it's not worth it, that's cool. God knows I've got enough on my plate."

"Alright."

"Alright you'll set it up?"

"Leave it with me."

"If there is a chance that it's connected... I mean, even a small one, it might be critical. I was at the first crime scene Noah. Tamara Sweeten. I saw what that bastard is capable of. You said you gave the file to Ethan?"

"Yeah, few hours ago. He didn't seem that interested."

"He's just busy. Let me know if you want to take it further, even if Ethan doesn't. Maybe I can help."

"Will do. Thanks."

"No problem, see ya."

Noah put his phone down, and looked out his living room window into the darkness.

If Jacoby was right, and he was most of the time, Noah was taking a huge gamble on pursuing Avery Hart's case instead of his own, but he wasn't ready to let it go.

When he woke, he made a call.

Chapter 7

WHEN AVERY ENDED THE CALL, she darted to her room, and threw on a pair of jeans. She took time to put on some mascara, and as she did, her mind and her heart raced.

Inspector Cotter asked her to go back to a place she avoided at all costs. A place she became the person she was.

When push came to shove, her curiosity outweighed her fear, and she agreed to meet him at the place where she ventured into the woods ten years before. She had been past the forest multiple times on her way to and from school since then, but she never went into the woods. Even when Josh would kindly ask her to come fishing with him, Josh who rarely asked for anything from her, and she would always refuse.

You gotta get back on the horse, he'd say, but Avery knew it wasn't the horse that scared her. She had been swimming several times since that day in pools and lakes. The water never bothered her. It was the thing that chased her over the edge that she couldn't stand the thought of.

When she arrived at the spot, she parked her car, and waited. No other cars were parked on the road, and she realized she was early. The sun was high in the sky, birds chirped, and a soft breeze blew through her window.

She wondered how far he would make her go, into the woods and into her memories.

After the first few times she told Jacoby and the accompanying officers in the hospital what had happened, it felt like everyone had changed the story for her, into something that felt right to them. The truth was still inside her, but the story she told since the end of her therapy sessions was different.

She flipped her visor down, pouted, applied lip gloss and threw it back in her purse. She remembered the day Sadie helped her pick just the right colour for her skin tone. She trusted Sadie for more than just makeup tips.

Sadie knew the truth about her attack because she was there for her through everything. Everyone else got the 'new' version of the story. She wondered what version she would tell Inspector Cotter when she saw him pull up behind her.

"Sorry I'm late." He called as they got out of their vehicles and met on the sidewalk.

He wore plain clothes, jeans and a long sleeved shirt, and she wondered if he was on the clock.

"No, I'm early. Thanks for meeting with me." She glanced toward the tree line. "Can I ask why you wanted to meet me here?"

"I wanted to get a better handle on your case. I read your file, and handed it in to the inspector on the case. I know you've been through this with the police, but I'd like to go through it with you if you're still up to it?"

Avery turned toward the trees. Until that moment, she felt like there was no backing out, but Inspector Cotter gave her the opportunity to turn around.

"Let's just go for as long as you're comfortable." He said, and his warm eyes seemed to look straight through her.

She nodded, waved him off with a smile, and took her first steps toward the forest. She wondered if he thought she was fragile, as he fell in step behind her.

He cleared his throat. "So, do you have anywhere else you have to be today?"

"I've got a class at one." She let him fall in stride beside her, though the path began to narrow.

"Oh, we should have plenty of time then. I don't want to rush it." he stopped, held out his hand, and let Avery go ahead of him. "What class are you taking?"

"I teach actually. Photography 101 over at the college. It's just a course, not a program."

"So you're a photographer *and* a teacher?"

Avery was sure he was trying to distract her, and make her feel more comfortable, but her legs still shook beneath her.

"I am."

"So you have one of those dark rooms at home?"

Avery laughed. "No, I wish. I live in an apartment, so I don't have the space. It's all sent out. Everything I do is digital."

They walked for another minute.

"Start anytime you're ready. Just take me through that day."

Avery kept her eyes on the ground to watch her step. The dirt and leaves beneath her feet were soft after the recent rain, and the whole forest smelt earthy. She pulled all her hair over her shoulder and held it in her hands.

"I was walking home from school alone. I didn't know anyone here yet. I thought I was taking a short cut by going this way, North West, toward my subdivision."

"What time was that?"

"School day ended just after three. It was probably after four when I realized I was lost and the sun was setting. I remember it wasn't dark, but with the shadows from the trees, it was hard to tell where I was going, and where I'd already been."

"Was it cold?"

She glanced behind her, surprised at the question. "A little. It hadn't been during the day, but it was getting chilly." The hairs on the back of her neck

42

stood on end, and she rubbed her hand over the goose bumps on her arm. "I took out my cell phone to call my mom, but there was no reception." Avery stopped.

"Do you know where you went next?"

Avery shook her head.

"That way." He pointed north. She looked in the direction, and began to walk. "You hear the sound of water yet?"

She shook her head. "I was going a bit faster than this. I was panicked." They picked up the pace. "It must have been around here."

"What?"

"When I heard it coming toward me."

A soft breeze cooled the back of her neck, she released her hair from her fists, and draped it over her shoulder.

"Okay, just stay in that spot and close your eyes."

Avery closed them. "It was like it came out of nowhere. All of a sudden, it was running at me." Her eyes opened, and Inspector Cotter stepped in front of her. The closeness made her heart beat faster, but she didn't want him to move away.

"What did you see? Close your eyes."

She looked up at him and sighed. The smell of his cologne was intoxicating.

"You don't have to close..."

She closed her eyes and caught her balance as she rested her hand on his arm. When he didn't move it away, she tried to remember.

"It was a long way away. Maybe thirty feet. By the time I was running, it was less, but when I saw it..." Avery closed her eyes tighter.

"You're doing good." His gruff tone was amplified with her eyes closed.

She could listen to his voice all day.

"It was something that didn't look human running toward me." She opened her eyes and stared at the ground.

She let it go. The secret she kept that sounded absurd to everyone else.

She looked up at him, and waited for the realization that she was crazy to wash over his face.

He looked down at her and kept eye contact. "Alright, so you ran?"

Avery took a deep breath, let go of his arm, and began walking in the direction he pointed toward.

"I was running, and I was pretty fast, but they were too. I kept looking behind me." She ducked under a tree branch she couldn't remember before. "Are you sure this is the way?"

"The place you were found isn't far off."

"So I kept looking behind me, and I could see this white face, and these dark eyes." Avery felt a chill again and stopped. "There was this sound, rustling leaves, and it got louder and louder as it came towards me. But then it wasn't as loud."

"How so?"

"I don't know. It was like people running towards me, and then it stopped, but I never saw anyone else."

"This isn't in the report."

"I didn't remember it until now."

"So there might have been more than one person here? You've said 'they'."

Avery shrugged, and looked around until she noticed something.

"There." She pointed. He followed her to a small clearing. "I ran through there, just before I went over."

They stood in place, and looked in the direction they'd been walking. The clearing led to more trees, and then a drop off. The fact that there was a ledge seemed so obvious to her that she couldn't believe she missed it.

"I wasn't looking where I was going because it's so flat here, and because..."

She stood in silence and turned to the ledge. She expected him to say something, but when she turned around, he was looking at the ledge too.

Maybe he didn't hear me before.

The wind blew gently through her hair, as if to calm her, and she gathered her courage.

"Because I thought a monster was chasing me," she blurted out, "but I couldn't be sure. I couldn't help myself. I had to look back and see what it was."

"And now?"

"I know it wasn't a monster, but the face, it was so real. I call it a face. I know it was a mask, but it was scary. I was terrified."

He looked from the ledge back to her. "Do you want to go now?"

Avery turned and walked toward the ledge. She passed the clearing, and turned to see the inspector still standing where they were.

"You can come."

He studied her for a moment before he walked toward her and she waited for him. "I just didn't want to..."

"Interrupt my train of thought?" She looked at him, and he stopped beside her. "You thought I might have a break through? That this trip down memory lane would help you decide if I was legit or not? What?" As soon as the words left her mouth, she wished she could take them back.

He flinched, but shook his head, and looked out to the ledge only a few feet away.

"I didn't want to follow behind you so close to here. I didn't want to scare you."

Avery looked down at the ground and cleared her throat. "Oh."

"Listen, I wasn't expecting anything from this. I just wanted to get a better handle on the case, alright?"

"This is where they stopped. I kept going but they stopped right here."

"So about six feet from the ledge?"

Avery nodded and took another step toward it. "It doesn't look as high as I remembered."

"It's pretty high. You fell roughly fifteen feet."

46

"It felt like I was falling forever." Tears came to her eyes again, but instead of brushing them away, she let the wind dry them before they could fall.

The wooded area was lush beneath them, and Avery listened to the river below. The trees were various shades of green, but that September, they had started to change colours. There were other things that made their trip into the woods different from her last, but the thing that kept her there was the feeling of safety.

"You must have been scared." He stepped beside her and looked down.

"I was."

I'm not with you.

He stepped in front of her and touched her arm to guide her away from the edge.

"It's lucky you only broke your arm."

"I wasn't scared of drowning, or hurting myself."

He studied her, but she focused on the ledge.

"Of falling?"

"I was scared that whatever it was, whatever was chasing me, would follow me right over the edge."

Chapter 8

AS THEY WALKED BACK through the woods, Avery was quiet. Noah wanted to say something to fill the silence. He thought about making small talk, but he didn't want to make light of the situation. He wanted to get to know her more, but the situation made things awkward, and he knew he had to be professional.

Even if he had suggested their meeting off the clock.

"I think the fact that there could have been two people here points to the conclusion that this isn't related to the case you saw on the news. There's also the possibility it was just the one person who came after you. Point is, the mask could have been something both of them bought, but our killer made his look different. Unique."

"With the blood?"

"Yeah," Noah had heard the killer smeared the blood of his first victim, Tamara Sweeten, on his mask, but it was just a rumor around the department, "and maybe a few other things. I think I understand what happened here as much as I'm going to anyway."

"That's funny." Avery almost laughed.

She tossed her hair over her shoulder and shook her head.

Noah turned back to her. "What's that?"

"I think this is the first time anyone's really tried to understand what happened to me, aside from my best friend."

"Well the police file suggests they did an in depth investigation. You don't feel they did?"

"Oh no, they sure did. They questioned me again and again. I did the police sketch, and they interviewed my family, as well as some of the people who live by the woods. They questioned Josh almost as much as they questioned me."

"So?"

"So no one ever really listened to what I said. They did the first time, but after that, they just heard what they wanted to hear, and the rest they made up. I was chased by some hooligan, obviously their words, in a mask. Someone was playing a joke on me, and it went too far. They determined the person stopped short of the ledge because they never meant to drive me off of it."

He stopped walking, but she continued past him. "Wait, you think parts of this investigation were made up?"

"No," Avery sighed as they reached the tree line. "I think they thought I was the one who got it wrong. That my account was some sort of fabrication that they needed to breathe some reality into. There was no evidence of an attacker at all, and I used to wonder if they even believed me about that. Jacoby pretty much suggested I needed professional help. That's why I worried I made a mistake calling you."

They walked to the sidewalk, and when he turned to face her, he noticed she finally met his gaze with a smile.

"But you're glad you did?"

She nodded.

"I'm glad you called, Avery, I mean initially. I'm not saying this is connected to the case at all, but there's still a chance it might be. I feel confident that the inspector in charge will be able to determine if your information is helpful."

Avery shoved her hands into her jean pockets. "So what's the next step?"

"I'll do what I said I would and let you know one way or the other." Avery squinted at him through the sun, and the light turned her hair a sunny golden blonde. "You don't believe me?"

"It's not that," He opened his mouth, but she continued. "Do you think I should speak to him? The inspector in charge?"

He shook his head. "That won't be necessary. He'll make the decision, and if he needs to talk to you, he'll call you in."

"The killer, he always finds his victims in the woods?"

He watched her look down at her feet and wished he knew how she felt.

"Yes."

"I don't think it's just a coincidence."

They stood in the warm glow of the sun and he studied her face. She licked her pink lips and he had the urge to kiss them.

"We'll see." He shrugged his feelings off. "Thanks for meeting with me alright? I'll be in touch."

She nodded, and shook his strong hand with her soft one. He realized too late that he'd held on for too long, as she pulled away.

"Thank you for trying Inspector Cotter. That's what I meant to say before."

"You can call me Noah, alright?"

She smiled and nodded, and he watched as she got back into her car.

As he got in his, he slipped his sunglasses on, and watched her shut her door. If nothing comes of this, he thought, maybe she'll finally feel like she got a fair shake. She made it clear, short of saying the system failed her, that she didn't trust the police. If she really felt like she was being heard, Noah thought his time with her was already worth it.

He waited until she pulled out before he followed behind her. He knew it was time to get back to the office, and start in on his new case, and after their time in the forest, he hoped he could finally concentrate on something other than Avery.

Chapter 9

SHE LOST TRACK OF how many times she refused to be taken from her room to be discharged in a wheel chair, and as the nurse reminded her again that it was protocol, Officer Minicozzi began to lift her from the bed.

"Hey, what are you doing?"

"You've gotta get in the wheelchair somehow," he laughed, "and I don't want to stand around all day waiting for you to realize it's the only way you're getting out of here."

She struggled until he sat her down, and she crossed her arms as the nurse placed her feet on the foot rests.

"In a rush Officer Minicozzi?" She looked up at him, as the nurse wheeled her to the elevator, and batted her eye lashes.

"Actually, we're on a schedule. Wouldn't know it with you around." He winked at her and she rolled her eyes.

She thought Officer Minicozzi was attractive in an older man kind of way. She flirted with him while they had her on drugs, until she saw the ring on his finger. Fiona soon came to believe Mrs. Minicozzi was one lucky lady. Through all the flirting she had done, he hadn't made one pass at her, and his friendly nature with her could barely even be called flirting.

"Will I have crutches right away?"

"Not yet. They'll be sent to you." The nurse told her as they exited the elevator.

"Actually," Owen called, as he held the elevator for the next group, "we'll be coming to pick them up."

"Sure." The nurse said, and waited for the officer, before pushing Fiona out the door. "Should I wait for you to pull up?"

"Nope." He pointed to the blue SUV ahead. "That's our ride. Thank you ma'am."

She nodded, and to Fiona's surprise, he picked her up again.

"Would you put me down?" Fiona laughed, as she watched an officer she recognized open the passenger door for them.

He was tall and thin, with thinning brown hair, and a brown suit.

"Here, easy." Officer Minicozzi hoisted her up onto her seat, and before she could say anything, he shut the door.

When the other officer got into the back seat, Officer Minicozzi climbed into the driver's seat.

"I wasn't kidding when I said we had a schedule. We have to check in as soon as we get you home, and if we're late, I'll lose my job." They pulled out onto the road.

"Hi Fiona, I'm Ralph. How are you feeling?"

"Hi." Fiona glanced at him from her rearview. "Alright, I guess."

The smoky smell of cigarettes and cigars filled the vehicle.

"I'll be staying with you for the night. Then Owen here's gunna come by in the morning. That's how it'll go for the next while."

"Great," Fiona looked at him, "so I'm under house arrest?"

"Not exactly." They exchanged glances.

"You won't be going anywhere for a while with your leg like that, so you'll be under our watch until..."

"Until what Officer Minicozzi?"

She honeyed her voice on purpose when she spoke to him.

"Call me Owen alright?"

And that was why.

"Alright." She smiled as they merged onto the highway. "Until what?"

He rolled his eyes. "You ask too many questions."

"*Excuse me* for wanting to know what's going on in my life."

"Anybody ever told you you're a handful?"

She looked at Owen, but he kept a straight face. In the back seat, she caught Ralph smiling.

Chapter 10

AVERY OPENED THE DOOR to see Sadie holding up a six pack of wine coolers and a bag of licorice.

"Tell me again why we can't have girl's night every night?" Sadie smiled, and Avery waved her in with a grin.

"Because we have commitments and we are grownups now, whatever that means." Avery closed the door behind her, and locked the first, third, fourth, and fifth locks.

"I don't" Sadie wrinkled her nose, and pushed the coolers into the fridge, "fine, I do, but I'm not grown up."

Avery walked over to her ottoman, opened the top, and revealed their movie selection. Sadie knelt down; her mint green skirt fanned out around her, and sorted through the options.

"How was your day?" Avery stood by the sliding glass doors.

"Slow. No clients. Yours?"

"Good. Class was good. I gave them their second week project. They have to take a picture of something that is considered ugly by society's standards, and make it appear beautiful using black and white."

Sadie looked up from the movies. "Sounds like something you'd do."

"Hmm?" Avery looked outside at the glowing lights of Crown River, then down at her friend, and tried to decide if she was going to tell her about everything that was going on.

"I don't want a rom-com, but I'm not picking some slasher flick either."

"It's your pick." Sadie smiled up at her, and Avery decided then she couldn't do it.

At least not without a drink.

Sadie rifled through the movies, and Avery picked up the framed picture she had on her end table. She studied the two girls with long blonde hair in their bathing suits at her parent's cottage. It was taken the first year she met Sadie, and they spent every summer together since. They were often asked if they were sisters and that's how they came to describe their friendship.

Sadie had listened to her whenever she decided to talk about her attack, and it always turned into Avery talking non-stop about the actual event, or her therapy sessions, or people who made fun of her for it (it made front page news for a week in the town paper). She didn't want to bring the mood down, especially when she knew it was out of her hands. If it amounted to nothing, she'd only feel guilty for obsessing over it and wasting Sadie's time.

She wished she could at least discuss Noah with her, but the thought was interrupted when Avery heard the twinkling notification sound on her phone. She plunked herself down on the couch and checked it.

"That Spencer? Are you still talking to him?" Sadie set another movie in her maybe pile.

"No and no. It's a Facebook message...from Charla Kent."

"What?" Sadie turned to face her. "Shh-ar-la? From high school?"

"Yeah."

"I didn't know you had her on your Facebook."

"I don't. You can message someone even if they aren't."

"What did she say?"

Avery read the message aloud. "Hey Avery, I know this might seem random, seeing as how we've never actually talked, but I just wondered how you're doing, and what you're up to these days? It's been ten years since high school, and I've been catching up on old times with our classmates. Wondered if you'd like to do the same?"

"Is that it?" Avery nodded, and read the message over to herself. "Wasn't she a -- a..."

"Bitch? Yeah."

"Yeah." Sadie smiled. "I still don't get why she'd message you."

Avery shrugged. "Maybe she sent lots of people the same message. Maybe she's trying to get a reunion started?"

"She didn't send me one."

"I don't know." Avery slipped her ring on and off her index finger "I mean, she was never a bitch to me, but her group..."

"Yeah, I remember."

Sadie was the reason Avery made it through high school in one piece and she let her know it all the time.

"You think I should respond?"

"I mean, if you want, but do you really want to see all those girls again?"

Avery stared at the message and contemplated deleting it altogether. She didn't care what any of those girls were doing since high school, or if they'd changed. She left the site and checked her messages.

"I'm gunna grab some coolers, want to set the movie up for when Josh comes?" Sadie went to the kitchen and her skirt flowed behind her.

Avery turned the TV on and grabbed the Blu-ray disc from Sadie's 'yes' pile.

"I love Into the Wild!"

"I know, that's why I picked it." Sadie called. "Want ice in yours?"

"Sure. You don't mind watching it again?"

"No, I haven't seen it in a while, and I never get the chance to..."

Avery stopped listening to Sadie the moment she saw the sketch of the mask on the screen. The same sketch as the night before, and this time she turned up the volume to hear the story.

"... Wendy was found shot and stabbed to death in Birch Falls Park. "

Avery noticed Sadie staring at her with their drinks in each hand. "You alright?"

"The identity of the previous victim has not yet been released, but she is believed to be a resident of Birch Falls. Police arrived at...."

"Avery?"

"I've gotta tell you something." Avery grabbed a drink from her hand and took a big gulp.

"Okay. That bad?" Sadie set her drink down on the coffee table and sat beside Avery on the couch.

Avery told her about seeing the sketch of the mask the night before, and how it resembled the one that was worn during her attack. She told her about her trip to the station to see Noah and their trip to the woods by the Crown River.

"So you think it's the same mask?"

"I'm not sure, but it looks so similar, and I've never seen another one like it since."

"What's going to happen now?"

"They're looking into it."

Sadie grabbed her drink and took her first sip. "Have you told anyone else?"

Avery shook her head. "Well, just Josh."

"You should call the inspector to see if there's any news."

"He wouldn't tell me if there was. He told me to leave it to the inspector in charge of the case."

"And now another girl is dead. That's three, right?"

Avery shrugged. "Noah's done everything he can, and I think it's two. One girl escaped. That's how they have that sketch."

"Right. Maybe it's fallen on deaf ears. I can't believe whoever's in charge hasn't contacted you by now."

"Sounds bad, but I'm used to them not really listening to me. Noah has though, he's different."

They both turned back to the reporter. "Please call the tip line with any information that could be helpful to the investigation."

"You should call." Sadie set her drink down and licked her pink stained lips. "Don't you think?"

"It won't help. The police have all my information."

"No, not the police. The news. That'd make them pay attention."

Avery stared at Sadie and realized she was being serious.

"I don't want to be in the news. I don't want the attention."

"The killer has to be stopped. People need to pay attention, or they'll end up like these girls. Hunted down and mutilated. That's so sick."

"They've already spoken to the girl who escaped. She's their best chance of finding him."

"Okay, just say it's the same person who attacked you ten years ago. That was before any of the murders happened. Maybe the killer was testing things out, experimenting with you? Maybe they were just getting started? It could mean the killer is from Crown River. That's important for not only the police to know, but the community."

"What if I'm just laughed at again? What if no one takes me seriously? I can't do it again Sadie."

"I take you seriously. To save even one life by bringing awareness to this, and maybe even getting a straight answer about what happened to you in high school, could be worth it."

Sadie grabbed her phone from her purse, punched in the hotline number, and held the phone out to Avery.

"All you have to do is press send. You can stay anonymous if you want."

Avery took the phone and hit the button. "I can't believe I'm doing this."

"I'm here for you no matter what."

Chapter 11

NOAH HAD JUST GOTTEN off the phone with the last person to see his drowning victim, and he was about to meet with them when he heard the news from around the coffee pot.

Another girl found shot, stabbed, and left in the park to be found. There was no question, as word circulated through the office, that it was the work of the masked man.

On his way to the parking lot, he saw Owen getting out of his car, and jogged over to meet him.

"Hey, did you just come from Birch Falls Park?"

"Yeah, I guess you heard."

"It's all over the news and the boys were talking about it in there."

"So you saw the news?"

"No, why?"

"That girl Avery Hart, she contacted the press. Told them everything."

"What do you mean?"

"Told them about how she thinks someone with the same mask was after her ten years ago. Apparently she tried to stay anonymous, but they researched her case, and they know it's her. Ethan's pissed."

Noah shook his head. "Why would she do that?"

Owen shrugged. "He asked me to be there tomorrow when he brings her in for questioning. He read your file. I don't think he was going to contact her-- until now."

"Is he pissed with *me*?"

"No, actually, he wants you in there with us when we call her in."

Owen gave him the details, and when Noah left to interview the jogger who claimed to have seen Mr. Hornby on the path, his mind raced.

How could she have done something so reckless?

He was trying to help her, and she thought she should handle things on her own. He wondered if there was a possibility that she could be in real trouble for compromising the investigation.

She has Ethan's attention now.

She put herself out there.

She put herself in danger.

Chapter 12

AVERY HID OUT IN her apartment all day after the news broke.

When she went to leave that morning, a news crew bombarded her at the door, and she decided to stay in her apartment until they went away. Her cell phone rang, with everyone from the local TV station, who tried to schedule a TV appearance with her, to her own parents leaving several messages. Sadie slept over, but left early that morning for an appointment, and Avery was left alone to wonder if she made the right choice by getting her story out.

She thought about what Noah, and everyone from the police department would do, when an officer called her.

She was so nervous, she almost shook as the officer scheduled a time for her to come in the next afternoon, and reminded her not to speak about the case again. By the time Avery got off the phone, her hands shook, and it was hard to swallow.

She would have never thought to call the news on her own, and she wasn't blaming Sadie for pushing her, but the circumstances for being called in to meet with the inspectors wasn't ideal. Someone from the department was ready to talk to her, but she couldn't appreciate the fact that she had gotten what she wanted only *after* she made the phone call to the news.

The fortune cookie told her she would get something she always wanted, and if this was what it meant, being careful what she wished for swirled in her mind.

As she checked her recent messages for the fifth time that day, she remembered her commitment to Veronica. She deleted another message from the local news, and was shocked to hear her dad's voice on the next new voicemail.

"Avery, I need you to call your mother back. We're coming down if you don't. You need to call that reporter back, and let them know this is a big misunderstanding, and I'm sure I don't have to tell you why. You're not a little child anymore, and I thought we put all this behind us, and if you haven't already called the police to apologize, I suggest you get on it. They have more important things to worry about than a prank that happened to you when you were young and naïve. Are you still that little naïve girl Avery? I hope not. Just put an end to this and call us back."

She shook her head as she deleted the message and dialed the shelter. She wasn't surprised at her dad's lecture, or the fact that he could make her feel like a stupid kid again so easily, but she was surprised that he'd called at all.

"Hey Veronica, it's Avery."

"How are ya girl?"

"Umm, I've been better."

"I saw the news." There was a pause, and Avery heard a few dogs barking in the background, "You take all the time you need alright?"

"Thanks." Avery exhaled. "You know I won't stay away for long."

"I'm counting on it. You'll be missed, but Josh took your shift already."

Avery smiled. Of course he did. "Thanks for understanding."

There was a lingering feeling of regret as she set the phone on her nightstand and pulled the covers over her head.

Her cell chimed, and she reached her arm out from under the covers to find it.

The Facebook message was from Charla Kent.

Could we meet for coffee tomorrow?

Avery sighed, and gripped the phone in her hand, letting the glow of the screen illuminate the darkness under her blanket. She wondered if Charla had seen her story in the news. She'd love that.

"What do you want from me?" She asked as she looked at the screen once more.

If she would be downtown at the police department tomorrow anyway, she might as well meet with the girl, and if she wanted to make fun of her some more, Avery could show her she no longer had any power over her.

I can meet you at Joe's Cuppa tomorrow at noon.

Great, see you then Avery.

Her message popped up right away in response and it surprised her. It surprised her more that she agreed to the meeting, but the phone rang again, and the local news reminded her that they weren't letting up.

She thought about telling Sadie about coffee with Charla, but couldn't bring herself to talk to anyone, and turned her cell off. She curled up in a ball and wished she had never seen the police sketch of the mask.

Wished she could let go of the past as easily as everyone else seemed to.

Wished that she didn't feel so trapped.

As she willed herself to sleep, she thought about Noah, and wondered if he would be there the next day, and hoped for the first time that she wouldn't have to see him.

Chapter 13

THE JOGGER TURNED OUT to be another dead end on his drowning case.

Noah was getting used to those, and as he left Joe's Cuppa with his breakfast, he decided to talk to the vic's wife, Mrs. Hornby, one last time before meeting with Ethan, Owen, and Avery.

Avery. He couldn't even picture her face without getting angry.

"Hello," Jennifer Hornby answered the door, looking disheveled, "Oh, Inspector Cotter. Any news?"

"No Mrs. Hornby, I've come to see if there was anything else you'd thought of." He looked into the house and waited, but Mrs. Hornby stood still in the doorway.

"I've really told you all I know."

"May I come in? I was hoping to get the phone number for your husband's sister."

"Oh sure, wait right here." Mrs. Hornby closed the door behind her, and left him on her porch.

Noah noticed a neighbor peek through their blinds at him, and he waved to them. As he turned his attention back to the house, he noticed a truck parked further up the driveway.

"Hi, sorry about that. I'm not having a good day."

"It's fine. Mrs. Hornby, is there someone else here?"

She looked at him confused for a moment.

"Oh, Grant's hunting buddy came to visit. Funeral's tomorrow."

"That's nice you've got someone here for you."

Mrs. Hornby smiled, and pressed her lips together, as she handed him a piece of paper.

"These are their numbers. Nice folks, the Hornbys. They live in Toronto, but they'll be here for the funeral if you wanted to talk to them in person."

"No, a phone call will be fine."

Mrs. Hornby nodded, and clutched at her housecoat. "Anything else?"

"That's all, thank you for your time."

After he got in his car, Noah looked over the paper she'd given him. When he got to his office, he sat down and called the first number on the paper.

"May I speak to Kim?"

"Speaking."

"This is Inspector Cotter from the Crown River police department calling. I'm sorry for your loss, but I was wondering if I could ask you a few questions about your brother?"

"Yes?"

"Do you have any idea who would want to harm him?"

"No, not at all. I mean, we don't live that close, or talk all the time, but he was a good man, Inspector. That's all I know for sure." He heard a quiver in her voice.

"No enemies to speak of, and no way anyone would benefit from him dead?"

"No, and I hope you're not wondering about his wife. Her family is loaded. She doesn't profit from his death. She loved him."

Noah gave his condolences, and left a message for her parents to give him a call if they knew anything, before ending the conversation.

He got on his laptop, and checked the local funeral home's site. He found the times for Grant Hornby's funeral and visitation, and decided he'd try for more leads there the next day.

On his way to meet with Ethan, he worried about his temper getting the better of him with Avery, and coming off as unprofessional. He went out of his way for her, and the first chance she got, she disrespected his authority.

Avery is on her own after this.

Chapter 14

AVERY CHECKED HER PHONE for the third time and realized it was twelve thirty. As if being bullied and made fun of in high school wasn't enough, she was about to add being stood up by one of the most popular girls in school to the list of ways she had been humiliated.

Just as Avery grabbed her purse, Charla Kent slipped into the seat across from her. Her brown curly hair sat on her shoulders, and Avery couldn't remember ever seeing her hair curled. She wore a blazer and bright red lipstick on her pouty lips.

"I'm sorry I'm late. I..."

"I think it was a mistake, coming here." Avery went to stand, but Charla held her manicured hand in front of her.

She looked the same as she had at graduation, well dressed and put together.

"Please stay." She looked around and lowered her voice, "I really need to talk to you."

Avery sat back in her seat, dropped her purse to the floor, and crossed her arms. "Go ahead."

Charla let out a breath. "I don't know how to say this. I was late because I wasn't sure I could face you."

"You couldn't face me?" Avery raised her brow.

"I know it's been a long time since high school." She played with her gold locket necklace.

"Yeah, a long time since I've been treated the way I was. So what, you came to tell me you're a better person now? Realized you and your friends shouldn't have treated me like that? That's nice, but not necessary. I've moved on."

Charla tucked a ringlet behind her ear. "I've thought about you a lot."

"Okay, now you're sounding creepy." Avery leaned back in her chair and studied Charla.

Her green eyes welled up with tears and Avery felt her body tense up.

"I'm trying to tell you something, and you're not making this easy, but I have to. I can't..."

"Please just tell me."

"When you had your accident, it wasn't really an accident. It was an attack, and I know because I was there." Charla spoke quickly, and Avery worked to keep up. "We decided it would be fun to scare you, and it was Jolene who wore the mask. Do you remember her? Anyway, we never meant for you to get hurt, and when you fell off that ledge, I just..."

Avery covered her mouth with her hand.

"I've felt so bad ever since, but Jolene threatened that if I said anything, told anyone, that I'd get it worse than you. I never talked to her after that you know. She became a big pot head, and I..." she looked Avery in the eyes, "no matter what good things have happened to me, I just carry this burden. I had to get it off my chest, and apologize, but I know no amount of..."

"How? How did you do it?" Avery squinted and studied her, wondering if it was another joke at her expense.

Charla licked her lips, and stared down at the table. "Over the lunch hour, Jolene came to my place. She said she was in your gym class, and she thought you were a bitch. She was probably jealous of you, who knows? She said we should scare you and I... I suggested an old mask we had in our garage. It was just supposed to be a joke."

Avery shook her head, but Charla continued.

"We followed you home, and I just thought we'd jump out from behind a fence, or a car. Jolene got so excited when you went into the forest. We followed behind you, and finally, she just broke into a run. I tried to follow her, but I couldn't keep up. That's when you..."

"You're serious. You really did this?"

Charla nodded. "I'm ashamed of it, of how you were hurt, and how I caused that. We caused that."

"It was all just a prank." Avery said under her breath, and tears welled up in her eyes as the words sunk in.

"It was meant to be. I was going to come clean to you before all this with the media, I even messaged you, but then I saw you on the news, and I had to contact you. I had to make sure you knew the truth, once and for all."

"I can't..." Avery's hand shook. "Why?"

"Jolene didn't like you, and it was just" she looked down at her hands, "it was supposed to be funny. I can't believe she pushed you off that ledge."

"She didn't. I fell."

Their eyes met, and Charla raised her brows. "I don't understand."

Tears streamed from Avery's eyes, and she wiped them away. "Did you laugh?"

"What? No." Charla answered immediately and shook her head. "I was horrified you got hurt. I regret it, and I'm so sorry Avery." A tear ran down her cheek and dripped off her chin.

Avery wiped the last of her tears, and grabbed her purse as she stood from the table.

"Please, Avery..." Charla looked up at her.

Avery pushed her chair out behind her, hurried out of the café, and rushed to her car. The fresh air cooled her face, and when she got in, she sat in silence.

Everything she went through was over a prank.

It was just a prank.

Something that was done by two girls her age and planned only a few hours after meeting. Something about her, Jolene didn't like, and that was it. She chose her as a target. It all sounded so immature, and simple, and different from how she had always pictured it.

Years of therapy bills, and wondering, and fear for *that*.

She put her hands on the wheel, and tightened her grip to stop her hands from shaking. She wondered if she was in shock, and if she should be driving, but realized she had to get to her meeting.

She had to tell the police what she knew to be true.

Why couldn't Charla have come forward earlier? Avery knew the what ifs would hold her back, but she couldn't help but wonder how different her life may have been if she wasn't seen as the spaz of a new girl, a victim, and an outcast.

Chapter 15

WHEN AVERY GOT TO THE reception desk, she was led down a few short hallways by an officer who looked familiar.

"Avery, my name's Officer Owen Minicozzi. You might not remember me, but I was on your case."

Avery nodded. "I thought you looked familiar."

"Yeah, haven't changed much except for the beard I guess." He gestured to their left, and before she got to the door, she saw Noah and another man through the window.

The other man was short and balding, and stood with his chest puffed out. They were talking, and Avery was relieved they hadn't noticed her.

Officer Minicozzi ran his hand through his hair. "And maybe a bit of salt and pepper."

"Officer Minicozzi?" He turned to her just before he opened the door, and leaned in as she whispered, "How much trouble am I in?"

He looked at her for a moment and then back into the room. "We'd better get in there."

When Avery walked in first, Owen closed the door behind them, and pulled out a chair for her that faced the men.

A smile faded from Noah's face as he turned to her. She sat down and avoided his glares by looking at the other man.

"Ms. Hart," Noah said, "this is Inspector Ethan Ascott. The case you compromised is his."

The gruff voice that had drawn her in to Noah sounded colder than before.

She couldn't meet his eyes with her own. "I want to say I'm sorry, but first, I have to tell you..."

"Please, Ms. Hart." Inspector Ascott pulled his chair out, and dropped into his seat. The other two men remained standing. "It's my understanding that you believe the mask used to scare you ten years ago, is the one a serial killer is now using. I also understand that you began by following protocol, but then you felt the need to take matters into your own hands, jeopardize my investigation, and the lives of..."

"I know who attacked me."

Ascott stopped, and stared at her.

"Who?" Noah asked.

It was the first time she made eye contact, and his brown eyes were no longer warm and welcoming as they had been.

"It..." Avery looked down at her hands folded in her lap, "it was a prank all along. I just met with an old classmate of mine, Charla Kent, and she admitted that she and her friend meant to scare me as a joke, and things went...too far, further than they expected." Avery cleared her throat and looked up at Noah. "I do still believe the mask is the same."

"Whose mask was it?" The hardness slipped from his face, and he studied her.

"Charla's. She said they got it from her garage that day."

"Did she say where they put it after the incident?"

Avery shook her head. "I left her at Joe's Cuppa right before I came here. She knew the details, so I believe her. She didn't talk about the connection to your killer though," She looked at Ascott. "We didn't get that far."

Her hands shook again, and she knew Noah had noticed them.

"I read your file Ms. Hart. I think we need to bring your old school mates in for questioning." Ascott looked up at Noah and nodded.

"I have Charla's contact info, but not Jolene's."

"Yeah, well, we're going to have to get them down here now. Owen, call them and tell them it's urgent. We'll have them escorted if need be."

Officer Minicozzi nodded. "Did you want their families in too?"

"Might need to speak to Charla's parents. We'll see. Better get their addresses as well."

"Can I bring you back a drink?" Officer Minicozzi asked Avery, and when she shook her head, he left the room.

"We'll need to keep you here while we talk to them." Ascott stood up, and started for the door. "Cotter."

Noah followed him out, and Avery watched them talk through the glass window. Ascott hurried down the hall as Noah came back into the room, and sat down across from her.

He brushed his hands through his hair, and rubbed his neck before he spoke.

"Why did you do it?"

"I called the news because I believed I had an important piece of information, and I still do, so I'm sorry if you felt like I went behind your back." Which was exactly what she did, and she knew it, but she could barely admit it.

"You've got the media hounding you now. They followed you here, and they're waiting outside. You made things harder for yourself. You made things worse for all of us."

"Let them follow me. I don't care. I'm not giving them a statement. I already told them what I know. This could help."

He shook his head. "You don't get it."

"I'm sorry, I guess I don't." She shrugged and shook her head.

Noah leaned forward in his chair, and rested his elbows on the table.

"Quite frankly, you put yourself in danger."

"How?"

"By linking yourself to this killer. If he saw the news, and thinks that we might be onto him, *we're* screwed. If he's mad that you tried to associate yourself with something that you have nothing to do with, or that you found out the truth, *you're* screwed."

"What do you mean?"

He sighed, and checked the clock. "I'm not trying to scare you. I just wish you hadn't done that. What gave you the idea?"

"I just," She looked at the clock, and then down at her hands to avoid his gaze. "I've always felt like no one was listening to me, and these girls are being murdered...brutally murdered, but no one contacted me."

"What about me? I was trying Avery," His gaze softened somehow.

She wanted to look at him. She wanted to look into his eyes like the other day, and tell him what it meant to her, that someone finally listened. She wanted to apologize, but she felt her cheeks burn, and she couldn't admit she broke whatever bond they had begun form because she didn't want it to be true.

"You did but... you couldn't help me."

"I was trying," He held his hands up, "I honestly was. We do things a certain way here because it's smart and it's safe. I see you don't trust the system, and you might have a valid reason not to, but you've got to realize you made a mistake."

She opened her mouth, but she couldn't get the personal apology she owed him out.

"Do you really think what you did helped anyone?"

She could feel him staring at her, and as she looked up from the table, she knew he was just as stuck in his position as she was.

"Charla tried to talk to me, get me to meet with her, and I wouldn't. After she saw the news, she tried again. If she hadn't seen the news, and tried again, maybe I wouldn't have been able to tell you the truth, and give you a potential lead."

He squinted at her before he turned away, but she caught him looking back out of the corner of his eye, and he pressed his lips together.

"Ascott will be making you sign something that makes you liable for any information slips from the case. You'll be legally accountable if this happens again. Do you understand? They'll explain it to you before you sign, but this can't happen again."

"I understand."

He nodded once, and stood. "Good."

She wanted to apologize before he left the room, but he was gone before she could force herself to speak.

Chapter 16

OFFICER MINICOZZI CAME BACK in the room with a glass of water, and set it in front of Avery.

"I know you didn't ask for a drink, but you'll probably be here a while."

"Thanks." She managed a smile.

"Listen Avery, can I call you Avery?" She nodded. "I understand why you felt like you needed to contact the news. I was there when Jacoby interviewed you, and I remember him assuming a lot of things because you were a kid. I really hope there is a connection here, that can somehow validate the choice you made."

"You do?"

"Anything to catch this guy. Just don't tell them I said that." He snuck a peak at the window, and then winked at her.

"Officer," Avery began.

"Owen."

"Do you think they will search the garage?"

"If that's where the girls say they put the mask. It might be somewhere else, hidden. You said you didn't ask about the mask, but she said she saw you on the news."

"I guess we would have gotten to it, had I stayed."

"Ah." Owen looked up at the glass window as Ascott waved him over. "Excuse me."

When he left the room, Avery stood and went to the window. She watched as Owen and another officer led Charla and Jolene down the hallway, past her. Jolene hadn't noticed her, but she inadvertently caught Charla's attention.

Avery couldn't tell what look she gave, but she didn't care. Her life had always seemed so neat, put together, and effortless, but underneath she hid her secret from everyone. Charla's guilt must have eaten at her, Avery thought.

She wanted to go home, curl up in bed and most importantly, never see those girls again.

Chapter 17

"OFFICER MINICOZZI TOLD YOU why you are here, so let's just get started." Ethan crossed his arms and looked down at Charla.

Noah noticed she was trembling, and wondered if it was guilt for what happened to Avery Hart, or something more.

"I met with Avery today..."

"Actually, we'll start from the beginning." Ethan sat down across from her. "It was the first day of school that Avery Hart was attacked, and put into the hospital. What is your relationship with Ms. Hart?"

"Acquaintances. Classmates. We were never friends, and I'd never even met her that day. She was new to the town, so I'd never seen her before either."

"Were you involved in her attack?"

"Yes. Jolene, she was a friend of mine, came home for lunch with me that day. She talked about this girl from class who she didn't like. Said she wanted to play a prank on her. Scare her a little."

"Why?"

Noah wouldn't have asked that question, but he waited eagerly for her answer.

"Why would she want to do that or me?"

"Her. Jolene."

"I don't know. I think she was jealous of Avery."

"Okay, so what did you say to her when she asked you?"

"I don't remember, but I thought it sounded like fun. I told her to follow me to the garage, and I dug around in some boxes, and found this old mask we had."

"Where was the mask from?"

"I don't know."

"Where had you seen it from?"

"It was just in the garage. I figured it was an old Halloween costume of my dad's." Charla shrugged. "I'd seen it in there before when I was looking for other things."

"Okay, so then what happened?"

"She got excited when I showed her the mask. She said she had an idea. She wanted us to follow Avery home after school. I thought we might not even get to do it if her parents picked her up, but we followed her from her locker outside, and she started walking."

"Who had the mask at this point?"

"Jolene. I don't think it was ever a question of who would be wearing it. It was her beef with Avery, not mine."

"Okay, continue."

"So we followed her to the forest by the Crown River, and when she went in, I got nervous. This wasn't just popping out from behind a bush, or fence. It felt like we were stalking her. She started looking around, and walking faster, and I knew she was lost. That's when Jolene put on the mask, and started after her. I couldn't keep up."

"Why didn't she notice you?"

"I was back farther. Like I said, I couldn't keep up. It got to the point where they lost me all together." Charla cleared her throat. "I knew they were heading for the river, and when I heard a scream, I knew it wasn't Jolene. She ran back at me with the mask still on, and she even scared me. She ripped it off and told me to run. I know it sounds silly now, but I thought someone was after us, so I did. When we got out to the sidewalk, she just started walking like normal." Charla stared off.

"What did she tell you?"

"She wouldn't say anything. She just told me to keep our prank a secret. Later, on the news, my parents saw what happened to Avery, and told me, asking if I knew her because we went to the same school. I lied and told them no. That night Jolene called me, and said if I told anyone what happened, she'd do the same to me." Charla had tears in her eyes. "I thought she pushed Avery into the river. I never spoke to her again, but I always felt guilty, so I contacted Avery. I wanted to tell her the truth."

"And?"

"She wouldn't meet me. Then, I saw the news, with the sketch, and the mask looked similar. Avery told them she thought they were the same. Then I needed to tell her the truth. She met with me, and I told her just now. She didn't take it well, but I didn't expect her to. She always seemed sensitive, so I didn't expect for it to go well, but she's really hurt. Then I got a call from you guys, and I knew."

"Knew what?"

"It's the same mask."

Ethan looked back at Noah. "Who took the mask home with them?"

"I don't remember." Charla looked up at them with her bright green eyes, and Noah thought he could have guessed she was the popular type, even if they had just met.

She was poised, and calm, especially under the circumstances, but Noah noticed her smudged eye makeup. She wasn't as collected as she put on.

"Think hard."

"I think I did. I think I put it back in the box it came from and piled more on top of it."

"Sounds like something you do remember."

Charla looked up at Ethan. "What happens now?"

"Now we talk to Jolene and see if everything matches up. Then, we find that mask."

Ethan knocked on the door inside the room; Owen opened it, and led Jolene in. Noah ushered Charla out, and Owen pointed to a chair where she sat. Noah looked into the next room before walking back in, and saw Avery looking back at him.

He could make out her blue eyes from where he stood, and the sadness they carried made him feel like he'd drown in them if he got too close. Charla was right—she was hurt. Overwhelmed probably, he thought, and wondered if he should have gone easier on her.

"Should I go in or stay with her?" Owen asked, and tilted his head to where Charla sat in the hall.

"Naw, we've got it. Thanks though." Noah closed the door behind him, and stood beside Ethan once more.

"I thought it would be fun to pull a prank. It's not against the law officer." Jolene smirked.

"Inspector." Ethan said, and shifted his glance to Noah. "And it's against the law when someone gets hurt."

"She's the one who overreacted. Ran right off the ledge herself. Is she telling you I pushed her? Did Charla tell you that?"

"Who took the mask with them when you parted ways with Charla?"

"She did! She's the one that suggested we use it in the first place."

"You're sure about it?"

"You calling me a liar? I haven't lied about one thing since I sat down. Avery was a stuck up bitch in high school. Probably still is. She was so scared she put *herself* in the hospital. Now do I need to get a lawyer?"

"What you need to do is stay here until we say otherwise." Ethan opened the door for Noah, and shut it behind them, as Owen approached.

"Charla, do your parents still live in the same home?"

Charla nodded.

"We need to search the house for the mask."

Charla looked up at them. "You think it's the same one the killer is using?"

"Can't discuss that." Ethan looked up and down the hall, "When we get there, you tell your parents if they don't give permission, we'll be there with a warrant faster than they can lock the doors. Officer Minicozzi will go with you."

Charla nodded and followed Owen back to the reception desk.

"Should we get her parents in here now?" Noah asked.

Ethan looked back into the room where Jolene sat. "If we find it, this could be huge."

"You think it could be her dad?"

"Maybe. Regardless, we'll have a better chance at finding the manufacturer if it's not the same one, and that could lead us to the killer."

"Should I let Avery go?"

"Better tell her the girls have confessed, but she's not able to press charges. No action can be taken."

Noah nodded. "What about Jolene?"

"She can go too."

Owen came back with Charla in tow.

Ethan looked at Noah. "You coming?"

Noah tried to suppress his grin. "Sure, be there in a sec."

As they walked down the hall, Noah opened the door to Avery's room. "You're free to go, alright? Charla and Jolene confessed. Can't do anything about it now though. Legally, too much time has passed."

Avery stood from her chair. "I don't care about that. What about the mask?"

"We'll find out soon." He paused, and grabbed the door knob. "You need a ride home?"

She shook her head.

"Alright. Take care."

Noah went to the next room and opened the door to find Jolene on her cell phone. "You can go now."

He didn't wait to hear what Jolene said, and hurried down the hallway toward the parking lot.

Chapter 18

AVERY SKULKED DOWN THE HALL to her apartment, and noticed Sadie had been sitting by her door. She scrambled to her feet, and hugged Avery tight.

Avery unlocked the door, Sadie grabbed her bag from the floor, and they both stepped inside. As Avery locked up behind them, Sadie went to the kitchen and placed the bag on the counter.

"I brought sandwiches. I figured you hadn't eaten."

When Avery finished telling her about her meeting with Charla, and everything that happened in the police department, she started in on her sandwich.

"It should surprise me that they were the ones behind your attack, but it doesn't. I'm more surprised that Charla actually confessed, and apologized to you."

"Hmm?" Avery chewed in a rush.

"Well, maybe she's changed."

"You think I should have forgiven her?"

"No, I'm not saying that." Sadie sighed, and ate a bit of her sandwich. "You wish they could have been punished? Charged?"

Avery shook her head. "I just don't think they're good people. Karma will give them what they deserve if it hasn't already."

"It's good that you know the truth now, you know?"

Avery nodded, and poured them each a drink.

"Thanks for this." Avery popped the last bite into her mouth.

"No prob." Sadie wiped her mouth with a napkin. "It's so quiet in here. Do you ever get lonely?"

"Nope. You're here most of the time." Avery smiled. "Sometimes Josh and Asher."

She realized it was quiet, and that the baby next door hadn't had a fit in almost two days.

A new record.

"Think it's serious?" Sadie smiled.

"Josh and Asher? Well yeah, they moved in together."

"Maybe they just didn't want to live at their parents anymore?"

Avery shrugged. "He said things are going well."

Sadie smiled and looked around the kitchen. "So you don't mind being alone at all?"

"No, I love being on my own right now. No parents to observe and judge my life, lots of time to myself, what's not to love?"

"I'm glad my mom's cool with me staying in the basement. Until I build up a better clientele, I can't afford to live on my own, or else I'd live with you."

"Oh yeah?" Avery smiled.

"Well, financial issues aren't the only reason it wouldn't work. I'd have nowhere to set up my massage table here."

"How about the fact that I don't mind living on my own?"

"I don't know." Sadie smiled, and looked around. "I couldn't do it. You should get a cat. Or a dog. I'm surprised you haven't brought one home from the shelter yet."

"I couldn't take just *one*, and besides, no pets allowed here."

"I just think of you alone here, and..."

"I'm fine Sadie. Honestly, I'm better than I've been in a while. Just feels like a weight has been lifted, you know?"

"Still, you've gotta be a bit confused. I am."

"It's a weird feeling. Can't describe it. I just hope they find that mask. Maybe it'll lead them to the killer."

A knock on the door startled them.

Avery looked through the peep hole and saw Josh on the other side.

"Hey, just wanted to pop by with Louie before he gets placed." Josh closed the door behind him, and moved out of the way so Avery could lock it. "I'm gunna miss this pooch."

"Oooh!" Sadie squeeled. "Puppy!"

Josh laughed and brought Louie to Sadie in the kitchen.

"I see the news crew finally left you alone." Josh smiled, but when he saw Sadie's face, it faded.

"Thanks for taking my shift, by the way." Avery wiped up the crumbs from the counter, "Listen, I've gotta catch you up on today."

Avery told him everything, and Sadie listened intently, cradling Louie in her arms.

"I'm sorry Avery. Kids can be so cruel."

"These girls were more than cruel. They were..." Avery shook her head and shrugged. "They weren't worth my time, until now."

"They were bitches," Sadie looked up from Louie. "Except Charla never really said anything to you, you know? She probably just talked behind people's backs."

"How does it feel to finally know the truth?" Josh asked.

"Weird." Avery plunked herself down on the couch, and they gathered in the living room.

Josh sat down beside her. "Listen, I think this is good news. It will help you move on, you know? Honestly, it means there's less of a chance you're connected to this killer."

Sadie sat on the floor and played around with Louie, who had already grown in the days since Avery saw him.

"It wasn't like I was hung up on it." Both Sadie and Josh looked at her. "What?"

"I think maybe it affected you more than you know..."Josh turned to Sadie.

"Sadie?"

She gave a half-hearted smile, and shrugged as she picked up Louie.

Avery crossed her arms.

"Listen, it's over now." Josh waited for a response, but when she was silent, he stood. "I've got to get Lou to his new foster parents."

Avery swallowed, and leaned back on the couch. "It's okay. I feel like being alone right now."

Sadie handed Louie back to Josh. "Call me if you wanna talk, alright?"

Avery nodded and Josh brought the pup to her.

"Want to say goodbye?" He held Louie up to her face, and she exhaled and kissed his chubby cheek.

"I hope I don't see you again Louie. You know I mean that in the nicest way. I hope you get your forever home."

Josh cradled the pup in one arm, and waved before the left. He followed Sadie out, and as the door closed, Avery got up and locked it behind them.

She went to her sliding door, and stepped out onto the balcony to watch the sun set. As it touched the horizon, it left the sky an orangey-pink. She thought about what Josh and Sadie implied.

As soon as they had left, Avery knew they were right.

The incident ten years ago still affected her, but as the remaining sun dipped below Crown River's landscape, she decided it didn't have to be that way.

Tomorrow was a new day, and she needed a fresh start more than ever. It was the first day she could move on without questions about her attack. About who wanted to hurt her, and if they were still out there. She thought it would comfort her to think of the guilt they carried, but she didn't take pleasure in Charla's pain, and Jolene seemed like she didn't lose a wink of sleep over it.

She thought about Noah, and imagined him and his colleagues searching for the mask at that very moment.

Chapter 19

NOAH AND ETHAN LOOKED AT EACH OTHER and shook their heads. He followed Ethan out of the musty garage, through the house, and back to the kitchen.

Owen caught Noah's attention for a brief moment, and let out a sigh.

"Mr. and Mrs. Kent, when was the last time you saw the mask in question?" Ethan slid the photo of the police sketch along the table in front of them.

"We told Officer Manicotti here that we don't even think it's the same as ours." Mr. Kent slid the photo back across the table. "Mine didn't have blood on it. That's for sure Officer Manicotti."

Owen rolled his eyes behind them and Noah tried not to snicker when Mr. Kent confused Owen's last name.

"When was the last time you saw your mask? The one we believe looks similar to this one?"

"I don't know. I wore it one time at a Halloween party."

Mrs. Kent glared at Charla, but when her husband didn't answer, she gave them her attention.

"I think it was back in eighty-eight. Or maybe it was eighty-five?"

Mr. Kent shook his head, but his wife stared back at Charla, who sat across from her dad at the table.

"And you never saw it again?" Noah could tell by Ethan's voice that he was exasperated by the Kent's.

"Charla seems to be the last one to have seen it." Mrs. Kent poured coffee into a few mugs.

"I told you mom, I'm pretty sure we just put it back in the garage."

"I don't know," Mr. Kent threw his hands in the air. "Maybe we sold it in a garage sale or something?"

"Hmm," Mrs. Kent tapped the spoon against the mug, "I think Maggie might have pictures of it. That's my sister. We used to go over to her place for Halloween. She always had real fun parties, and we'd make it every year... before we had Charla."

Noah caught Charla rolling her eyes, and looked away when she noticed him watching her.

"Are these photos on Facebook?" Noah asked.

"No, Maggie's not on that thing. I don't think she is anyway." Mrs. Kent pointed at Charla. "She'd know better than me."

"No, Aunt Maggie isn't on Facebook."

"Could you call her and see about getting those photos?" Ethan asked.

Mrs. Kent nodded, and went to the phone after she placed their mugs in front of them.

Mr. Kent slurped his coffee, but no one else took a sip.

"Maggie, you got a minute?" Mrs. Kent leaned against the wall.

"Could the killer have taken the mask from us somehow? Gotten into our garage?" Charla asked Ethan.

"I can't say. It might not be the same one, but we haven't found any masks resembling the one in the police sketch. If we can get..."

Mrs. Kent raised her voice over Ethan's. "The police are here Maggie. It most definitely cannot wait."

Ethan lowered his voice. "It's important we find this mask."

"I'll hold while you look." She pushed the speaker of the cordless phone against her chest. "She's not sure if she's got them. She's gotta look around." She put the phone back to her ear.

"Charla's not in trouble is she?" Mr. Kent asked.

"No." Ethan barely turned away from Mrs. Kent.

"You know how kids can be Officer Manicotti." He smiled at Owen.

"Fine. Hold on." Mrs. Kent tipped the mouth of the phone away from her. "Should she call me or you if she finds the pictures?"

"Please have her contact this number." Ethan handed her his card. "We're done for now. If you remember anything, or find anything, please call that number."

Mr. Kent stood, and led the men to the door. "Hope you catch that sicko."

When they got to their cars, Owen suggested getting some drinks, but Ethan declined.

Noah followed him in his car to their usual watering hole, and they took a seat in their back booth.

"Missy mad you're staying out?" He asked, as the bartender set two pints in front of them. "Thanks Joe."

"I might not be on the clock, but this is still a business meeting, of sorts." He took a long chug of his beer, "I gotta relax before I go home."

"She's gunna know you've been drinking."

"I won't lie if she asks." Owen shrugged. "But she won't."

"How's Fiona doing?"

"The docs wanted to keep her sedated, but she won't take the pills. Ralph's on duty at the house right now, but she still doesn't feel safe. She hasn't come right out and said it, but I can tell."

"When were you last over?"

"With Ethan this morning."

"Can't really blame her for being afraid. The killer shot her and chased her through the park. When did she go home?"

"She was only in the hospital for a week. I'm sure you heard, but the bullet tore right through the side of her leg. Missed the major arteries. No infection either. She's lucky."

"She using her crutches yet?"

"Not while I was there. Ralph says she's been in her room since she was told about the first murder-- the girl before her-- and now Wendy O'Connor."

"Listen, you don't think Mr. Kent might..."

Owen shook his head. "He's not our guy. Mrs. Kent fits the profile better than him."

Noah coughed, and choked on his beer. "Tough as nails. You see the way she looked at her daughter?"

Owen nodded. "It could have been that someone took the mask, a friend or family member, but I doubt it."

"So what do you think?" Noah sipped his beer.

"I think Mrs. Kent's sister better get us those pictures. It's our only shot at some sort of a trail, unless..."

"Unless he kills again."

Noah thought about Fiona, and how she barely got away. He was sure another victim wouldn't be so lucky, and an uneasy feeling swept over him when he thought about Avery.

They both sat, listening to the music for a while, before the bartender looked their way. They were the only patrons in the bar, and had been since they arrived.

"She didn't want to go in the program?"

"Fiona? Nope. Stubborn girl." He took another swig of beer, "Avery, she's a pain in Ethan's ass, but she's pretty isn't she?"

Noah smiled, sipped his beer, and hoped he wouldn't have to say anything.

"Charla too." Owen shrugged and laughed. "Girls like that are trouble. I know-- I've got one of my own."

"I think Joseph's waiting on us." Noah looked toward the bar again.

Owen swallowed the rest of his pint. "I better call Missy before I leave. She'll probably be having cravings about now."

"Oh yeah?"

"Olives."

"Huh."

"Of course it could be different. That's why I've gotta call first." Owen laughed. "The joys of being pregnant."

"Hey, she's the pregnant one, not you. You'll call me if Charla's aunt finds the pictures?"

"Sure buddy." Owen took out his wallet.

"Naw, this one's on me." Noah threw a few bills down on the table. "Say hi to Missy for me."

Owen smiled and clasped his hand on Noah's shoulder.

"Will do Noah."

Chapter 20

AVERY GRABBED THE PHONE FROM her nightstand and checked the time. She'd barely gotten any sleep, and was feeling guilty about kicking Josh and Sadie out. She knew she overreacted, but she didn't think she was any more scared of the dark than the average person who lived alone.

She got up from bed and shuffled down the hallway toward the kitchen.

She couldn't see more than a foot ahead, and her heavy steps were the only sound. She was thankful for the quiet nights without the neighbour's baby crying, but as she got halfway down the hall, she heard a noise. It sounded like it came from her balcony, and she rushed into the bathroom.

She shut the door behind her, her hand hovered over the lock, and turned on the light.

When she looked in the mirror, her face was pale, and she stood still.

She waited to hear the sound again, and when it didn't come, she began to giggle.

They were right. Sadie usually was. I'm a chicken.

She made a mental note to try to remain calm when things made her nervous, turned off the light, and opened the door.

There was nothing there.

She started toward the kitchen, while mentally reprimanding herself for giving into fear, and promised to apologize to Sadie and Josh.

When she got to the living room, she felt chilly, and her attention was immediately drawn to the breeze she felt.

The sliding door curtains blew in the wind and cast shadows from the moon into her living room.

Avery gasped, took a step back, and then she heard whistling.

Was it coming from the hallway, she asked herself, as she began to back up to the door.

Or the balcony?

When she turned to look through the peephole, she realized it was coming from her bedroom.

Her hands flew to the top lock, and she turned it to the left. Onto the third as the whistled tune continued.

Six locks in total, only four actually locked. She learned the trick from a TV show, but now the locks slowed her down, and the whistling grew louder.

She fumbled with the last lock as she looked down her hall and saw it.

The man in the mask from her nightmares was back for her.

He turned the corner and strode down the hallway toward her. The hair from his mask flew behind him, his face streaked with blood.

Avery turned the door knob, and as she pulled to open it, the man slammed his hand across it.

He pushed it shut, and as Avery struggled to hold the knob, he grabbed her before she could turn around. He covered her mouth, and pushed her to the ground.

Her body collided with the tile, and she gasped for breath. The man mounted her, each leg on either side of her torso, and she tried to scream.

No noise came out.

She saw dark eyes through the holes in the mask, only visible as he lowered his face to hers, and she grunted as he covered her mouth once more.

Out of the corner of her eye, she saw a silver glint. The man pulled a knife out of his pocket, and when she saw the large blade, she bit his hand.

He yanked it away and it came back just as fast to smack her across her face.

Her cheek stung, and he wrapped his hand around her neck. Her eyes opened wide as he raised the knife and she scrambled beneath him.

The choking sensation flooded her with fear, and for a moment, she was frozen in his grasp.

She turned her head to the right to look for something. Anything to get her away. As she turned to look to her left, he eased his pressure on her neck, and she lost sight of the knife.

He lifted her tank top, revealed her stomach, and she felt the side of the cold blade as it ran along her skin.

She let out a muffled scream, and the dark eyes flickered to her face for a moment, as a deep chuckle escaped from behind the mask.

She jabbed her knee up toward him, but it didn't connect, and he brought the blade to her neck. He shook his head and tears rolled down her cheeks.

He started to whistle again, just before the knife sliced into her stomach for the first time.

She howled until he guided the blade out of her flesh and she tried to cover her stomach with her hands. He grabbed them both together, held them tight above her head, and focused on her stomach again.

He pushed the knife into her stomach and sliced through the flesh again and again.

The pain ripped through her, and the whistling pushed her over the edge, as she cried out into the dark.

Her stomach muscles clenched, and warmth ran down her sides as the blade cut into her.

Avery screamed and cried so hard; she wasn't sure when the sirens had come. She felt him cut her so many times, she couldn't take it anymore. When the sirens grew louder, he released her hands, and suddenly, she felt lighter as her eyes began to close and the pain faded away.

Chapter 21

NOAH SHOT UP FROM his pillow when his cell phone chirped. It was a text from Owen.

Charla's aunt, Maggie, found a picture.

Noah rubbed his eyes, looked at the time, then texted back.

Have you seen it?

She's bringing it in tomorrow at nine.

I'll be there.

Noah slid his phone onto the side table and sat still. He wasn't sure he'd be able to get back to sleep, and his mind raced, as he wondered if the mask was the same.

He got out of bed, put on his slippers, and shuffled down the hall to his office. He sat in front of his laptop, and checked his email.

His dad emailed, no doubt asking when Noah would be back home to visit. He began to read, when his cell phone rang.

"Cotter."

"Listen Noah," Ethan huffed, "There's been an attack. I'm not positive yet, but I think it's Avery Hart."

"What?" Noah sat up straight and a lump formed in his throat.

The killer. It had to be.

"EMS unit's taking her to St. Andrews."

"Is she alive?"

As the words left Noah's mouth, he ached to be told she was going to be alright.

"She was when they got there, but she's lost a lot of blood. I don't know anything else. I'm on my way."

Noah ran his hand over his face. "I'll meet you there. Wait, Ethan?"

"Yeah?"

"Is it him?"

"I don't know. Get down here."

Noah snapped his phone shut and bolted to his room. His mind raced with the possibilities of what happened, but he was sure he knew why.

The killer attacked her because she involved herself in the investigation so publicly. Whether he knew about her before then was only a slim possibility, and although she didn't understand at the time, she called him out from a place of fear.

He had asked her why she went to the news, and her reason seemed valid enough to her. As Noah got dressed, he wished he could have saved her from that, and from the domino effect she had caused.

When he left his apartment, he slowed down to check his phone for an update. When there was none, he sped to the hospital.

Chapter 22

"AVERY?"

She could hear a soft voice, and as she opened her eyes, a blurry figure came into focus.

"It's me."

Avery jumped, but when Sadie grabbed her hand, she relaxed.

"I should go tell the nurse you're awake again."

"Again?" Avery whispered, and her dry tongue brushed across her lips, which felt like sandpaper.

She felt an itch on her stomach, and went to rub it, but Sadie pulled her hand away.

"Don't."

Avery cleared her throat and licked her lips again. "Did they get him?"

"Who did this to you?" Sadie whispered, and squeezed Avery's hand.

Avery stared back at her, as the night came back to her in flashes, and a tear slid down her cheek.

"The man in the mask. Did they... they didn't catch him?"

Sadie shook her head, and a nurse came into the room followed by Inspector Ascott and Noah.

"It was him." She croaked, as the nurse bustled around them, and checked the machine to her left.

"The killer with the mask?"Ascott asked, and stood at the foot of her bed with Noah beside him.

Noah looked over her body, and met her eyes with a look that made her heart flutter.

"The man in the mask, only it wasn't exactly the same. The blood. There was so much blood." Avery looked down at the bandages around her stomach, and pressed her hands over it. "He cut me."

"You were in surgery dear," the nurse smiled down at her.

"Am I okay?"

"Honey, you're gunna be just fine. How are you feeling?"

An image of the blade shining in the light came to her. "I feel sick."

"The medication might do that. You've had a lot of stitches. You're a lucky girl. It's mostly superficial. The doctor can tell you more when he comes. Miss," She looked at Sadie. "You need to leave while the inspectors talk to Ms. Hart. Remember, only two people at a time."

Sadie looked from the nurse to Avery. "Do you want me to stay?"

Avery saw the nurse put a hand on her hip, and she shook her head. "No, it's okay. Wait outside for me?"

"I'm not going anywhere." Sadie smiled. "Your parents should be here soon, alright?"

Avery nodded, and watched Sadie follow the nurse out of the room.

"What happened?" Ascott asked, as Noah came to her side and took Sadie's seat.

"I got up to get a drink, and I saw my curtains, they were open." Tears flooded her eyes. "My sliding door was open. I knew someone was in my apartment, because I always lock it."

"What floor do you live on?"

"The fifth." Avery took a deep breath, and wiped at her eyes."I tried to run, but I had trouble at my front door, and then I heard him. I heard him whistling. Next thing...he's coming at me." Her voice quivered, and the tears took over.

"You're doing good Avery." Noah smiled at her, but she could tell somehow it was fake. She felt self-conscious, helpless, and struggled to get a breath. "Should we get the nurse?"

Ethan shook his head. "Avery, just take your time."

"I...I..." Avery knew she was hyperventilating, and tried to catch her breath, but the deeper she breathed, the more her stomach ached.

Noah touched her arm; his fingers cool against her skin. "Let's call the nurse."

"No," Avery choked. "I can do this." She shook as she tried to take shallow breaths. "When he was on top of me, he smelled bad. I can't describe it, but it was hard to breathe, and when I could, he smelt bad. He cut me. I kept screaming, and he just kept cutting me. Then I heard sirens."

As soon as she had it all out, she stopped shaking, and rested her head back on the pillow. She looked down to see Noah's hand still on her arm, which continued to cool her skin and warm his fingers. He glanced down to the place where she watched him, and pulled his hand away.

"Was it the same mask you saw when you were younger, that day in the woods?"

"I think so, except...maybe that's why he smelt bad?"

"The blood." Ethan finished for her, and she nodded.

"Did he say anything to you?"

"No. He was just whistling, and I think he was laughing...when he cut me." She started to cry again at the realization that he took so much joy and amusement out of the torture he inflicted on her.

"Okay, Avery. That's all we need for now. I'll be back to question you later. You work on getting better alright?"

Avery nodded to Ascott and her attention flickered between the men.

"Officer Minicozzi is right outside if you need anything, or remember anything, alright?" Noah stood from his chair.

As soon as they were out the door, Sadie came back in with a tea in her hands.

"Did you hear what I told them?"

Sadie nodded and handed her the cup.

"Good, because I don't know when I'll be able to talk about it again. I just can't..."

Sadie pushed the chair closer and sat down.

"It's okay." Sadie nodded and watched, as Avery held her stomach in her hands.

It ached from the intensity moments before, and Avery closed her eyes, and tried to push the pain away.

Chapter 23

"Dr. Freebush, I'm Inspector Ascott. I need to ask you a few questions about your patient, Avery Hart."

"Now?" The lines in his forehead multiplied, "An officer was just by."

Ethan looked to Noah, and back to the doctor. "I'm sure you've got important things to do, but talking to us could also save lives. It won't take too long. What were her injuries?"

"I'll show you." They followed Dr. Freebush into the room down the hallway. "These pictures are after the stitching, but before we bandaged. Due to the blood loss, I had to close the wounds as quickly as possible."

"I understand." Ethan closed the door behind them and the doctor pulled a file from the wall organizer.

"They are mostly superficial, and I know what you're wondering. Why was it such an emergency to stitch her up if the incisions weren't deep right?" The doctor handed Ethan the file.

Ethan opened it so Noah could see, and passed him the first page. Noah stared at the picture of Avery's stomach slashed open in so many places. Ten wounds, each roughly four inches long.

Ethan turned the paper out of Noah's sight, upside down, and then on its sides.

"We'll need a copy of this."

"Of course. The nurse's station can do that for you before you leave."

Ethan nodded. "Would you say the person who did this wanted to kill her?"

"Slowly maybe. He might have been trying to make her bleed out. It's difficult to speculate. If this was all he meant to do, then no. I don't think it was meant to kill her. We can't know the answer to that."

Noah watched the doctor take the chart back. "Is Avery alright otherwise?"

"The psychological effects might be worse than the physical. With a week's rest, she'll heal fine. No infections, as long as she takes her anti-biotic. No permanent damage, except the scars."

Ethan extended his hand to the doctor. "Thank you Dr. Freebush. I'll let you get back to what you were doing, as soon as we get a copy of that picture."

"It'll be ready at the nurse's station when you are." The doctor left the room, and they followed.

"What do you think?" Noah asked and grabbed the picture from Ethan.

The marks were in no particular pattern or order from what he could see.

Ethan rested his hands on his hips. "If we're dealing with our killer, the mask has something to do with it. Avery means something to him. If it's because of the way she called him out on the news, that's one thing, but he didn't kill her and he could have. He might know her, or know of her from before, from her attack."

"You think he knows Charla in some way too? Knew what she did?"

"We've gotta get back to the department. Charla's aunt Maggie's coming in, and we've got to see if the picture matches the description. If it does, someone from Charla's family knows where the mask went. It's our best lead."

"Right."

"Oh, by the way," Ethan lowered his voice, "the man after Fiona whistled too. It's our guy."

As Ethan hurried to the nurse's station, Noah let his last words sink in, and popped his head back into Avery's room. Sadie turned her attention to the door, and cleared her throat.

"She's sleeping again."

"I'll be back, okay?" He asked. "Will you tell her that?"

Sadie nodded, and Noah nodded at Owen, before following Ethan out.

Ethan held the door open to the parking garage. "I think we might need more security on Fiona. She won't like it, but she might have to go away for a while. Avery too."

"Meet you back there." Noah called, as Ethan headed for his car.

As much as he hoped Maggie had a picture to show them, he wished the girls wouldn't have to look at the face of their attacker again to prove it was one in the same. They'd both been through enough, and although Owen and Dr. Freebush were right about the girls being lucky, Noah knew they weren't out of the woods yet.

Chapter 24

"I'M SO SORRY, AVERY." Sadie sat beside her, and gestured to a vase of flowers by the wall. "They brought you these and they said they'd be back."

"Sadie, it's okay. I'm not surprised they didn't stay. I don't blame them really because I wasn't even awake."

"They're your parents." Sadie shrugged. "I'm apologizing for me too by the way."

"What? Why?"

"I should have stayed with you last night."

"You couldn't have stopped this from happening. You would have been hurt too, or worse."

"I'm the one that got you to call the news..."

"Sadie, do you know how nice it is to wake up here and not be all alone? I appreciate how much you care about me. Don't blame yourself."

"I do care about you." She sighed, and wiped her eyes. "You've been the closest thing to a sister to me since high school. I love you, girl."

"I know you do." Avery smiled.

"I'm so sorry this happened to you. I'm not letting you out of my sight."

"That's not realistic. You have to go to work."

Sadie pursed her lips, and looked down at the bed.

"I...are you scared Avery?"

Avery watched the sun dip behind a few clouds and the room went gray. She thought about the masked man running toward her, down her hallway.

Sadie rubbed her lips, and sighed. "I don't want you to be scared Avery. You've been scared for a long time now."

A knock on the door turned their attention, and Avery smiled when she saw Josh in the doorway wearing the same brown jacket he always wore and a vase of flowers in his hands.

"I hope I'm not interrupting." To see him carrying something so feminine caused laughter to rumble inside her, but before she could start, her stomach warned her that the medication was wearing off.

"No, that's fine. Those are beautiful. Thank you."

Josh put the vase down on the windowsill beside the flowers her parents left her.

"Hey Josh." Sadie stood up and looked down at her. "They said you could go home as soon as tomorrow. Will you let me take you home?"

"Yeah, thanks."

Sadie left the room and her bohemian skirt flowed behind her.

"Asher's getting you some real food." Josh took Sadie's seat. "I couldn't wait to see you, so I just ran up by myself."

"That's sweet."

"I hate to see you like this again."

Avery cleared her throat, and even that slight movement sent pains through her midsection.

"Are you okay?"

"The doctor says I'll be fine. Like Sadie said, I can go home tomorrow."

Josh looked her in the eyes and then scanned down to the foot of the bed. "I told Veronica you'd be away for a while. The flowers are from her too. Her idea."

Avery smiled. "Tell her thank you."

She wondered how much Josh wanted to know about her attack. The details were too hard for her, but he hadn't addressed any general curiosity either. When an awkward silence followed, she decided to leave it alone.

"How's Louie doing?"

"He's with his foster parents now." A small smile greeted Josh's lips. "They seem like nice people. Anyway, when I told Veronica about, you know, she said you shouldn't stay away for too long."

"I know, I know. We heal the animals, and they heal us." Avery smiled, and thought of the first time she heard the saying, back when she first started volunteering at the shelter.

Josh had gotten her into it at first, and her parents supported her when she told them she wanted to become a vet. Since she'd changed her mind, they showed no interest in her involvement.

"I hate the thought of you livin' on your own right now."

Avery hadn't thought about returning home, but his words made her queasy.

He squinted at her, and rubbed his beard. "I want you to try to lay low and stay out of all this. Can you do that?"

"He's going to do it again Josh. I know it sounds crazy, but not when you think about it. There are police inspectors following the case. They were here a while ago. He left me alive."

"I don't like it Avery. You shouldn't be involved in any of this."

"Well I am now."

"Sadie should have never told you to call the news."

"Josh, it's not her fault. I did it."

"I know, I'm sorry. Sadie feels terrible," He rubbed his eyes. "You must be exhausted."

"Yeah." Avery fumbled with her gown. "The choice was mine Josh."

He wiped his mouth and kept his hand on his chin. "If you go home, I don't want you to ever be alone. You've got Sadie and me and Asher. Maybe your parents..."

They shared a look, and Avery licked her lips.

"If there is ever a time when someone won't be with you, you call me. Day or night, I don't care. Until they find out who did this, I... do they know how he got in?"

"Through my balcony. I don't know how he got on it though."

"Did you leave it unlocked?"

She raised her brows. "No, I'm sure I didn't. I never have."

"Well, depending on what the police find out about how he got in, maybe you shouldn't go home at all."

"I don't know..."

"Avery," his Adam's apple bobbed in his throat, "why do you think he did this to you?"

"I don't know for sure, but...it just felt like he was there on a mission. It's hard to explain, but at first, when he cut me," She saw him wince, and her heart ached for the way he sympathized with her. "He was going really slow. When he heard the sirens, he went faster, like he was trying to finish it, whatever *it* was."

"It doesn't make sense."

"I don't feel safe Josh, but I feel a lot safer because of you, Sadie, and the police. I just want them to find this guy."

"What if it wasn't who they think it is?"

Avery looked to the window, past her flowers, and through the tree leaves that rustled in the wind.

"I'm sorry Josh. I'm feeling kind of tired."

"I'll get Sadie. I'm glad she called me. When Asher gets here, I'll just make sure to leave the food for you."

Avery nodded. "Tell him thank you. And thank you, Josh."

He nodded and left the room.

When she was sure he was gone, she let her tears fall, and turned to face the window. If the police couldn't catch the man who did this to her, she wasn't going home.

It didn't even feel like home anymore.

Chapter 25

"THIS WAS THE ONLY PICTURE I could find, but I knew I had at least one." Maggie Henderson sat across from them, and handed Ethan the envelope.

Noah saw the family resemblance between Maggie, her sister, and Charla. Maggie had the same piercing green eyes as Charla, and the same mousey brown hair as her sister.

Ethan took the picture out and held it up for Noah to see. It was a dark picture, but there was a woman they recognized as Charla's mom, dressed as Marilyn Monroe, and her dad wore a mask with plain clothes.

Right away, Noah recognized the mask, and they compared it to the police sketch that Fiona gave them. Next, they placed it beside the one from Avery's case file. Although there were small changes, Noah believed it was the same one.

"Thank you Mrs. Henderson." Ethan set the photo down. "Have you seen the mask since this photo?"

She shook her head. "I'd remember if I did. Masks like that scare me, especially on Halloween. I like to see a person's face."

"So you never saw it at the Kent's after that Halloween?"

"No. I think my sister was saying she thinks they might have sold it at a yard sale. I don't know how she can't remember though. I'd have made it my mission to get rid of the thing."

"Did your husband come with you?" Noah asked, and picked up the pictures.

"No. He's away on a trip. If you don't have any more questions, I've got to be heading home to be there when he comes back. We live in Cedar Ridge."

"Here's my card." Ethan slid it across the table. "Please call me if you or your husband remember anything else."

When Maggie left, they both sat in the room and stared at the photos Noah laid out on the table.

"They look similar." Ethan mumbled from behind his hand.

"I don't think it's safe to assume they are the same, but to be honest, I think we should work with that theory."

"Okay, that means the mask was used for the first time at this Halloween party in the eighties. Then it was put away, and not seen again until Charla found it in the garage, and decided to use it as a prank with Jolene on Avery. She says she brought it back home, probably put it in the box where she found it, and then it wouldn't have been seen again until the sale."

Noah pulled Avery's sketch beside the Halloween picture. "So if it was bought in a yard sale, there is a large possibility that someone from the surrounding neighborhoods purchased it."

"And yet, after seeing the sketch on the nightly news, no one in any of the towns and cities within the surrounding regions has come forward in recognition."

"Maybe the Kents threw it out?" Noah leaned closer to Maggie's photo. "If it wasn't sold at the yard sale."

"Maybe."

Noah pulled Fiona's sketch closer to Avery's. "It was during the time between Avery's original sketch and Fiona's sketch that the murders started, right?"

"Right. So you think Avery's attack could have been the...what, inspiration?"

"Or the beginning of these attacks in some way." Noah ran his fingers through his hair and massaged his neck. "Who else knew the details of the attack? Did Charla tell anyone about using the mask?"

Ethan crossed his arms. "She said she didn't. Said Jolene threatened her."

"We'll have to ask again. Otherwise, the attack was seen as a prank on a high school student. No one believed Avery about it, so that leaves Charla and Jolene. Charla had the mask. We need to talk to her again."

"Noah, I haven't officially asked you to come on the case, but I think it's in our best interests to work together."

"Thank you Ethan." They shook hands and Noah beamed. "I appreciate this. Thank you."

"We'll bring Charla back in this afternoon then, and ask her some more questions. Until then, could you visit Avery, and see if there is any other info she's got on her attacker? I'm going to see Fiona to do the same."

"Sure thing. I've got a funeral to go to before that."

"Oh, I'm sorry."

"No, not for me. For a case I'm working on. Drowned man in Crown River."

"Ah right. How's that coming?"

Noah shook his head. "Nothing yet."

"I'll get Owen to call Charla in."

"See you then."

Noah decided to call his dad when he got home to tell him about his promotion. He could already guess the first thing his dad would say.

I wish your mom could see you now.

It was what he told Noah after each big accomplishment since his mom died. Noah thought the same thing each time too, but when Noah said he wished she was there after getting into college, his dad had cried. Since then, instead of sharing his thoughts, he hugged his dad. The phone call would be more difficult, but Noah still couldn't wait to tell him the news.

He was on the biggest case Crown River had ever seen.

Chapter 26

WHEN NOAH REACHED THE FUNERAL HOME, he paid his respects to Mrs. Hornby, and noticed a long line waiting to talk to her behind him. He asked if there was anyone else he could talk to who knew Grant Hornby well. She pointed to a man who was headed for the exit door and whispered his name.

"Darrel Beelson?" Noah called when he was just a few paces behind.

"Who wants to know?" The man in the brown suit turned around and gave Noah a dirty look.

"I'm Inspector Cotter from the Crown River police department. I need to ask you a few questions about your friend Grant Hornby. Mrs. Hornby said I should speak to you. That you knew him best." The last part he added and hoped he would flatter the man.

"Oh," Darrel took a step towards him, "Alright, but I need a smoke."

Noah followed him out to the back parking lot, where the group dispersed.

"Do you know anyone who would have any reason to want to kill Grant Hornby?"

"Nope," He lit his cigar, "Grant was a great guy. Great friend to everyone."

"What was your relationship with him?"

"Friend for years, maybe close to twenty. We didn't keep track. I met him up at a friend's cottage. My buddies like to go up north during hunting season. That's where we met. Friends ever since."

"Did you see him any time other than at the cottage?"

"Yeah, barbeques in Birch Falls or Cedar Ridge every year. Never missed it. Jen Hornby's potato salad is amazing."

"Any of your friends not like him?"

"Nope. Like I said, he was everyone's buddy." Darrel took a few puffs of his cigar in the silence that followed. "Probably wasn't cut out to be a hunter though. I think he just went up to hang out with us."

"Why do you say that?"

"He never caught anything. Never killed anything. He was a softy. Wouldn't hurt a fly, although he pretended to try."

"I see."

"You ask me," Darrel pointed his cigar at him, "I say it was random. Some sick asshole just saw him alone, and did it. Makes me sick." He shook his head.

"Can I get the name of your friends whose cottage you all meet at? Where was it?"

"Bob Pope. Cottage is up, just north of Cedar Ridge. He's here somewhere, or he was. We're all meeting up for drinks later at Jerry D's. You could ask him questions yourself then."

"Thanks for your time Mr. Beelson." He shook his hand.

On his way to the hospital, a weird feeling passed over him.

He decided to take the opportunity to question all Grant Hornby's buddies at once.

After that, he was out of leads.

Chapter 27

WHEN AVERY OPENED HER EYES, she saw Sadie and Noah in the doorway. Neither had noticed she was awake, and they spoke in low voices. Sadie turned to Avery, smiled, and left the room. Noah came and took a seat beside her.

A brief silence hung in the air, and the smell of his cologne wafted toward her.

"I hear you're going home tomorrow."

"Yeah."

"Are you ready for that?" He leaned in toward her.

"I think so. The doctor thinks so, and he's giving me some pills for the pain, so I think..."

"No, I mean, are you ready to be back in your apartment?" Avery stared at him. "If you're not, that's okay. Sadie said you could stay with her for as long as you need to."

"I just wish I knew how he got in. I did everything, everything I could think of to make it safe."

"I found out on the way over. The people in apartment fifty one, the ones on your left? They were away on holiday for the week. He broke into their apartment, and hopped the balcony onto yours."

She thought about their crying baby.

I should have known something was different with all the peace and quiet.

"They're fine. It was either lucky they were gone, or he's been watching you, and knew they weren't home."

"But how did he get in through my sliding door?"

"There are a few ways it could have been done, but the officers at your home believe it was simply lifted out of the lock."

"What?"

"All he would have to do is grab the handle and lift the door to unlock it, and slide it over on the track without making much noise. I understand, most folks on a high floor of a building would feel safe, but he got around it, so the sliding door was the easiest way to get in."

Avery balled her sheets in her fists, and concentrated on them. Her stomach pains increased, as she used her muscles to lift her head.

Noah's eyes darted around the ceiling. "Avery, you had six locks on your front door."

"Silly me. I thought they'd be enough."

Could he hear the pain in her voice, she wondered, or did he interpret it as irritation altogether?

"Well, if you're not ready to go back, just let Sadie know, and you're set, alright?"

Avery nodded. "Did you just come to question me?"

"Actually, I was wondering if you remembered anything else about last night?"

Avery let out a huff of warm air, and rested her head back on her pillow. "Not really. I remember a bit more detail. I've been going over it a lot."

"Would you mind going over it one more time with me?"

"No, that's fine. I woke up thirsty, and went to the kitchen to get water. Before I got there, I heard something, and ducked into the bathroom."

"You didn't tell us that before."

"I've been on some heavy meds." She tried to curve the edge to her voice, but her abdomen growled at her.

"Okay, go on."

"So I locked myself in the bathroom, but then I thought I was just being silly, so I went out to the kitchen again."

"How long were you in the washroom for?"

"Not more than a minute."

"Okay, so that's how he got past you to your bedroom."

"I guess so. I saw the sliding door open, and the curtains blowing. I tried to get to the door, but that's when he showed up, coming at me from my bedroom. The mask was more like the one on the news, than the one I saw ten years ago, but I still think it's the same one."

"Avery, the doctor says you were cut ten times."

"I didn't even know that, or if I was told, I didn't remember. I haven't seen my stomach yet."

Noah took out his phone, and Avery resisted the urge to ask him to leave, as he typed something.

"Then what happened?"

"He knocked me to the floor, and held me down with his weight."

"How big was he?"

"Solid, but I wouldn't say fat. He pulled out a huge knife, and I was sure he was going to stab me. The first cut was nothing compared to the rest. The first two, he took his time, and he was enjoying it. He laughed. I told you that right?"

Noah covered his mouth and nodded.

"Then, there were sirens, and he just started slicing into me. So fast." She closed her eyes, and when she opened them, she focused on the ceiling, instead of Noah's face. "The pain was too much at that point. I think I passed out."

"You were unconscious when the paramedics arrived."

"You think he meant to cut me ten times? It would explain why he stuck around, even when the police were on their way. Who called the police?"

"Your neighbor across the hallway. He said he heard muffled screams that woke him, and he called right away."

"I couldn't scream at first. At first I was just shocked." Avery let out a huff, "I bit him."

"What?"

"I thought I was prepared for anything. I feel like ever since I was attacked, I've just always been ready. Locks on the doors I checked so often, I convinced myself I have OCD. Never really trusted anyone, or let myself be too vulnerable. Never walked anywhere alone at night, and never went into that forest again, except with you." She turned her head to look at him, and he waited.

"I thought of everything, but it wasn't enough. I choked, but then I saw my opportunity, and I bit his hand."

"You're alive, Avery. It might be because of a concerned neighbour, or because the man who attacked you didn't plan to kill you, but it's probably because you screamed eventually. You fought back. You did everything you could to shout. How hard did you bite him?"

"It was hard to even get his hand in my mouth because of the way he was covering it. It seemed like it hurt him, but I don't know if there was blood."

"Okay." He got on his cell phone again, and Avery looked back up at the speckled ceiling tiles. She scrunched the bed sheet in her hands, and fiddled with them. "I was fooling myself, thinking I was safe. That I was in control. I was just scared."

"Avery, you can't think like that. Like a victim."

"That's what I am. That's why my parents came to see me for the first time this year. It's why you're here."

"Feeling sorry for yourself isn't going to help you right now."

"I brought it on myself." She muttered, but Noah heard it.

He stood from his seat. "You made a mistake, calling the news, but like you said, it might have helped our investigation too. We have a lead on the mask. I think we owe it to you. It wasn't right how you went about it, I'm not encouraging it, but you've helped us too."

"You said I might have screwed myself, back at the police department."

He sighed. "I did say that, and I'm sorry. It's not your fault. I was angry."

She could see him staring at her from her peripheral.

"Well, it's fine."

"You have to let people help you Avery. Let Sadie have you at her place."

Avery closed her eyes, and envisioned going back to her apartment. Even in her imagination, she couldn't bring herself to open the door.

"I don't think I can go back."

She felt his hand wrap around hers and she turned to him as he spoke. "I didn't just come here to find out more about the victim in my case, Avery. I came to see how you were."

The words made her heart beat faster and for the first time since her attack, her thoughts were solely on something else.

"I'm sorry."

"I told you not to blame your..."

"No, I'm sorry for breaking your trust when I called the news station. It's not even that I didn't trust you."

Noah stared into her eyes, and she wondered what he saw in them.

"You can trust me Avery."

"I do now. I just wanted you to know."

He nodded, but as she squeezed his hand back, he pulled it away. "I've got to get back."

"Thanks for coming."

He nodded again. "You take care."

She watched him stride out the door, and wondered if she had crossed the line, at the same time she hoped he would come right back.

Chapter 28

NOAH COULDN'T STOP THINKING about the energy that went through him when Avery squeezed his hand. He knew he shouldn't have told her he had a personal interest in visiting her, but through the pain in her eyes, he saw a spark of interest when he spoke those words. If he hadn't let go when he did, he couldn't have convinced himself that she didn't see his true feelings for her, the way he felt hers for him. He told himself he towed the line, but if she felt the same energy he did in that moment, they crossed the line together.

On his way to Ethan's office, the thoughts muddled in his head, and he bumped into Owen.

"Hey, welcome to the case." Owen shook his hand, and Noah couldn't help but smile.

"Thanks man. It'll be great getting to work with Ethan."

"No love for me huh?" Owen laughed.

"I guess it's cool that we get to work together again." Noah faked a yawn and Owen laughed. "No man, I'm actually tired. Haven't slept in a while."

"Well, you're gunna want to get in that room. Charla came, and her aunt too."

"Why's Maggie back?"

"You're gunna wanna hear this for yourself." Owen opened the door, and they rushed down the hallway, to the room they questioned her in earlier that morning. Owen followed behind him, and closed the door.

Noah was startled to see Maggie Henderson in tears, while Charla sat beside her, and rubbed her back.

"Noah." Ethan nodded to the chair behind him. "Mrs. Henderson, could you start from the beginning?"

"I went back to my sister's, to say goodbye, and that's when Charla told me you guys wanted to speak with her. She told me she was going to tell you sooner, but... she didn't think it was relevant." Noah struggled to understand her through her sobs.

"I told Aunt Maggie about what happened with Avery." Charla looked up at Noah, with her hand on her aunt's arm. "That same year, when she came to visit, I had to tell her. I was feeling guilty, and Jolene and I weren't talking anymore. I didn't have anyone to talk to, and I saw how it affected Avery, more than just physical, you know? Everyone in school knew she went to a psychiatrist. I just couldn't keep it a secret. Aunt Maggie told me to go to Avery's family and tell them, but I couldn't."

Noah looked at Ethan, and shrugged. "Mrs. Henderson, you're shaken. You did the right thing in telling her to come forward. You're not in trouble."

She shook her head, and looked at Charla, who took her hand and held it. She swallowed hard, and wiped her eyes.

"I think my husband..."

"Mrs. Henderson?" Ethan asked.

"I think my husband might have killed those girls." She choked, and shook more tears from her eyes. "I don't know for sure, but I think he did."

"What? Uncle Arnie?" Charla turned to her, but Maggie stared down at her hands. "Aunt Maggie, what are you saying?"

"I told him, your uncle, what happened. I told him about what you and Jolene did. About putting her in the hospital, sending her to the psychiatrist."

Noah hadn't noticed Owen leave the room, but when he came back in, he brought a box of tissues. Maggie took a handful, and hung her head.

"Aunt Maggie, how? How could Uncle Arnie have done this?"

"Mrs. Henderson, why do you think your husband is a killer?"

"I never thought he was before today, I swear." She raised her head, and looked at them with wide red eyes. "When my sister phoned me about it, it got me thinking. After meeting with you, and talking to

Charla. I just know it. I was scared to even think it, but I'm more scared to go back there. To go home." Her hands gripped the tissue covered in black mascara stains.

"Please, Mrs. Henderson, you're safe. What leads you to believe your husband did this?"

"I told him about what Charla and her friend had done. I told him, about the young girl they frightened, and I remember he was interested. Kept saying poor girl." She sniffled. "I knew he felt sorry for her, for Avery, and it was strange. It almost made me angry."

Noah and Ethan exchanged a glance. "Why?"

Maggie's big eyes stared up at him, and she covered her mouth with her hands.

"It's alright Maggie."

"He... beats me." She looked down at her hands when she spoke, and Charla took her hand off of her arm.

"No." Charla shook her head.

"It's not something I've talked about. This is hard..."

"Aunt Maggie?" Charla studied her.

Ethan broke her concentration. "So he's violent, and that's why you think..."

Maggie nodded. "And I couldn't understand how he could hurt me, and feel bad for this girl he didn't even know. He never felt bad about anything he did to me, and there he was asking questions about it. He wasn't acting interested—he was mesmerized by the story."

158

"What did he do to you?" Ethan asked, and Noah noted his subtlety needed work. "How has he hurt you?"

"There's not enough time to tell you." She shook her head. "He's hurt me too many times to count."

"Why didn't you tell me? Oh Aunt Maggie." Charla hugged her, and Maggie put her head down again. "I'm so sorry."

"I...I dealt with it. There were times I wanted to leave, but I couldn't."

"Does my mom know?"

Maggie shook her head. "No one knows, and if they suspect it, they haven't told me, but they wouldn't suspect it, because Arnold..."

"Mrs. Henderson?"

"He's a master manipulator. He's well liked, funny, strong, driven. Everyone thinks he's a good guy. No one would have guessed." She turned to Charla. "I'm sorry Char."

"Don't be sorry." Charla shook her head with tears in her eyes. "I just...I wish I'd known. I still can't believe..."

"Mrs. Henderson?"

"My husband is away more often than not. Sometimes it's business, he's a salesman, and this time it's hunting. He loves to go hunting." Ethan and Noah exchanged looks. "I looked up those murders after I spoke to you this morning. I didn't go home; I went to my sister's. The man you're looking for, every time there was a murder or attack, Arnold was away."

"How did you figure that out?"

"It wasn't hard. When he's home, I don't go anywhere without him. When he's gone, he's always back when he says he'll be. Says I'm lucky I can depend on him that way." She shook her head. "When he goes away for longer than a day or two, I take a trip to the city. Every time. I always take an opportunity to go to the city library, and sit and read there. I never check any books out, but I mark it down in my calendar when I get to go, so I can look forward to it. I don't actually write it, I just highlight the date in my cell phone." She slid the phone across the table, and Ethan picked it up. "It's all there."

"Mrs. Henderson, where is your husband now?"

She looked at the clock on the wall. "He should be back home any minute."

Ethan stood from the table, and Owen followed him out.

"He's going to know something's wrong when I'm not there." Maggie called to them.

Noah stayed back, "Is there anything else Mrs. Henderson?"

"He went on another trip. Did he do it again? Did he kill another girl?"

"No, but a girl was attacked." He looked at Charla.

"Avery?" Noah nodded and Charla's mouth hung open. "Oh my God."

"She's going to be alright."

"Isn't that proof enough?" Maggie turned to Charla, who stared up at her. "I told him about her and now he's tried to kill her."

"Listen, Mrs. Henderson, can you stay with your sister for a while? You can't go back home now."

"She can." Charla nodded. "I'll call my mom."

"No, let's just tell her when we see her, alright?" Maggie rubbed her nose with the tissue.

"It'll be a while until we can let you go. We'll get it sorted out."

Charla nodded again, and looked at Noah. "Are they going after my uncle?"

"Yes."

"Good."

Chapter 29

"INSPECTOR COTTER'S A HOTTIE. Know if he's single?" Sadie stood by the window, and sniffed at the flowers she had received.

Avery watched her pull her hair up into a pony tail and wished she could have a real shower.

"He dresses well too. He can't be single." Sadie tightened her pony and turned back to Avery.

"I have no idea. It's not like it would have come up." Avery sipped her juice as Sadie shrugged. "He doesn't wear a wedding ring."

Avery wondered if her curiosity had anything to do with the talk she noticed them having in the doorway.

"These flowers are gorgeous."

"I know. It was sweet of Josh to come see me, never mind bring flowers."

"You can't be surprised that Josh came to visit."

"No, I guess not. Thanks for calling him. I guess you filled him in too. He didn't really say much or ask much about what happened."

"Listen," Sadie pushed the food tray away from the bed, toward the door. "I asked my mom, and she said she'd love to have you at our place. You can stay with me for as long as you want. I'm not taking no for an answer."

"I don't know."

"I'm taking you as soon as you're well enough." She took a seat beside Avery. "Listen, I spoke to Inspector Cotter, and we think you should move."

"To where?"

"Anywhere but the apartment."

"You and *Inspector Cotter* really got to brainstorming, didn't you?"

"I just think it's a good time to start fresh."

"You don't get it. I can't have a fresh start. He found me. He's after me now. I can feel it."

"Inspector Cotter said..."

"Whose idea is this? Yours? No, it was probably his right? Well it's my decision."

"Avery, you're being ridiculous. He asked me if I could have you over for a while. I told him I already planned on it."

"You're not just going along with him because you have a thing for him?" Avery asked and Sadie glared at her. "Then why did you ask if he was single?"

"For you!" Sadie stood from her chair, went back to the window, and closed her eyes. "I was asking for you."

Avery watched as she paced back and forth beside the bed to regain her composure, until she turned back to her.

"It's no secret I haven't been the biggest fan of your past boyfriends." She said with her hands up, and Avery rolled her eyes. "But I've supported whoever you date because I want you to be happy. They never seem to make you very happy though. Hell, when's the last time you felt appreciated? Cared for?"

Avery went to open her mouth, but took a breath, and waited.

"It's not about Inspector Cotter, but I had to say something because of the conversation I had with him earlier. He expressed more concern and care for you than I've ever seen a boyfriend of yours do. Coming from someone you barely know, I mean, I think that says something." Sadie took a deep breath. "There. I had to say it, and I hope I didn't hurt you." Sadie looked at her hands. "I'd better go get a tea."

"Sadie, wait." She watched her best friend stand there at the foot of the bed. "You didn't hurt me. I know you've never liked any of the guys I've introduced you to, and I've always wished you got along better, but I didn't know you thought all that."

"Did I say too much?"

"I think about some of those things...sometimes. I've even thought about Noah like that—imagined how it could be. Now though? It's the furthest thing from my mind, okay?"

"I just thought it seemed sweet. The way he looks at you—" Sadie went to sit beside Avery, when they heard a knock on the door, and Sadie went to get it.

When she came back, she was alone.

"I don't know if you want to see her, but Charla Kent would like to see you."

Avery wondered how she found out about the attack, and was sure Noah had somehow told her, unless she had already made the news.

"I guess you can let her in. Could you give us a bit?"

Sadie nodded, and moments later, Charla walked into the room and stopped a few feet away.

"Avery, I'm so sorry." Her face was drained of any colour.

"Why? You didn't do this."

"Can I sit down?"

Avery nodded to the chair and Charla took a seat. Her red lipstick had worn off and her eyes looked tired. She set her purse in her lap and grabbed onto it with white knuckles.

"Please don't feel guilty. It's not your fault. Listen, I appreciate your apology, alright, but I think this whole thing is bigger than us now. Bigger than what happened so many years ago."

Avery noticed tears welling up in Charla's eyes.

"I think it's my uncle, Avery." She shook her head and stared off out the window. "I think my uncle's the killer."

Chapter 30

NOAH ARRIVED AT THE HOUSE to find two unmarked cars parked by the boulevard. He looked down the street, and saw Ethan's car parked discreetly near the corner.

The Henderson's lived on the outskirts of town in a bungalow on a quiet street.

"He wasn't here." Owen met Noah at the door. "I've gotta get to Fiona."

Noah nodded, and patted Owen's back as he swept by him.

"Noah, in here!"

He went past another officer, towards Ethan's voice, into a room at the end of the hall. Ethan stood by the window beside a desk in what Noah assumed was the study.

"The place is clean."

"You think he has another residence?" Noah asked, and scanned the room.

Bookshelves lined one wall, an old couch against the other. The room was clean and the house smelled like lemons.

"If he's our guy, yeah. I think he got tipped off when his wife wasn't home. Maybe he went out to look for her, but if he's our guy, I think he knew something was up."

Noah nodded and looked at the desk. Solid oak, with a laptop, and maps strewn across it. The shelves behind the desk held a clear mixture of romance novels, hunting books, and magazines.

"What's the next step?" Noah picked up a picture frame from the desk.

A picture of the Hendersons when they were younger.

He studied Maggie's face, and although she smiled, he saw a hint that something was wrong. The smile seemed fake.

He wondered if he would have thought that before he learned the truth about their abusive relationship.

"If he comes back, I've got a guy at the neighbour's house on the lookout." A techie slipped past Noah, and sat at the desk in front of the laptop.

"Think he'll be back?" Noah asked.

Ethan shook his head and his eyes scanned the room. "We're doing a search through everything here, and then we're meeting up in Room C. Go on home, and see if you can sleep until then."

"Where's Maggie?" Noah handed the frame to Ethan.

"She's staying with her sister and Charla. I've got a car sitting on their house. Just sent Owen to Fiona's."

"I saw him going when I came. You think he'll go for her? What about Avery?"

"I've got the phone tapped at Charla's. Maggie's been calling Uncle Arnie, but no response. She says it's unlike him. I put out an APB on his truck. Black Silverado. If he's on the road, he won't get far."

"Assuming he did come home."

"Yeah," Ethan strode out of the room and Noah followed out the front door. "I've got Ken searching the computer, specifically for other properties in their name, and we've gotta go back to Charla's to ask Maggie more questions. Get home Noah. I need you sharp, alright?"

Noah nodded and started down the driveway. "Hey, you get my text?"

"Yup. If Avery bit him hard, there'll be a mark."

"It's something."

"Good job Cotter. I'll see you in Room C."

On his way to his car, he realized Ethan didn't answer his question about the security for Avery and Fiona. He was sure Fiona was well looked after, and Avery wouldn't be alone, but he decided to check on her again as soon as he could.

On his way home, he thought about going to the hospital, but it was hard to keep his eyes open. When he got home, he curled up in his bed without changing, and drifted off.

Chapter 31

AVERY TRIED TO PULL herself up in the bed, but the shooting pains from her stomach made her slump back against the pillow.

"I'm just...I'm so sorry." Charla had a dazed look in her eyes, and Avery wondered how hard it must have been to say those words.

"Why would he come after me Charla?"

"I don't know." She shook her head, tears streamed down her cheeks. "My aunt told him what Jolene and I did to you."

"You think that made me his target?"

Charla wiped her cheeks, and chin. "I can't think of another reason why."

"Where is he now?"

Charla cleared her throat, and her voice cracked when she spoke. "I don't know. We don't know. The inspectors are looking for him though. Do you have a safe place to stay?"

Every muscle in Avery's body clenched, as she took everything in.

Charla shook her head again and stood. "I should be home, but I needed to come and see you. I had to tell you because you have to stay safe. There's an officer here... when do you get out?"

Avery looked out the window, where storm clouds brewed. "I'll be fine."

"Seriously, you need to be careful. Until he's caught, you can't be alone, okay? Call me if you need me." Charla set a business card down on the food tray.

"Why would I call you? You don't even know me." Avery looked up at Charla and wondered why she really came.

"I know I got you into this. I owe you, think of it that way. If you ever need me, for whatever reason..."

"Oh, so I call you for help, and you get to feel less guilty about what happened when we were kids?"

"No, that's not it."

"If it's your uncle, you've got just as much to deal with as me, if not *more*. I thought someone was out to get me all these years because of what you and Jolene did. We were kids though. You told the truth just days ago, and for just a moment, I thought I got this fresh start in life. Then I'm attacked, maybe by *your uncle*?" She shook her head in disbelief, "And now the issue I've been dealing with is worse than ever. We each have our own issues to deal with."

Charla stood still while Avery's eyes burned through her. "I'm sorry."

She turned on her heel, and hurried out of the room.

"It's not your fault." Avery whispered.

Chapter 32

Fiona

"IT'S NOT YOUR FAULT." Owen shrugged, and leaned against the door frame with a mug of tea in his hand.

Fiona took a deep breath, and threw her brown hair into a messy bun. "There's got to be something else. Something that could help catch him."

"So this is what you've been thinking," he walked toward her, and sat the mug on her night stand. "Up here torturing yourself. Haven't you suffered enough?"

She grabbed her mug of tea and looked away from him.

"I've got to be of some use. I might be your only shot at finding him."

Owen walked back out of the room, but stopped at the door. "We might have a lead."

"What? Since when?"

He turned back to face her, with a small smile. "You know that girl Avery Hart from the news? Well, she thought her attack might have been related to our guy, and it looks like the mask might have been the one used in his attacks thereafter."

"Why were you holding out on me?"

"You know I shouldn't be telling you everything. You're on a need to know basis."

"You *should* be telling me everything. I can help."

"You need to rest." She could tell he was trying not to look down at her leg, so she smiled.

"Please?"

"Girls from her school tried to play a prank on her the day she was attacked and her injuries were an accident. They used a mask that looks similar to the sketch you drew; we found a picture of it."

"Can I see it?"

"Not right now. The picture belonged to one of the girl's aunts. She thinks her husband is the killer."

Fiona stared at him, wide eyed, and her heart beat faster by the second.

"Is he?"

"We're trying to find out. The timeline matches so far, but we can't find him so..."

"So that's why you're here. To watch out for me."

"It's just my shift. Anyway, it's looking good. No promises or anything, but when we find him, we'll bring him in. Feel any better?"

"I feel like that's a lot to take in."

"Listen, I'll be downstairs, so just ring if you need me. Don't tell anyone I told you anything alright?"

"That's fine, but can you talk to Inspector Ascott? Let him know I could help to identify him?"

Owen walked backwards out the door. "I'll do my best. We don't expect anything from you, help or otherwise, alright?"

When he left, she soaked in all the information he'd given her, and by the time she took a sip of her tea it was cold. She unscrewed the lid from the small container by her bedside, popped a pill into her mouth, and swallowed.

She could hear Owen in her living room, watching the news with the volume just low enough so she could only make out some of the words. She knew it was a story about Wendy O'Connor.

Fiona missed her yoga, and her pilates. She missed being able to walk on her own and drive whenever she wanted.

She did not miss her daily jog in Birch Falls Park.

Fiona placed her mug on the nightstand and rested against her pillows. She watched the sunset, and the glow filled her teary eyes until they burned, but she kept them open. Since her attack on that path, she felt like she appreciated all the little things in life more. Enjoyed them more, not only for herself, but for Tamara Sweeten and Wendy O'Connor.

Chapter 33

NOAH CHECKED HIS WATCH on the way to Room C, and hoped the meeting wrapped up in time to get to the bar before it closed. Beelson hadn't given him a time, so he was taking a chance regardless of when he got to Jerry D's.

"Noah, good, just shut the door." Ethan stood at the dry erase board with a timeline of facts. The techie from the Henderson's home stood at the table beside a woman he didn't recognize.

Her chestnut brown hair sat in loose curls around her shoulders. Her ankles were crossed neatly under the table, with dark red heels, and Noah tried not to stare at her long legs hidden under her pencil skirt.

"This is Ken, our tech expert," Ethan didn't turn around from the board, and Ken nodded his shaved head at Noah, "and Special Inspector January Stevens. She's been going through the Henderson's belongings, trying to find anything significant."

Noah nodded and shook their hands.

"This is Inspector Noah Cotter. I've just brought him in on the case. I've filled them in on the previous work on the Hart case, with you and Jacoby."

"Have I missed anything?" Noah stood at the table and glanced around the room.

January shook her head, and Ken looked to Ethan. Room C reminded Noah of a board room, with water and coffee in the middle of the table, and ten leather chairs that saw around it.

"Just getting started." Ethan finished writing something, and they both sat down. "Ken, what've you got for us?"

Ken hit a few buttons on his keyboard with his chewed down finger nails.

"The Uncle, Arnie rarely uses the laptop. It's primarily used by Aunt Maggie. The only searches I've found worth any notice were business trips that have all checked out. When he was on business, his company confirms it. When he was hunting, according to Aunt Maggie, it lines up with our vic's timeline."

Noah pursed his lips at Ken's reference of their names. They were the family names Charla called them, and he wondered if there was significance to them for Ken.

"What does he do for work?" Noah poured himself a glass of water and wondered if he should sit down with them.

"He's a salesman. Travels around as a representative for prescription eyewear." Ken pulled out a sheet of paper from his file. "However, he was not at any of these job sites when Tamara Sweeten, Fiona Wolfe, Wendy O'Connor or Avery Hart were attacked."

"So where was he? Hunting?" Ethan asked.

"That's what it says in Aunt Maggie's phone." Ken nodded to January.

When she spoke her voice was calm and calculated. "A murder or attack was committed on each of the days Maggie Henderson has marked down that Arnold was away. She never specifies if it was business or pleasure, but since we know it wasn't business..."

"January, what else did you find?" Ethan crossed his arms.

She stood from the table, and lifted the lid off the banker's box in front of her.

"Everything in this box has told me something about Maggie, Arnold, and the two as a couple. These pictures," She took out two frames, as well as several loose photos, and spread them on the table, "are what interest me most."

Ethan pulled one in front of him. "Their wedding day?"

"Mhmm, they've been married for thirteen years, together for twenty-four."

"What's this one?" Ken asked, and held it up.

"A picture of one of the themed parties they were famous for."

Noah pushed around several pictures on the table.

"And this one," She picked up another photo, "is of the Henderson couple on their honeymoon."

"Am I missing something?" Ken pushed his photo away.

"There are only a few photos of the Hendersons even touching. No hand holding, no kissing, no brushing of body parts. They're disconnected. What kind of married couple doesn't touch each other?"

"Most that I know." Ethan smirked, and Ken chuckled. "So their relationship was distant. Doesn't make him a killer. Give me more."

"They didn't get married until they were together for over ten years. That rarely happens, and when it does, it's usually high school sweethearts. They met after high school though, when they were both twenty."

"So what does that mean?" Ethan shrugged, "Other than a case of cold feet and commitment issues?"

"It supports the abuse theory, but I think there's something else going on here. I just can't figure it out." January handed a photo to Ethan. "Then, there's this. You know what kind of gun that is?"

"A Ruger No. 1 Varminter K1-V-BBZ. Fits the type that could have shot our vics. Can't know for sure 'til we get it though. It wasn't at the house."

The men pushed through the photos and Noah watched January search through the banker's box.

"Ken? Have you had contact with Charla Kent?" Noah asked.

"I just got off the phone with her. Ethan asked Jan to set up another appointment with her, but I guess she was too busy..."

January rolled her eyes.

"Why do you ask?" Ethan said.

"You call them Uncle Arnie and Aunt Maggie."

Ken furrowed his brow, and looked to Ethan. "You call them that too."

Ethan let out a deep breath. "You're not in trouble Ken, just answer the damn question."

"Well," Ken started to play with his pen, "I don't know. I guess she kept saying their names like that, so I do too."

"She's still calling him Uncle Arnie? After everything she knows?" January asked.

"Yeah." Ken dropped the pen.

"I guess it could just be she's used to calling him that?" Ethan shrugged, and studied the photo with the gun again.

January sat down and Ethan handed the photo to Noah. He saw a group of three men standing together with their hunting gear in front of a cottage or cabin. He held the photo closer, and squinted.

Darrel Beelson.

"Ethan. I know this guy."

"Uncle-- I mean Arnold Henderson?"

"No," Noah pointed to Darrel. "Him. He's the guy I went to talk to at the funeral. He was a friend of my drowning vic."

"Your vic knew Arnold Henderson? Are you sure?" Ethan leaned over the picture.

"Yeah, and I bet I know who the guy in the middle is. I'll tell you on the way." Noah jumped out of his seat, and headed for the door, without waiting for Ethan to follow.

He heard footsteps behind him as he reached the end of the hall.

"Wait up, where are we going?"

"Jerry D's."

Chapter 34

Fiona

"HEY FIONA, I'M LEAVING EARLY, but Ralph just got here." Owen called up the stairs.

"Okay, see you later!"

She heard her front door shut a moment later, opened her laptop, and began to read.

Avery Hart was attacked in her apartment this past Saturday in the early hours of the morning. There is reason to believe there may be a connection with the masked serial killer, as just days ago, Avery called in to Channel 12 news, and claimed she may have been attacked by the serial killer ten years ago. After her initial statement, we were not able to follow up for any comments, but we have news that she is being released from the hospital as early as today.

Why didn't Owen tell me, she wondered, as she clicked on a site from her recent browsing history. Wendy O'Connor's memorial site.

She checked Tamara Sweeten's page often, and found most of the grizzly details of each of their murders on news sites online.

She knew the same things would have happened to her had help not arrived in time.

They would have found her body along the path.

Carved.

Fiona read each of the articles carefully, trying to get to know the girls, and to find any similarities she could between them.

Tamara was black, a college student, and had a job in her local mall doing part-time retail work. She could find nothing in common with her yet, but she searched every day. Wendy was white, with dark hair like Fiona's, but those were the only features they had in common. Wendy was a receptionist at a car dealership, and was engaged. Fiona was the oldest target at twenty-eight, but not by much, and she was the most established in her career of the three.

The thing all three had in common was jogging or running. The fact that they were all attacked on a path in their respective towns made Fiona lean toward the possibility that it was a crime of opportunity.

She entered Avery Hart's name into her Google search engine, along with Crown River. She found a few news articles on the first page, which related to her attack, and then something related to a college website that she clicked.

A photography course, she thought, that Avery teaches. She clicked on her Facebook page, and found the first photo she had seen. Light blonde hair, blue eyes. Fiona studied her face for a while, closed the laptop, and sighed.

Where do you fit in, Avery?

She heard the front door slam shut.

"Ralph, you in here?"

"Yep, what's up Fiona?"

"Would you help me down the stairs?"

She heard him march up to her room, and when he reached her door, she smiled.

"I can bring you whatever you need."

"I just want a change of scenery, alright? Maybe do some yoga in the living room."

"You? Do yoga? Sorry, but doesn't that involve twisting yourself around?"

"It's just meditating really," She smiled wide, "and stretching. It'll be good for me."

"Alright. Sure." Ralph grabbed her crutches, as she swung out of the bed, and walked beside her down the hallway. "Careful."

The stairs seemed daunting, and before Fiona could attempt them, Ralph picked her up.

"Ralph!"

"What?" He smiled, as he walked down the stairs carefully. "If *dreamy Officer Owen* can do it, so can I. Hold on."

When they reached the bottom, she used the banister to steady herself, and Ralph raced back up the stairs to grab her crutches.

"Do you mind leaving me for a bit? Go out front, or down to the basement? I like to do my meditation alone." She batted her eye lashes at him.

Ralph shrugged, and felt his pocket. Fiona knew he was a smoker, and it probably killed him to wait out the better part of a shift without one.

"Back in fifteen."

When he was gone, she eased her way to the living room, and set the crutches against the couch. She eased herself down on it, and relaxed for a moment, before she brought her hands by each side of her legs, and pushed herself off the seat, held up by her arms.

She dipped down, pushed herself back up, and took a deep breath.

Up and down.

She closed her eyes, and pictured a field in Ireland, where her parents were from. Green as far as the eye could see and a calm sky above.

Up and down.

She needed to remain focused.

Up and down.

Keep motivated.

Up.

Strong

And down.

To walk on her own again.

And soon.

Chapter 35

"DOESN'T LOOK TOO BUSY." Ethan checked his cell phone again. "Owen should be here soon."
Noah watched a few smokers out front checking out two well dressed women as they walked by.

Noah turned to Ethan. "What's the plan?"

"I thought you had a plan."

Noah studied the photo and slipped it onto the dashboard.

"Well, the plan is to confront Beelson about this photo, and prove a connection between him, Hornby, and Henderson. We can find out where Arnold Henderson is, and if they don't know, they might know something else. I thought you called Owen to help bring them in for questioning?"

Ethan craned his neck to see which car had entered the lot. "I don't know if interrogating them is the best way to get information. I understand you're eager and it's a great lead, but I've had experience with this kind of thing, alright?"

"Okay…"

"I was thinking maybe you could go in and kinda feel them out first."

Noah looked at the building, and back to Ethan. "What?"

"You could talk to them about old times with their dead friend Hornby, who they've all come to celebrate and remember. Make them think it's just about finding his killer. Act buddy-buddy with them."

"You think that's a good idea? I'm still an outsider. What if they don't want to talk to me?"

"Beelson will right? He's the one who invited you. You're in Noah."

"Alright." Noah looked around the lot. "And when Owen comes?"

"We only use him if we need him. I send him in, and he'll be watching if you need any help. If you're able to stay friendly, do. Nothing's gotten in the news about Arnold Henderson yet, but we don't have much time. Hornby knew him, and Beelson definitely does. Maybe Henderson has something to do with Hornby's drowning."

Noah nodded. "I think he found out that Arnold Henderson was killing people. It's the most logical explanation I can think of for now."

Ethan shrugged. "Who knows, but we've gotta consider it. You need to get in there."

Noah opened the car door. "Any advice?"

"Just try to get them to co-operate peacefully." Ethan added, before Noah was out.

Noah entered the bar, and spotted the group immediately. They sat in a round booth, far from the door, with somber faces.

Beelson noticed him right away, and Noah wondered if he had been expecting him, when he waved him over.

"Boys, this is Inspector..."

"Cotter. I'm sorry for your loss." Beelson nodded once, and a man he didn't recognize took a swig of his drink.

"This is Bob Pope, the one who owns the cottage we all go up to, the one I told you about. This is Scott Parker. Another friend of ours." Beelson scooted over in the booth and Noah sat beside him.

"Not sure if Darrel told you about our conversation." Noah said.

"Just that you're tryin'a find out who did it." Bob burped, and scratched his beard. "I'll tell you the same thing Darrel did. Nobody'd wanna kill Grant Hornby."

"I'll be honest. When Darrel filled me in on how you know each other, and your hunting trips, it choked me up. You've been friends for a while now, and to have something happen like this, I mean, you've gotta be asking yourselves why."

Bob looked at Darrel. "Just don't make sense."

Noah shook his head. "And it's my job to try to make sense of it. To try to bring justice to this horrible act. From what I've heard, Grant Hornby was a great guy, and it doesn't make sense."

"He *was* great." Scott echoed.

"Do anything for ya," Darrel nodded, "shirt off his back kinda guy. That's what I told Noah here."

"If it was random, I mean," Bob picked up his pint glass, "that's just about the worst thing. How do you catch the guy if it was random?"

"You don't." Scott put his drink down. "You haven't got any suspects, have you? Why'd you come if you don't have anything to tell us?"

"Listen, I didn't want to interrupt your night and paying respect to your friend. When Darrel told me I could come, I figured you'd want to help catch the bastard. I didn't want to ruin your night though," Noah went to stand, but Darrel grabbed his sleeve, and pulled him back down.

Scott shook his head. "No, we'll help however we can."

"We owe it to Grant." Bob raised his glass, and they all took a drink.

"You mind if I record it?" Noah asked, and pulled out his phone.

Darrel stared at the phone for a moment, but Bob shook his head. "Just do whatever you can. If we help catch the guy, God, we could give Jen some closure."

"She deserves it." Scott nodded, as Noah pressed record.

"I spoke with Mrs. Hornby before."

"She's a mess." Darrel shook his head. "Naturally."

"What'd she have to say?" Bob asked.

"Same as you all. Didn't think she could help. I want to do the best job I can here boys. Please state your names, and your consent to this taping." They all did. "Darrel, do you know of anyone who had issues with Grant Hornby?"

"No sir. Everybody loved him."

Bob and Scott answered the same.

"Do you know of anyone who would stand to profit from his death?"

Scott looked to the others. "Just Jen, but she's got her own money. Her family's stinkin' rich."

Bob gave Scott a look, and he stopped. "It wasn't her."

"When you all went up to Bob's cabin to go hunting, who all went?"

Darrel looked to the others. "There's us three, Grant, sometimes Bob's friend Arnie, and what was that guy's name again Scott? That friend of yours you brought up that summer?"

"Ray."

"Right, and that's it. We'd all go hunting, but like I told ya, Grant wasn't much for it."

Bob laughed. "He'd always pretend to shoot at an animal, but he'd scare em' off. Bastard."

They all burst out laughing, and Noah shared a genuine smile with them.

"Did he get along with Arnie and Ray? Last names?"

"God, I don't even know Ray's last name." Scott kept laughing long after the rest stopped. "Guy's a weirdo and we don't talk anymore."

Bob took a sip of his drink. "Henderson. Arnie Henderson. He got along fine with Grant. Now he was pissed when Grant scared away the prey, but that was it. After that, he'd always ask if Grant would be coming up, and when he was, Arnie just wouldn't show. No issue there."

"Ray only came the one time. Don't even know if Grant was there." Scott finished the beer, and refilled his glass from the pitcher. "Hell, I wasn't up as often as these boys."

"Back to this Arnie guy," Noah said, "he come out often?"

"Like I said, as long as Grant couldn't make it, he was there. Half the time it was one, other half the other." Bob burped again and Noah watched his eyes glaze. It gave him an idea.

"I see." Noah raised his hand, and pointed to the pitcher, when the bartender looked their way.

"Thanks man." Darrel smiled and clapped him on the back. Same glazed look.

"No problem. So did any of you ever hunt anywhere else?"

"Bob and I hunted up at another friend's cottage one time." Bob nodded, and Darrel continued, "When Arnie was up at Bob's with us, Grant never hunted somewhere else. He'd never hunt without us, but Arnie did on his own."

Noah took a sip of his drink. "Know where that'd be?"

"North of our usual hunting grounds by my cottage. That's for sure." Bob looked at the empty pitcher, and then over to the bartender who was pouring them another.

"Anyone know where?"

"Naw, he never said specifics." Bob grabbed a few beer nuts and shoved them in his mouth.

"He'd always tell us about his trips without us. Always claimed he'd bagged lots, and we figured he was lying, but then he never told us where. We think he was holding out on us. Keeping the more populated areas to himself." Darrel shrugged.

"When was the last time you saw Arnie?" Noah asked as the bartender brought them their drinks, and from the corner of his eye, he saw Owen enter the bar. He took a seat on a bar stool, and didn't make eye contact. "Maybe I should speak to him."

"Listen," Bob said, pouring himself a tall drink, with lots of head, "it's been a while. Like we said, they were never around each other."

"They were both there last month at the BBQ, the one they brought their wives to." Scott said, greedily eyeing the pitcher. "They're the only ones shacked up. Bob, Darrel and I here are bachelors."

"So a recent barbeque. Was Grant acting differently then? He get into any fights?"

Scott started laughing and slapped his hand on the table, and the other patrons, including Owen, turned to them.

Darrel shot a look at Scott. "Nothing happened, so no big deal."

Noah continued to stare at Scott. "Where was the BBQ?"

"Arnie and Maggie's." Bob smiled. "Maggie makes the best potato salad."

"No way," Scott shook his head. "Jen does."

"I've gotta take a piss." Darrel started to slide out of the booth before Noah even moved, and Noah nodded to him.

He caught Owen's nod to the bartender out of the corner of his eye, and watched Owen slide a bill down for his drink and leave.

"So nothing unusual happened at the barbeque?"

"Like we just told you. *No*." Bob wiped his mouth with his hand. "Listen buddy, we came to remember Hornby, not investigate his death alright? That's your job."

"I think we're done here." Noah looked at his phone. "Thank you for your time."

Scott nodded, and Bob shook his head. "Thanks for the drinks."

When Noah got to the parking lot, he found Owen standing outside waiting for him.

"Hey man, wait here alright?"

Noah knew the topic of the barbeque made Beelson act differently than the rest of the group, but he couldn't say how. When they started talking about the barbeque, Noah noticed a change in his demeanor, and decided to play a hunch.

Owen nodded, and they leaned back against the front of the building.

A few minutes later, Darrel walked out, with a smoke in his hand.

"Hey, I thought you left?" He said, and when he saw Owen, his forehead wrinkled.

"You wanna tell me what you know, or should we go downtown?" Noah asked.

Darrel looked between them, lit his cigar, and shifted his weight from foot to foot.

He took a few puffs, and shook his head. "I swear I didn't hurt him. Let's get that outta the way first."

"Don't waste my time." Noah said.

"The barbeque last month? The one where everyone brought their wives? I caught Jen Hornby getting it on with Arnie in the hallway."

Noah looked to Owen, who squinted at Darrel. "Okay."

"They were finishing up, or whatever, and then he whispered something to her. She shakes her head and she slips him a note. Course, she had to go an' do that." Darrel puffed his cigar again, and shook his head. "I wasn't gunna tell Grant, cause there would be no proof, and it'd be their word against mine, but then when I saw that letter, I knew I had to tell him."

"What happened next?"

"She was cryin' I think, so she went to the bathroom, and Arnie took the note with him, down to the basement. I went outside, and found Grant, and I told him." Darrel ran his fingers through his hair. "He was my best friend. I told him what I saw, and about the letter. He just stood there, watching the house, but then when she came out, and then he came out...he looked at me, and told me to distract Arnie. I tried to stop him, but nobody could've." Darrel choked on a chuckle.

"What's funny?"

"If you were there, you'da thought he was going after Arnie, to hit him or something, but I knew him better."

"That why Scott was laughing?"

Darrel nodded. "He was going to find that note. I did what he said, and kept Arnie busy. When he came back out, he acted like nothing was wrong. He walked right over to Jen and *kissed her*. I didn't know what to make of it. Arnie watched them too, but he didn't do anything either."

"Then what happened?"

"Nothing, that's it. Grant never said anything to me about it, and nobody else knew anything."

Owen cleared his throat. "He was your best friend, and you never spoke about it again?"

Darrel shrugged. "We don't talk about that shit. Come on. It was none of my business. Maybe they had one of those open marriages? Shoulda kept my mouth shut in the first place."

"Why didn't you tell me this before?"

Darrel rolled his eyes. "No one was supposed to know, and nothing ever came from it."

"Grant found out his wife was cheating on him, and he dies a month later. You didn't think that was important?" Noah crossed his arms. "I don't buy it."

"I didn't want to get involved. I shouldn't have told him."

"Problem is," Owen clapped his hand on Darrel's back, "now we know you're a liar."

"I swear I didn't kill Grant. I've told the truth about everything. I thought Jen was still seeing Arnie, but she came onto me when I came to pay my respects. I'm not a good friend, but I'm not a killer either."

"Listen to me Darrel," Noah stepped close, "where does Arnold Henderson go hunting?"

"I don't know. I swear. I don't think he killed him though, I mean, nothing ever came from it. They barely knew each other, and Grant seemed over whatever happened with Jen and Arnie."

"Owen, take him."

Owen nodded, cuffed Darrel Beelson, and walked him towards Ethan's car.

"I'm telling you, I told you everything I know now."

They both ignored him, and slipped him into the back seat, as Ethan got out.

"Arnold was having an affair with my murder vic's wife, Jennifer Hornby."

Ethan walked to the front of the car to meet them. "How'd you find out?"

They all looked in the car, where Darrel Beelson sat staring back at them.

"You think Arnold caught him? Maybe he found something related to the murders? The mask?"

"Nope, he was outside with Darrel the whole time. He might have realized things had been moved though, or maybe someone else saw Grant going downstairs. Arnold might have been paranoid, but I think he killed Grant Hornby because he at least *thought* he knew."

"About the affair or him being a serial killer?" Owen asked.

"Either." Noah shrugged, and looked back to Darrel. "Both? We'll get a statement from him, but he says he doesn't know where Arnold is."

"Alright. I'll meet you back at the department. It's time to make a statement to the press."

Chapter 36

AFTER RALPH BROUGHT HER UP to her room, Fiona went back online, and checked her email.

Another from her mom and dad, begging her to move back to Ireland with them. If they only knew, she thought, and was thankful they were in the dark about her attack. Her ex fiancé, Sam, had been her emergency contact the hospital used when she arrived in the ambulance.

The next email was from Jill, asking when she could come by. She missed going to yoga with her, and she wanted to bring her a care package whenever the police would allow it. Fiona wanted to tell her to come over, but the truth was, the police hadn't banned her, or Sam, or anyone from visiting.

She had.

The last email was from Sam.

How are you feeling? Anything I can do?

Their break up was recent, and with muddled feelings, she didn't blame him for wanting to be there for her. She wished she had someone close to look after her, instead of these officers she barely knew, but this was safer. She shut her laptop, and pushed it beside her on the bed.

She lifted her good leg in the air as far as she could, and slowly set it down. Without moving her wounded leg, she let the muscles clench and relax with the motion of the other. It felt weird, but she kept going, eventually lifting her wounded leg slightly, and then setting it down to raise the other. She continued until beads of sweat fell from her forehead, and then she relaxed.

When she could breathe normally, she sat up and grabbed her crutches. She hobbled to the bathroom, and turned on her shower.

It was her third time showering with crutches, and she couldn't get used to it.

The hot water relaxed her aching muscles, and she finally felt clean, when she heard a knock on the door.

"Yeah?" She shouted, and turned the water off.

"It's just me,"

Ralph.

"Listen, Inspector Ascott wants you down at the department tomorrow morning. You feel up to it, or would you rather he came here?"

"I can go." She shouted louder than before. "Thanks, Ralph!"

"Okay, sorry for interrupting."

She listened to the footsteps fade on the other side of the door, and turned the hot water she craved back on.

Maybe they've made progress.

She let the water wash away her worries.

Maybe they need my help.

She started singing the first song that came to her mind.

Maybe it's over.

Chapter 37

"I HEAR MY PICTURES HELPED." January smiled as Noah and Owen entered Room C.

Noah thought he saw a twinkle in her eye, and couldn't help but smile. Ken sat at the table in a black polo shirt, and typed away on his laptop, seemingly unaware of their arrival.

"Well, *one* did at least." Ken said.

Owen and January bumped knuckles and smiled at each other.

"Whoa, which of you smokes cheap cigars?" The smile faded from her face, and she glanced at Owen who shook his head.

"That smell is courtesy of Darrel Beelson." Noah pulled out a chair, "So was the new info we just got. We're going to fill the whole department in, put out a province wide search for him. I guess Ethan already told you guys everything. Where's Ethan?"

"Dealing with Darrel." January smiled at Owen. "How's Fiona doing?"

"She's doing alright. Ethan's bringing her in tomorrow."

Noah nodded. "Yeah, he wants to see if she can tell us anything more about Arnold, and form some type of protection plan for them."

"Them?" Ken asked.

Ethan strode into the room and slammed the door behind him.

"Darrel's lawyered up. He says he doesn't know anything else, and I doubt he does." Ethan went to the dry erase board, and started to write. "Doesn't know where Arnold would be, and was shocked to hear we consider him a suspect. He's clueless."

Noah read the board aloud. "Q Darrel Beelson, no leads."

"So that's where we're at folks. We talk to Avery and Fiona together tomorrow, but before that, we've gotta give the department a profile for Arnold. What do we have?"

"Here's the most recent picture." January held it up. "I've made hundreds of copies to hand out. Six foot one, Caucasian male, brown, thinning hair."

Ken looked up from his laptop for the first time and didn't miss a beat from where January left off. "Uses a rifle to shoot his victims, and a hunting knife to carve them up. Has at least twenty years of hunting experience and is known to frequent these woods." Ken set a stack of papers down on the desk. "Hunts in Cedar Ridge, but is thought to hunt in more northern regions, circled here, and possible regions north of there."

"His victims are female," Ethan clipped photos of the women on the timeline, "between the ages of twenty and twenty-eight, except for Grant Hornby. He's the only vic who was drowned, likely on purpose to avoid using our killer's method of operation so we wouldn't link the two."

"Tamara Sweeten," January said.

Ethan stood beside her picture. "The first vic was shot and stabbed at Crown River Park, body found near initial contact. The second, Fiona Wolfe, was shot on her jogging path in Birch Falls, but survived when a local man walking his dogs interrupted the killer. Around the same time, Grant Hornby is found drowned in the Crown River. Third victim, Wendy O'Connor. Shot in Birch Falls Park. Stabbed to death, and body found where initial contact was made."

"Avery Hart." January said as Ethan clipped her photo up.

Noah stared at her picture, and wished it wasn't up with the others.

"Went to the media about her past, and the possible connection to our masked killer, attacked in her apartment, cut ten times and left alive. What else do we know?"

Ken looked down at his laptop, and typed quickly. "Medical Examiner reports Tamara, Wendy, and Fiona were all shot with the same gun, all three in the leg. Tamara and Wendy's bullets both hit arteries, and they were both sliced up afterward. Avery was cut with the same hunting knife, however Avery's cuts were far less severe. It took Tamara an hour and a half to die after she was shot and two hours for Wendy. The hunting knife was the final cause of death in both instances.

Tamara and Wendy's bodies were moved back after time of death to their primary locations where they were first attacked. Still not aware of their secondary murder locations."

"Wait," Noah said, "they were moved?"

Ken nodded. "He keeps them for short amounts of time, not enough blood at the parks; no one knew they were missing until their bodies were found there with minimal blood surrounding them at the scene."

"What does this all tell us?" Ethan asked.

"Secondary murder location is close. Less than a few hours away from initial contact." Ken said.

"Likely crimes of opportunity." Noah interjected, and they all looked at him. "Victims unrelated."

January turned to the group. "He likes to torture them before he kills them, and unlike real hunters, he likes them to suffer after they've been shot."

The room went quiet.

"What are we hoping to learn from Fiona and Avery?" Owen asked and his voice startled Noah.

Ethan took a seat at the head of the table. "I'm hoping they'll be able to jog each other's memory. One of them will remember something they didn't before, or they'll be able to tell us more if we give them some more information. We also need to figure out what we are doing for them regarding security."

"Okay, what else?" January asked.

"We need motive." Ethan drummed the dry erase marker on the table, "and what made him start killing now?"

"One thing," Noah stood from his seat, "both Avery and Fiona were maimed using the usual tactics, but one was shot, while the other was cut. He meant to leave Avery alive, but certainly not Fiona. She was saved by a man with dogs. Avery was also saved by a man with a dog."

"Huh," January put her hands on her hips. "I didn't think it was the same person..."

"They weren't." Ken clicked his keyboard, and read, "Joshua Carter, thirty-six, found Avery Hart in the Crown River ten years ago. Steve Baxter, forty-nine, found Fiona on the Birch Falls pathway."

"Well, it's worth keeping in mind." January smiled at Noah and nodded. "I've got everyone coming in less than an hour to give a briefing. Until then, I was hoping we could look for some patterns to help predict his actions. Prevent this from happening to anyone else."

"We have to know why before we discover anything else." Ethan said, before Noah grabbed the marker from his hand, and went to the board where the map hung.

"If Arnold's our guy, he started off here, in Crown River, with Tamara." He drew a circle, and wrote her name. "Here is Fiona, just north of Tamara, at the north edge of Birch Falls. Then there's Grant." He drew an X beside his name. "He was drowned in Crown River. I'd say there was symbolism behind the location, but his wife confirmed he jogs that path every morning, so we shouldn't use him for the pattern. Next, Wendy. Then Avery here in Crown River." He circled the last place and wrote her name.

"So he's staying within the two towns." Ethan stood in front on the board, "Arnold Henderson lives here, twenty minutes North East of Fiona."

"Might change his pattern now that he's been found out. If he continues though, he'll be headed to Cedar Ridge." Noah circled the town just north of Birch Falls. "If not, could be anywhere."

January grabbed a ruler, and joined Noah at the board. "Let's look at the border between Birch Falls and Crown River. Any abandoned buildings, or property there? If he's been bringing the victims back, and dumping them on the same night, it can't be further than..."She placed the ruler at the midpoint, and made a mark, drawing a circle around the surrounding towns and cities.

"Either this guy is old school," Ken said looking up at the board, "or he's got a laptop of his own that his wife didn't know about, because there is nothing on his. It's clean."

"He killed Tamara on the night of their barbeque." Noah looked to Owen and Ethan. "That's the day he was caught by Darrel fooling around with Jen Hornby. She gave him a letter. Her husband found out about the affair that day too. Maybe she broke up with him?"

They all stared at him and he stood up straight. "I think *that* was his trigger."

Ethan nodded. "Makes sense, but why kill?"

"Because ever since Maggie told him about what Charla had done in the woods, he'd wanted to do the same thing. He's abusive. He likes the control. Maybe Jen Hornby breaking up with him made him lose the control he'd always had with her, and of course Maggie."

January nodded. "That's good, but it happened ten years ago."

"I think he thought about Avery's attack all this time. Do you remember how Maggie told us about it? She said he was enthralled with the story. That's why he got the mask. The rejection from Jennifer Hornby triggered his attack on Tamara."

"Noah's right," Ethan nodded, "let's run with this."

"So he's turned down by the woman he loved? Maybe that's too strong, maybe it was just sexual, but he was embarrassed. He was frustrated. Angry." January looked at the board, "Ready to lash out."

"Ready to kill." Noah said.

January looked at him and the twinkle in her eyes was back.

"Okay, let's give the profile, and get the info out." Ethan stood up. "We keep the motive to ourselves, and we meet back here tomorrow at noon after Noah and I talk to the girls."

Ethan put his fist in front of Noah's and Noah bumped his.

I'm in.

"Let's go get him."

Chapter 38

FIONA WOKE TO A crashing sound. She grabbed at the dark for her crutches, and when she found them, she hobbled slowly to the door.

"Don't move!" Ralph yelled, and Fiona heard something break.

She hobbled to the top of the stairs, and when the lights came on, she saw Sam standing at the bottom of the stair case with his hands up.

"Ralph, it's alright. I know him."

Sam turned to look up at her, with his hands still raised in the air.

"Sam, what are you doing?"

"I wanted to see you, and I still had your key, so..."

"Fine." She turned back down the hall, and heard Ralph tell him he had better follow.

By the time she sat back down on her bed, Sam stood in the doorway.

"Fee, what's going on?"

"I told you, I can't have visitors. It isn't safe."

"Why haven't you called me then? Or emailed me back? Am I not even worth an email?" He stood tall in the doorway.

She rolled her eyes. "Don't get all dramatic."

"You're back on your feet so to speak."

"Yeah. You're not surprised are you?"

He shook his head and grinned. "You smell good."

"Sam. Stop."

He swayed through the doorframe, and back out again. "I'm worried."

"I'm not for you to worry about." She looked down into her lap.

"Doesn't stop me from worrying."

"Sam," She looked up at him, and forced herself to speak, "we're done. We're over. What we had is in the past. You can't do this."

He stood still in the doorway, and shadows from the light in the hall made it difficult to see his expression.

"Are you okay?"

"I'm fine."

"Are you?"

"I'm fine," she raised her voice. "Just stop it Sam."

"Everything okay up there?" Ralph yelled.

Sam leaned away from the door, still holding the frame. She saw his face, and she wished she'd looked away. His eyes were glazed, and his lips pressed together.

"I guess it is." He swayed out of the doorway, and when he left her vision, it felt like he'd never been there at all. She didn't hear him going down the stairs, or the front door open and shut.

All she could hear was her heart banging in her ears, and she lay back down on her bed, and cried into her pillow.

Chapter 39

"WHEN DO YOU THINK Ethan will bring Aunt Maggie in again?" Owen poured his beer into the pint glass.

"You've been talking to Ken, huh? Soon. I'll bring it up if he doesn't. She knows more than she thinks she does. The wife always knows…"

"That's what you think. Missy doesn't know I come here."

Noah shrugged. "Maybe she does."

"I feel guilty for it. Didn't think you'd want to come along. Figured you'd had enough bar time for the night."

"Yeah, well," Noah drank his beer, "I was expecting some kind of info, but a break through like that?"

"You've brought a lot to this case. Ethan likes you. Ethan doesn't like people so easily."

"Call it beginners luck, 'cause I feel like I'm winging this."

"Maybe you're a natural then. I always wondered when we'd get to work together. Didn't think it would be this soon."

Noah watched the last patrons leave the bar.

"I never thought I'd be working here. After school, I thought you'd stick around in Toronto teaching. When you married Missy, I knew you were a goner."

Owen laughed, "A goner?"

"Yeah, I knew you'd be moving out to the 'burbs. Have a couple kids."

Noah had secretly thought it was about time for his friend to settle down, but teasing him about his happiness had become their *thing*. On the other hand, he thought, Owen didn't start getting grays until after he got married.

"What's wrong with that?"

"Nothing," Noah smiled, "I just didn't count on being moved out here myself."

"Come on, top of your class? You knew you'd climb the ranks."

"Maybe, but out here? If it hadn't been for the promotion, you'd never catch me moving to Crown River. My dad's still pissed."

"I didn't know he had an issue with it."

Noah looked down at his beer. "It's not a big deal or anything, but since my mom passed, I think we relied on each other a lot. Then when Lisa finally moved in, I thought that I could start out on my own.

Owen, I kid you not, he didn't even want me to move out after I got my job first job."

Owen raised his brows. "Really?"

"So, I mean, it was going to be difficult no matter when I moved out, but to move a couple hours away?"

"So what's the deal? You still talk?"

"Yeah, pretty often. He just wants to keep the family he has left together. Lisa's got a daughter, so now she's technically my step-sister, and she's got a husband and baby of her own. The whole family got together a lot. Now I'm just back for birthdays."

"You could go back more often if you wanted."

"Yeah." Noah turned his glass around in his hands.

"You gotta start your own thing anyway buddy."

"Exactly."

"Well, I'm glad you're here man." Owen raised his glass, and they clinked them together. "Looks like he's waitin' on us again." He pointed to the bartender.

"Listen, I'll see ya tomorrow."

Owen stood from the table. "I got this one buddy."

"Thanks man." Noah punched his arm, and grabbed his coat. "Hey by the way, what exactly did Ethan say about me?"

"Nothing. I can just tell he likes you."

"How?"

"You're still on the case."

Chapter 40

WHEN FIONA HOBBLED OUT of her home for the first time in over a week, she was greeted by Owen and Ralph.

"How you feeling today?" Owen asked, and stepped aside to make room, as she hobbled beside him.

"Glad to finally be out." Her eyes squinted against the sun.

Ralph walked ahead of them, toward a truck.

"We're going in that?"

"I'm sorry; this is going to be a little difficult to maneuver." Owen opened the passenger door to the truck for her.

"Oh," She looked up at Ralph in the driver's seat. "No big deal."

She leaned her crutches against the truck, and hoisted herself up on her seat. She was glad she'd been working on her upper body strength.

"All set?" Owen asked, as he shoved her crutches in the back.

Ralph nodded. "See you there."

They followed Owen in the unmarked car, and when he turned right out of her subdivision, they went left. She noticed another car turn left behind them.

"Did you bring any pain meds?"

"Yeah. I didn't know how long we'd be out, so I thought better safe than sorry."

"Good. I know you think you're ready to be out and about, but we'll see."

Ralph turned onto the main road, and headed north, away from the police department.

"Listen, if you don't want to talk about it, I understand, but that guy that was over last night..."

"I don't want to talk about it."

Ralph chuckled. "Okay, but I was just going to say, he didn't have to sneak in. Tell him to use the doorbell next time."

"He's my ex-fiance, Ralph. Not in my life anymore." Fiona checked her side view mirror. "There won't be a next time."

"Well, listen, next time someone wants to visit, just let me know. I could have shot him."

She knew he was looking for a reaction, but she turned to look out her window.

"That bad, huh?" Ralph scratched his head and sighed. "It's none of my business, but he really seems to care about you."

Fiona licked her dry lips, and swallowed hard. "Yeah, that's what I thought too."

They drove in silence, until they merged onto the highway.

"You're not even going to ask why we're going this way, or why we made you climb up into this truck, instead of the car Owen's taking?"

"No."

"So what's your guess?"

"You want to elude the killer, if he might be watching me. You wanted to put me into a vehicle he wouldn't think I'd be in, and go on a route he wouldn't think of taking because you have people on the lookout for him."

"Hmm. You're good. Who'd think we'd make you climb up in a big truck? Very perceptive for the meds you're on."

"I'm aware because I'm not on them right now. I stopped taking the pain killers regularly when I got out of the hospital. I've only taken three since."

Ralph glanced over at her. "Aren't you supposed to be on them for a while?"

"Are you aware that someone has been following us?" Fiona looked at him, and he smiled.

"Extra security for your transport."

"Well they should be a little more discreet, if even I can tell we're being followed."

Ralph smiled as they exited the highway. "Maybe we want him to be noticed."

"Can we turn on the radio?"

"Sure."

Fiona changed the station, rolled her window down, and breathed the fresh air in deeply.

Her heart fluttered when the department came into view.

Chapter 41

NOAH WATCHED THE WOMAN push herself along on her crutches; into the room he questioned Avery in with Ethan. She was fit, with dark hair, and faint freckles on her nose and cheeks. He thought she was beautiful without a doubt, but she glared at Ethan with an intensity that made Noah uneasy.

"Fiona, this is Inspector Cotter." Noah shook her hand before she set her crutches against the wall behind her, and sat down across from them. "He's with me on this case."

Owen stepped outside, and closed the door behind him.

"Whatever I can do to help, I'm ready." She smiled, and her eyes lit up.

Noah realized Fiona wasn't at all how he expected her to be. An insecure victim, who was generally nervous talking to the police or about her case in general.

"We really appreciate it," Ethan nodded, "I'm sure the victim's families do too."

Fiona nodded. "That's why I'm here."

"Okay, I want to make sure you know what's going on. We have a suspect in this case. He fits the profile, and we are looking for him now. When we bring him in, you might be able to help us in identifying him. We'll get to that later."

"How much do you know already?" Noah asked.

"Just what you're telling me. I know the killer is still out there. I know what he did to Tamara and Wendy. It would have happened to me too."

Ethan studied her. "We believe he also attacked a young girl named Avery Hart."

"I heard about her on the news. Is she alright? Wait, so it was the same guy who attacked her before?"

"No, but likely the same mask. We believe when she reached out to the news, it provoked the killer, and he attacked her. She's safe." Ethan nodded to the door, and Noah got up, and opened it.

"Owen, is she here yet?"

He shook his head, and Noah ducked back into the room, and listened as Ethan went on.

"*If* you were both attacked by the same person, it could provide some more insight into this case. We know you each had different experiences though."

"Who's the suspect," Fiona set her hands in her lap, "and what happened to her exactly?"

They heard a knock on the door, and Owen popped his head in the room.

"She's here."

Chapter 42

WHEN AVERY WALKED INTO THE ROOM, she wasn't expecting to see the unfamiliar face that stared back at her.

Owen told her they wanted to formally question her about her attack when she got out of the hospital, and her parents dropped her off as soon as she was released. The ride was quiet, and when they asked when she would be finished, she told them not to bother waiting.

"Avery, come sit down." Inspector Ascott gestured to the chair across from him, beside the girl staring at her.

Her eyes matched her hair, and her lips were pressed together. She wore yoga clothing, and even with no makeup on, Avery thought the girl was beautiful.

Avery sat down, and smiled at the girl, before she noticed the crutches.

"Fiona, this is Avery Hart." Noah looked at Avery with something that was almost a smile. "Avery, this is Fiona Wolfe. She was attacked by our suspect on her running path in Birch Falls. I know you've seen things about each other on the news..."

Noah opened his mouth and closed it again, and Avery debated reaching her hand out, but when Fiona continued looking at Noah, she focused on the inspectors.

"We are investigating each of your cases separately, but with the possibility that your attackers might be the same person." Ethan finished for him.

Fiona cleared her throat and glanced her way. "I'm sorry to hear about your attack. Well, both of them."

"Thanks, same to you." Avery tried to make eye contact, but Fiona looked back at the inspectors again.

Avery crossed her legs, and slipped her hair behind her ear. She noticed Noah stare at Fiona, and although she wasn't surprised, she felt a tinge of jealousy.

"We explained to Fiona that when we catch the suspect in question, you might be able to help us identify him." Avery noticed Ethan staring at Fiona too, and when she looked over, she saw Fiona squinting at him. "Did you have a question?"

"I'm just not sure why we are both here together. I guess I'm wondering what good it will do, you know, why it's necessary?" Fiona stared straight ahead, and Avery couldn't see her expression.

Noah leaned forward. "We had to bring you both in, because until we find our suspect, you both need protection."

"We need to make sure we've taken the proper security measures." Ethan said.

"I'm sorry," Fiona interrupted, and Avery heard an angry tone, instead of anything that sounded apologetic, "I was under the impression I was here to help *you*."

Inspector Ascott glanced over his shoulder to Owen, who tried to stifle a laugh.

"I don't know who gave you that impression, but we have your statement, and…"

"Hold on Inspector Ascott…" Fiona raised her hand.

"You can call me Ethan."

"Ethan." Fiona's tone sounded warm for the first time, "I am already being watched by officers around the clock. Are you suggesting that isn't enough?"

"In this situation…"

The door opened, and Owen took one step outside. In just moments he poked his head back in the room.

"Can I see you both?"

Noah and Ethan both looked up at him for a moment, before pushing their chairs out, and standing.

"Just stay here." Ethan looked between them, before they both left.

When Fiona looked up at the door, Avery could see her face was flushed.

"Where are you staying right now?" Fiona asked, without turning toward her.

"I just got out of the hospital. I'll be staying at my friend's place tonight, and tomorrow, I'm supposed to be going back home."

"Where's home?"

"My apartment in Crown River. You're in Birch Falls right?"

Fiona gave a short nod, and finally turned to face her. Her eyes were welling up, and she gripped the back of her chair tightly.

"I honestly mean no disrespect, but I don't want to live with anyone. I want to help them solve this case, and get justice for the girls who were murdered. I don't want to be handled with kid gloves, and treated like a victim. I also don't want to be lumped in with you when we've had two very different experiences."

Avery looked at her for a moment, and then back to the door.

"I don't know why they didn't tell me about their security plans sooner. They made it seem like I was free to go home if I wanted."

Fiona shrugged. "There's a reason they don't want you back there."

Avery looked down into her lap, and rested her hand against her stomach.

"It's probably best I don't go back. I don't know if I could have gone back anyway."

"Why?"

Avery looked up at her, and looked down at her leg for a split second. When she met Fiona's gaze, she bit her lip.

"That's where you were attacked?"

Avery nodded. "Your sketch made it on the news. That's how all this started. I recognized the mask, and I guess if you hadn't gotten away..."

"What happened to you? How did you get away?"

Avery went to open her mouth, and realized she was sweating. She wanted to tell Fiona her story, but she was taken aback by how blunt she was, and pushy too.

"I was attacked, like they said."

Fiona stared at her. "What did he do to you?"

Chapter 43

FIONA LISTENED AS AVERY told her story. She sat still as she took it all in. She felt pain when Avery talked about the cuts he made into her stomach, and it mixed with her own, as stabbing pains shot through her leg.

"They don't think he meant to kill me, or if he did, he ran out of time." She watched Avery take a deep breath, and wipe a tear from her cheek.

"I'm sorry."

"I guess it didn't last as long as it could have. The cutting." Avery tucked her blonde hair behind her ear, her hands sat gracefully in her lap during the story, except for when she spoke about the knife. Then they skimmed up her body instinctively to her stomach. "It just doesn't make sense."

"I don't understand. He always starts by shooting the girls. He shoots us, and then..."

"I guess he was working his way backwards with me, I don't know." She brought her hands from her lap to her mouth, and played with her lip. "I don't know much."

"This is what I meant. We had very different experiences."

Fiona looked at the thin rings on Avery's fingers, and watched as her pink lips turned darker as she fussed with them.

"Were you really going to go back to living in your apartment?"

Avery sighed. "I don't know. I really thought I was safe, and now..."

Fiona waited, but Avery said nothing. "Anyone live with you?"

"Nope. I live alone. You?"

Fiona nodded, and grabbed her purse. The pain was sharp, and she squeezed her strap, and waited for it to fade.

"So you were jogging? I saw it on the news..."

"Yeah."

"So he shot you first, and then, did he cut you too?"

"No. I don't want to talk about it." Fiona had waited as long as she could, and when she pulled the pill bottle from her purse, her hand shook. She grabbed a pill, popped it in her mouth, and swallowed hard. "You on any pain meds?"

"Not anymore. Just anti-biotics. It doesn't hurt much, really. Just itchy."

Fiona set her purse back down. "I try not to take mine. This is the first time I've been out on my leg.

Not as easy as I thought, but it was an easy choice. Mope around my house, or get out here and help find the sick bastard."

"Except they won't really let us." Avery shook her head, and looked down at her leg again. "I wanted to go back."

"Hmm?"

"I wanted to prove to myself that I could go back to my apartment. With the killer still free…"

They looked at each other, and Avery leaned in, and whispered, "Do you think he'll come back for us?"

At the next moment, Inspector Cotter came through the door, and shut it behind him.

"I'll get back to you both, alright? Officer Minicozzi's just outside. If you need him, just knock."

"What's going on?" Fiona asked, louder than she had intended.

"I'll be back soon." His hand was back on the door knob.

They both nodded, and looked at each other after he left. Fiona saw a fragile girl in front of her, and every tear that Avery had cried when she retold her story made her feel more uncomfortable.

She truly believed the girl in front of her needed help.

Protection.

What Fiona needed, she thought, was a gun, and a chance to be alone with her attacker.

Chapter 44

NOAH FOLLOWED ETHAN DOWN the long corridor, and waited by the door as he spoke to the officer who brought Arnold Henderson in.

"He was just out front?"

"Well, yeah," the officer stuttered, "I mean no, he was at the front desk. He stated his name, and right away I knew, so I placed him under arrest. His lawyer showed up before I could even take him 'round back."

"Did he say anything else to you?" Ethan looked past the officer through the window in the door.

"No, just his name, and that was it. I cuffed him right away."

"Alright, that's all." Ethan nodded to him, and he lingered a moment, before he strode away.

"He asked for you?" Noah spoke in a low voice.

Ethan nodded. "Well, his lawyer did. Apparently he's ready to talk. You ready?"

"Have to be. We don't have any real evidence, and we're not ready for this, but he's here now. We have to try to get the confession." Noah focused on the door; Ethan opened it, and revealed the two men who sat side by side.

"Arnold Henderson. I'm Inspector Ascott. I understand you'd like to speak with me?" They stood before the men, who looked serene.

"My client has some information he believes you've been looking for." The man dressed in the suit looked to Arnold who nodded, and ran his hand through his thinning hair.

Noah tried to get a good look at his hand, but without knowing which one Avery bit, it was difficult to tell.

"I saw on the news that you were looking for me on suspicion of multiple murders." He looked up at them. "You mind sitting down?"

Ethan pulled his chair out, and Noah followed, sitting directly across from him. His breathing seemed steady, and Noah watched, as Arnold crossed his hands in front of him.

No bite marks.

"So you're ready to confess?" Ethan asked. "I can get a copy written up to be signed."

"Oh, no Inspector. I'm actually here to tell you I'm innocent. You boys seem to have gotten it wrong." Arnold took a deep breath, sighed, and shook his head.

His lawyer looked at Ethan. "Do you have any evidence to suggest my client may have killed the women in question? Any witnesses? Or might this have been an innocent mistake on the department's part?"

"I'll ask the questions, mister?"

"Briggs."

"Arnold Henderson, where were you on July twelfth?"

Arnold looked at his lawyer, and when he nodded, he spoke.

"I was on a hunting trip."

"Where?"

"Just north of Cedar Ridge."

"Was anyone with you? Can anyone prove your whereabouts?"

"Yes, I was hunting with a friend of mine." Arnold nodded to Briggs, "Bob Pope."

Briggs slid a piece of paper across the desk. "Let me save you the trouble, Inspector. This is a list of each of the dates in question, when each of the victims in question were murdered. Mr. Henderson was with someone on each of these occasions, and I've included their contact numbers and addresses."

Ethan scanned the paper, and slid it in between them. Noah read it and recognized each of the names.

Grant and Jennifer Hornby.

Bob Pope.

"So I'm to believe that you were out hunting with Grant Hornby when Tamara Webber was killed, and Fiona Wolfe was attacked? Just days before he was killed himself?" Ethan shook his head.

Arnold opened his mouth, but Briggs spoke first.

"It doesn't matter what you believe. Facts are facts. My client was with Grant Hornby on the first two nights in question, and with Bob Pope the day Grant Hornby was murdered. He was also with Jennifer Hornby on the nights Wendy O'Connor was murdered, and Avery Hart was attacked."

"It's unfortunate Grant Hornby can't corroborate that." Ethan pushed the paper away. "I happen to know Grant Hornby didn't go hunting without a particular group, so excuse me if I can't buy what you're selling."

"You'll just have to do your job and bring Jennifer Hornby, and Bob Pope in, won't you?" Briggs smiled, and when Noah looked to Arnold, his expression began to frustrate him. No smile on his wrinkled face, but a lack of emotion. "So there is no concrete evidence against my client?"

Noah sat up straight, "Mr. Henderson?"

Arnold looked over at him, and raised his brows.

"Does your wife have any idea about all this?"

He could feel Ethan and Briggs watching him.

"I haven't been home from my trip to see her."

Noah maintained eye contact with Arnold.

"Of course, we'll need to see proof that your alibis check out, so you'll have to remain with us for further questions." Arnold looked to his lawyer, but Noah didn't give them a chance to respond. "Do you have a good relationship with your wife, Mr. Henderson?"

"No." His response was quick and short.

Noah looked to Ethan, and continued. "How would you describe your marriage?"

"Unfulfilling. I was having an affair with Jennifer Hornby. My wife doesn't know, but if she found out, I reckon I'd be in a bit of trouble, hey boys?"

"You *do* realize you've just admitted motive for killing Grant Hornby." Noah looked at Ethan, who was still fixated on Arnold.

Briggs shook his head, but Arnold went on.

"Grant was a buddy of mine, and trust me, he wasn't getting in the way of his wife and I if you know what I mean." Arnold smiled for the first time, and his big teeth filled his mouth.

Noah wanted to reach across the table and grab him.

He smiled down on those helpless girls from behind his mask while he...

That's where he made himself stop, and forced the rest of the image from being formed.

"Is my client free to go?"

"He'll remain here for the proper holding time. As Inspector Cotter has already told you, we'll be checking out your alibis—those of whom are still alive." Ethan pushed his chair back from the table. "We'll be speaking to him again, so stay close Briggs."

Noah stood, and resisted the urge to meet Arnold's gaze as he followed Ethan out of the room.

When they were through the long corridor, back toward the girls, Ethan turned to him.

"I'm sorry Ethan. I know you had things under control."

"No, that was good. You kind of surprised him."

"Really?"

"Yeah, it was the first time his expression changed. You noticed that right?"

Noah nodded.

"It's good to mix it up a bit. You didn't say anything I wouldn't have. Let that go." When they got to the doorway where Owen stood, Ethan clasped Owen's shoulder. "I need Jennifer Hornby, Bob Pope, Maggie Henderson, and Charla Kent here yesterday." He gave Owen the contact sheet. "Bring them in yourself if you have to."

Owen nodded and headed back down the hall.

"I'm going to see Ken and January. See if they've got anything else for me. Bring em' up to speed. You stay here with the girls, alright? Just keep them calm."

Ethan was back down the hallway before he finished speaking.

Before Noah went in, he saw both of the girls watching him.

He knew calm wasn't an option.

Chapter 45

"WE HAVE A SUSPECT IN custody, and we were just questioning him." Noah said, with all eyes on him. "He came in less than an hour ago."

"Did he confess?" Fiona asked.

Noah sat down across from them. "No. He's claiming that he is innocent, and that he can prove it. That remains to be seen."

"It's Charla's uncle, isn't it?" Avery asked.

A wave of realization swept over him; Charla had told Avery what she knew. He hadn't planned to go into any more detail, but Avery caught him off guard.

"Who's Charla?" Fiona grimaced and Noah shifted in his seat.

"She's one of the girls who pulled the prank on me ten years ago." Avery looked to Noah, and he nodded. "She's the one who had the mask they used. The one that I recognized in your police sketch. After I was attacked, Charla came and told me her uncle was under suspicion." She turned back to Noah. "He's their number one suspect."

"Why didn't anyone tell me?" Fiona scrunched her freckled nose.

"They wouldn't have told me either..." Avery started, but Noah held up his hand.

"Hold on a minute. You're both on a need to know basis. This is information that, in the wrong hands, could compromise the case."

Fiona rolled her eyes. "So what now?"

"We're holding him for questioning. He may still confess."

"Good." Fiona crossed her arms in front of her.

"How is it good?" Avery asked. "He's denying he did anything. You guys don't have any proof do you?"

"We will use all the information in our power to hold him longer. To prove he's the guy. We are bringing in his wife," He looked at Avery "Charla's aunt. We also have two more people to question who he claims he was with at the times of the murders. Until we figure out a plan, we need you to hang tight."

"That's it?" Fiona asked.

Noah ran a hand through his hair. "That's about as honest as it gets."

Fiona smiled for a split second. "While I appreciate your honesty Inspector Cotter, I don't feel comfortable with him here."

"I completely understand that." Noah nodded. "He can't get to you, rest assured. You're both safe."

"Thank you." She gave him a tight lipped smile and he returned it, although it made him uneasy.

"How are you both feeling?" He asked, just as Owen came in.

"Ladies," he nodded to them, "Noah? A word?"

Noah went to the door and leaned in as he whispered.

"Jennifer Hornby's on her way. So are Maggie and Charla. No answer for Bob Pope, so we sent someone to his house."

"Thanks Owen. You mind staying here?"

He shook his head, and they switched places.

"Tell Ethan will ya?"

Noah nodded, and before he closed the door, he stuck his head back in the room.

"Oh, by the way," he whispered and nodded to the girls, "they'll try to get more out of you. Don't let them."

"Have you met Fiona?" Owen whispered and chuckled.

Noah knew Owen would keep any details of the case quiet, but he wondered if he should trade places with Fiona to interrogate Arnold, with the way she had grilled him.

The thought made him smile.

Chapter 46

NOAH FOUND ETHAN WITH Ken and January in Room C.

"They're all on their way in except Pope."

Ethan nodded. "Bob Pope is divorced, so he lives alone. There isn't going to be anyone who can corroborate that Bob was with Arnold during the time period he states here. If he lies, we know he's at the very least covering for Arnold, with a possibility of him being an accomplice. Is Owen working on it?"

"He's got someone going to the house to escort him in."

"Jennifer Hornby is probably scared of Arnold. If she really thinks he might have killed her husband out of jealousy, she might not talk."

Ken shook his head, and looked up at Ethan. "She might not even know about the murders."

"We've got to convince her she is safe with us so she'll talk. If she's on Arnold's alibi list, she's there for a reason. What about Maggie?"

"She'll be coming in with Charla." January addressed the room. "You could take a chance and tell Maggie about the affair. Tell her we need her to assure Jennifer Hornby that she is doing the right thing by telling the truth, regardless of why she might cover for him. To put him behind bars so he can't hurt anyone..."

Ken shook his head. "Why is that taking a chance?"

January looked to Ethan and Noah, but they stared back with blank faces.

"I guess it's easier to understand if you're a woman. If we tell Maggie about the affair, she might not want to talk to Jen Hornby. Even though she has been beaten and abused by Arnold, she stayed with him for all this time. She could be regretting coming forward, and this could go either way. Either it's her chance to set things right, or it's her chance to go back to the only life she's known."

"You think she'll go back to living with him? Pretend everything's normal?" Ken huffed.

"She'll do whatever she has to to survive." January placed a hand on her hip and looked to Ethan.

"Maybe we can use this to our advantage then." Noah rubbed the scruff that had begun to form on his chin. "Maybe we tell her we already told Arnold the truth. That she gave him up."

"Did you?" Ken asked.

"No," Ethan pointed to Noah, "but that's still a card we can play. We can offer the deal to Maggie first. Tell her we've told Arnold that she gave him up—that he's furious, and that she has to help us put him behind bars. If she refuses to talk to Jennifer Hornby..."

"Then you tell Arnold that his wife and mistress have given him up?" Ken asked.

January rubbed her lips together and shook her head. "That's not good."

"Huh?" Ken stretched, "What?"

"You can't put her in danger like that."

"I think it's a good idea." Ken puffed out his chest, "Might be your only chance."

January rolled her eyes. "Of course you do."

"We'll protect her." Ethan leaned over the table. "She won't be in any real danger."

"It's wrong." January crossed her arms. "You'll do what you want, but it's bad enough telling her her husband knows she gave him up. You can tell her it's not true, but tell him she knows more than he thought? No way."

Ethan started to pace the room. "I know what you're saying, but we've got a shot at catching him here. I don't want to lose it. If we go ahead with this plan, and tell Arnold the women gave him up, we'll also need something to prove Jennifer Hornby would have known. Phone records proving that Arnold called her before and after her husband was murdered. Search her place. Maybe we can find a threatening letter. We know they wrote them to each other, or at least that she wrote him one. Maybe he wrote back. We need her cell phone records."

"Listen, I'm all for the search, but giving up Jennifer Hornby and Aunt Maggie? And then he goes free?" Ken raised his brows at Ethan. "What happens then?"

"Thank you." January huffed.

Ken made a face. "It's not our call. It's Ethan's."

"I'll send Owen to the Hornby's," Ethan looked to Noah, "and see what he can dig up. Ken, get me those phone records." He headed for the door, and Noah followed him. "January, come with us."

They rushed down the hall in a pack, toward the room the girls were in.

"What can I do?" January asked.

"We need you to talk to those women. First Maggie when she arrives. Try to get her to talk to Hornby. If she will, we'll let you facilitate that meeting. Really convince Maggie he already knows she gave him up. That way there's no turning back. If not, we move to plan B." Ethan stopped in front of the interrogation rooms and looked at Noah. "We tell Arnold Maggie gave us proof that he's our killer. We bluff."

Noah looked to January, and although she was disappointed, he saw a fire in her eyes when Ethan spoke about the plan.

"We won't have to use plan B. I'll get Jennifer Hornby to confess to what she knows."

Noah glanced over at where Avery and Fiona sat with Owen. "Should we have a plan C? So maybe we won't have to use plan B? I don't think we should tell Arnold the women gave him up. Telling Maggie that he knows is one thing, but actually telling Arnold she gave him up?"

January's face lightened and they both looked at Ethan.

Ethan nodded to the room. "January, tell Owen to get to Jennifer Hornby's home. I want him on the search for something we can use if we have to bluff. I don't want it to come down to that either, but we have to nail this guy. You get that right?"

They both stared at Noah, and when he nodded, January walked away.

"We've gotta make tough decisions here Noah. Glad you're on board."

Chapter 47

AVERY WISHED THERE WAS a window to look out. Another source of light besides the horrible fluorescent bulbs that gave her a headache.

"You know, if this guy is their prime suspect, and he gets loose, we're screwed." Fiona looked through the window into the hall.

Owen had only left minutes ago, but Avery wondered what was still keeping Fiona in the room.

"So Charla's the girl that attacked you way back?"

Avery nodded. "Ten years ago."

"She used the same mask that her uncle is probably using? That's messed up. Why you?"

"Charla told me she told her aunt what she did to me. Her aunt told her uncle I guess."

"And the sick bastard, what? Got off on it? Was inspired by it?" She pushed her chair out from the table, and crossed her arms. "That's crazy."

Avery hadn't thought about being a serial killer's inspiration before, nor had she thought much about what her attack had to do with the murders, but as Fiona's words permeated the air, she pressed her palms against her stomach.

Ten cuts for ten years away? Ten years it took to start killing?

Her mind flooded with questions and her stomach ached.

"Can we not talk about this right now?"

Fiona turned to her. "They brought us here to protect us, but they are keeping us here in case we can help too. I don't want to just sit here and wait. You didn't see his face at all? When he attacked you?"

Avery shook her head and tears filled her eyes. She didn't understand how Fiona could be so crass about her attack when she had been attacked too. It was the only reason she had shared her story—she could understand what happened to Avery more than anyone else.

"His voice? Maybe you'd remember his voice?"

"No." Avery turned away, back to the imaginary window, and rubbed her head. "He didn't talk."

"If you saw him, face to face, do you think..."

Avery turned to face her as tears ran down her cheeks. "Did *you* see his face before he shot you? Did *you* hear his voice as he chased you down? Did *you* hear him whistle before you saw anything at all?"

Fiona stared at her blankly, as Avery wiped the tears off her cheeks.

"I heard him whistle. He whistled before I saw him, like you said, and then after when..."

"When you realized you were trapped?"

"Maybe," Fiona leaned forward in her chair, "maybe that's something that could be useful to them?"

"I've already told them about the whistling. Could you just give it a break?" Avery stood from her chair, but her stomach ached worse than it had since she left the hospital, and she sat back down.

"Listen, I know you're hurting right now, so am I. We have to be strong. We can't just be the victims. We got another chance. Those girls he killed, whoever *he* is-- they didn't get the second chance we have. I'm doing this for them."

"You do what you've gotta do." Avery rested her head on her arm, and faced the space where her imaginary window was.

Fiona was on this crusade, Avery thought, for the girls who were murdered. She wanted to avenge them, and it seemed like she made it her mission to play detective.

Or she's deflecting her anger and hurt.

"He won't get away with what he did to them." Fiona said, and Avery didn't know if she was even talking to her anymore.

"Did to us." Avery whispered.

She imagined it was bright and sunny outside, and that she would get to walk outside and feel the sunshine on her skin, and Charla's uncle would be trapped inside the gray walls instead.

Forever.

261

Chapter 48

NOAH CHECKED HIS WATCH, and waited for a few minutes to pass as they had agreed. When he entered the room, Maggie Henderson was in tears, and her face was red. Charla sat beside her in the same supportive pose he had seen before.

"You want me to talk to that whore? Try to convince her to change her mind about covering up for him? You're outta you're mind."

"Maggie, it's the only way we can catch him in this…" January began and stopped to look at him, "Inspector Cotter."

"Inspector Cotter." Maggie looked up at him with pleading eyes. "They want me to talk to her. How long have you all known she was with my husband?"

Noah stood tall behind January. Charla rested her hand on Maggie's arm, but she didn't seem to notice, and continued staring at him. Ethan cleared his throat, and January spoke.

"There's more. I'm so sorry you have to find out now Mrs. Henderson, but your husband," Maggie made eye contact with January, "he knows you're the one who gave him up."

"What? What do you mean?" She looked to Ethan. "*You* told him."

Ethan looked at Noah.

"You told my uncle?" Charla stammered. "Why?"

Noah put his hand on the back of January's chair. "We didn't tell him. He already knew."

"Oh God. How?" Maggie squeezed her tissue in her fist and whispered, "How could he know that?"

January was about to speak, but Noah rested his hand on her shoulder, and the room was quiet.

"It's because I wasn't home when he got there." Maggie looked up at Noah. "That's gotta be it, right? And I was calling him over and over…" She stopped, her bottom lip quivered. "But he's locked up now, right?"

Noah checked his watch. "For a few more hours, and then we have to let him go."

"No." Charla shook her head and made eye contact with Noah. "You can't."

"We don't have enough to keep him here Maggie." Ethan spoke up, and his voice was colder than the others. "If you wait a while, you'd be driving back home at the same time."

"Now you're really talking crazy." Maggie looked back to January. "What do I need to do?"

"We need you to talk to Jennifer Hornby, and let her know the truth. That Arnold Henderson is a killer." Ethan said.

"If you do," Noah said, "you could help us put him away. Keep him from hurting anyone else. You heard about Avery Hart."

Maggie looked up at him with trembling lips and then looked at Charla. "Yes. I did."

"If Jennifer Hornby keeps living this lie, if she knows what your husband has done and doesn't confess," January shook her head, "there will be no proof."

"But..." Maggie's voice wavered, "what if she's scared like me?"

January held her hand out, and Maggie took it. "I know this will be difficult, but we need you to tell her you're on her side. Let her know that we can help her like we're helping you. Make her see the real Arnold Henderson. The abuser you've known for far too long. The man who you believe is a killer."

"What if..." Maggie started to stare off.

"Maggie." January spoke in a soft tone and she looked back at her. "He says he was with her the night of one of the murders, and I know that hurts Maggie, but two girls are dead. He killed her husband too. You've got to help us put him away Maggie. Can you do that?"

Maggie squeezed her hand back and then let go. "I don't know."

"You came to us for a reason." January leaned in toward her, "You told them what you believed to be true about your husband. You're doing the right thing."

"You can try Aunt Maggie. You can at least try." Charla and Maggie exchanged a glance, and Noah saw the pain they shared.

"Will you do it Maggie?" January asked.

"I don't have a choice."

"Good." Ethan nodded, and stood. "January, please prepare her, and get her whatever she needs."

January nodded, and they left the room.

"Can you believe she's going to do it?" Noah asked.

"We've got a real chance. I'm going to contact Owen. Can you see if Jennifer Hornby's here yet?"

Noah nodded, and they parted ways. Nothing they found at Jennifer Hornby's could be used as evidence, but it could lead them to something real, and Noah hoped Owen would find something to point them in the right direction.

He knew that if January was right, and Maggie could have potentially decided to return home with her husband out of fear, they did the right thing.

Lying to her.

The fact that she wouldn't survive going back with him should have been enough, but he was glad they didn't take that chance. The women would be protected, and the chance of putting Arnold Henderson away felt closer than ever.

Chapter 49

NOAH FOUND JENNIFER HORNBY with the officer at the front desk.

"Inspector Cotter." Her face lit up, and just as quickly, the smiled faded as he spoke.

"Could you bring Mrs. Hornby to the room?"

The officer nodded, and Noah followed behind them until they went into the room.

Ethan hurried down the hallway. "She here?"

Noah nodded. "Any word from Owen?"

"He just got there. Nothing so far."

They entered the room and the officer left.

"Mrs. Hornby." Noah nodded. "Nice to see you again. I'm sorry it's under these circumstances though. This is Inspector Ascott."

She nodded. "I'm just waiting for my lawyer."

"Alright," Noah sat down. "You aren't being arrested though. Just so you know."

"Okay."

"Have you spoken to Darrel?"

She looked at him blankly. "No."

"Mrs. Hornby," Ethan started, "You know why you're here, don't you?"

She looked from Noah to Ethan. "I should really wait for my lawyer before I answer any questions."

"I'm sorry for the loss of your husband." Ethan nodded. "Out of respect for him, I can't wait that long. Mrs. Hornby, we have Arnold Henderson in custody for the murder of your husband, and of two other women."

Noah watched her eyes well up. "Mrs. Hornby, we have someone who wants to talk to you."

She looked at him, her brows furrowed. "Arnold?"

"His wife, Maggie." Noah watched her eyes widen, as she pushed her chair back.

"No, no, I can't see her."

"Arnold already told us about your affair. His wife knows, and she wants to talk to you, not about the affair, but about this case." She shook her head. "She's afraid for you."

"Ha." Mrs. Hornby let out a burst of air, and tears fell down her cheeks. "She's concerned for *me*?"

"For you, and for all the other women out there who could be hurt or killed if Arnold is set free today, and he will be if you don't listen to her." Ethan nodded to the door, and Noah opened it.

Maggie stood behind January and peered out from behind her.

"Mrs. Hornby, I'm January. Thank you for letting us speak with you." Noah watched Maggie approach the table, slowly coming out of January's shadow.

She offered her the seat next to Noah.

The room was quiet for a while, and when Ethan began to speak, January shook her head.

"I'm sorry Maggie." Mrs. Hornby spoke first, and hung her head.

"I know you know my husband in ways no other woman should." Maggie cleared her throat. "But do you know what he does to me?"

Mrs. Hornby looked up at her with wide eyes.

"He beats me Jen. He has since we got married."

Mrs. Hornby shook her head, but Maggie went on.

"He abuses me in every way, mentally, emotionally..." She rolled up her sleeves, to show a bruise in the shape of fingers. "Physically."

"I'm sorry..."

"I'm not trying to make you feel sorry for me. If you did, you wouldn't have done what you did with him. I want you to know he's dangerous. I believe he killed those women, and probably your husband too."

Mrs. Hornby started to cry, and Maggie waited. "I..."

"If Grant found out about the *affair*," Maggie said the word affair like it was a swear word, "or about what my husband was doing with those girls...that's why he killed him. He killed your husband, Jen. You loved him once, didn't you? Are you going to let Arnold use you like this?"

271

Mrs. Hornby took a deep breath. "My husband knew."

All eyes in the room focused on Mrs. Hornby.

Noah lowered his voice. "He knew about the affair with Arnold?"

"I told him more than a week before he passed and he didn't even seem surprised. I decided to end it with Arnold a week before," she looked at Maggie, "at the barbeque. I wrote him a letter telling him it was over. After that, I had to tell my husband, but you know what? He forgave me."

Noah had a feeling Darrel had interpreted the letter correctly, and the way Grant had kissed her when he came back out of the house at the barbeque indicated he was happy with her, regardless of what Darrel told him.

This confirms the trigger, he thought, and nodded to Ethan.

The tears streamed down Mrs. Hornby's cheeks, and dripped off her chin. "I didn't deserve it, but he forgave me. Told me he thought it was his fault, that he'd try harder. We were happy...in his last week. We were..."

"Mrs. Hornby," January stepped toward the table. "If you're not with Arnold Henderson anymore, will you please tell us where you were on the twentieth and twenty-first of this past week?"

Mrs. Hornby dried her eyes with a tissue January gave her and cleared her throat.

"I was with Arnold Henderson." She looked at January, but her eyes flickered back to Maggie.

"After your husband's death, you must have suspected *something*. Was Arnold mad that you broke up with him?" January asked. "Did he threaten you?"

She stared past them to the door. "I don't want to…"

Maggie reached out across the table, and before Noah could react, she grabbed her hand.

"If you don't tell them the truth, he'll go free. He'll kill me. He might kill you. He'll kill again. You can stop this. You have to stop this." Maggie hissed at her.

They looked at each other for another moment, before the door opened, and Briggs stepped through with another man in a suit.

"You will *not* speak to my client without my presence ever again." The taller man reached out for Mrs. Hornby.

Mrs. Hornby stood, and Noah watched her shake as she walked to the door, but Maggie grabbed her hand again.

"Please. Please tell them. God, you have to tell them."

Mrs. Hornby shook her head, and tried to pull away from Maggie.

January pulled Maggie off of her, and they watched Mrs. Hornby leave with the men.

Charla rushed in after the room began to clear, and held her aunt in a tight embrace, while she whispered to her.

"Maggie, we'll have an officer escort you and Charla back to your sister's. A police car will be stationed there for your protection and we'll be in touch."

January led Maggie and Charla out the door, and Noah heard Maggie's cries fade further down the hall.

"Arnold got to her. He's got to have something big on her. Something bad." Ethan walked to the door. "It's onto plan B. We've got to do it soon. We can't have Mrs. Hornby telling Briggs anything he could tell Arnold. You call Owen again, and I'll meet you in Arnold's room. I'll make sure no one talks to him."

Noah looked across the hall, to the door the girls were behind, and dialed Owen's number. Avery's head rested on her arm, and he wondered if she was sleeping.

"Hey man, you got anything?"

"I might have something. Ken told me phone records show that Jennifer Hornby and Arnold haven't spoken on the phone for two weeks. They texted each other a few times since though. Arnold asked her to meet him. There was no reply. Then, after her husband's death, one message. It's too bad about your husband. Very sorry I'll have to miss the funeral. I'll be by to pay my respects very soon."

"You think that sounds threatening?"

"Knowing what we know, maybe, but as far as evidence, it's a stretch. Mrs. Hornby couldn't help us?"

"Wouldn't," Noah corrected.

"That's all I've got."

"We need something else. Now."

"I know, I'm trying alright?" Noah heard some rustling on the other end. "I've gone through almost everything. Ken accessed her computer remotely. Nothing on there."

"Keep trying. Without anything concrete…"

"I know, Noah." Owen's voice sounded rough, "I'm getting another call. Listen, I'm trying my best."

"At least Ken found the texts. It might be helpful. If you get something, call me directly."

"Got it."

Chapter 50

"I'LL ASK YOU TO DIRECT your questions to me now." Briggs checked his watch, and sighed.

Noah leaned back in his chair as Briggs straightened his glasses.

"We have just gotten confirmation..." Ethan began but Noah interrupted.

"We have the phone records Arnold." He looked directly at him, and Arnold stared back. "Jennifer Hornby."

Arnold continued to stare, but when Briggs set his hand down on the table, Arnold lost focus.

"If there is any such evidence, I..."

"We have proof of your texts to Jennifer Hornby after her husband was found dead. We have every word of those texts shared between Arnold Henderson and Jennifer Hornby."

Briggs squinted at him and then shook his head.

"Shame," Arnold pressed his lips together and his face appeared lighter, "that's what it was. I had to send my condolences."

Briggs turned to Noah. "Unless you have the evidence with you, Mr. Henderson is finished entertaining your..."

"We *do* have the phone records Mr. Briggs. Of course, it wasn't just your condolences, as you claim. You also said you'd be seeing her." Noah saw the clock in his peripheral, and realized their time was up. "You told her you'd come to see her. What was the nature of your visit?"

Before Arnold opened his mouth, Briggs held his watch up to Arnold.

"Time's up. We're done here. Mr. Henderson's free to go. Don't bother trying to speak with him without me again."

They stood and started for the door.

"Mr. Henderson." Ethan stood eye to eye with him. "I don't have to tell you to stay close."

Briggs opened the door. "Mr. Henderson has no plans to leave the country."

Ethan shook his head and smiled. "I don't have to tell you, because we'll be the ones staying close. Know what I mean?"

Noah couldn't tell for sure, but he thought he saw Ethan wink at Arnold before they left the room. When the door closed, Ethan turned to him.

"Why didn't you let me say the girls turned on him?"

"It wouldn't have been enough. He wasn't going to confess."

"It was all we had left while we still had him. You

can't pull that shit with me."

"I couldn't put those women's lives in danger Ethan. Come on, could you really have done it?"

"I meant what I said Noah. I'm keeping eyes on him." He shook his head. "You knew there were risks. You also know we are protection those women. If you had doubts, you should have asked me first."

"I did. I told you my doubts, but you wouldn't take no for an answer. What do you want me to say?"

"Nothing to me. You can tell those girls he walked." Ethan stalked out of the room, and Noah let the door shut behind him.

He made the choice he could live with, and he wouldn't apologize. If it cost him his position, or his place on the case, so be it.

When he left the room he saw Arnold at the far end of the hall, as he waited behind Briggs at the reception desk. Arnold noticed Noah, and waved to him. Noah stared him down until Briggs tapped his arm, and he turned to leave.

Chapter 51

"HE JUST GETS TO LEAVE?" Fiona stared up at Noah.

Her eyes burned through him, but Avery's threatened to make him second guess the decision to use the women in Arnold's life as bait. Both expressions made him feel worse than Ethan's words had.

"We didn't have anything to hold him."

"But he's your number one suspect, right?" Avery asked.

"We've got to have evidence, and when he came to us..."

Noah heard the door open behind him and turned as Ethan entered the room.

"Listen ladies, our suspects are *our* focus. You don't need to worry about your safety. It's our priority." Ethan pulled his chair out, and motioned for Noah to sit down with them. "We've got people who are ready to work around the clock to make sure you're both protected."

"And what about the girls of Birch Falls, or Crown River, or where ever else he's going next?" Fiona grabbed her crutches. "Who's going to watch out for them?"

"The public is already on high alert. We have announced that Arnold Henderson is a suspect, and between our unit and the media, he won't be able to get a moment alone. Like I said, it isn't your concern."

"Like hell it isn't." Fiona pulled herself to her feet.

"So we are just supposed to go home? Go about life as usual?" Avery crossed her arms. "I--I can't do that."

"I sure as hell can't." Fiona began to hobble towards the door.

"Hold on a minute." Ethan stood in front of her. "We are doing everything we can to catch the killer. You've got to trust us."

Noah saw Fiona roll her eyes, and then looked at Avery. She seemed to be deep in thought, lost in whatever place she went to.

"Avery?" Ethan asked, and she looked up at him, "Can you do that?"

"Do what?"

"They want us to trust that they've got everything under control." Fiona looked back at her.

Avery stared at Noah, and his heart raced as he waited for an answer.

"Hey, she can do what she wants," Fiona turned back to Ethan, "but I'm not counting on anyone to save me."

Ethan put his hand on the door knob.

"Am I free to go?"

Ethan stepped away, and let her struggle past him, leaving the door ajar behind her.

"Avery, where do you want to stay? Your place? Sadie's?" Ethan looked quizzically at Noah. "Her friend's place."

"I'd rather stay with Sadie for now."

Noah nodded and stood. "We will have a unit at her place at all times. If you want to go somewhere, let them know, and they'll go with you. If you see anything suspicious, or are worried about anything at all, call us. You've got my number."

Avery nodded, and followed them out. Fiona had limped just down the hall, and was sitting on a chair outside one of the rooms.

"Where's Owen?" She called to them.

Ethan started down the hallway toward her, but stopped. "You need a ride back home Avery?"

"No, I'll just call Sadie."

Ethan hurried back down the hall to Fiona. "Ralph will be here to take you."

"So how are you feeling? Your stomach?" Noah asked.

"I was hurting a while ago. Doesn't hurt much now, but I feel sick." Avery took a step closer to him, "I know you tried to get him to confess. I know you did your best."

"My priority is the safety of everyone involved. You believe me right?"

"You're going to get whoever did this... just a matter of when."

"Thank you for trusting me."

Avery looked down at her hands as she fiddled with her purse strap.

"I better call Sadie."

Noah nodded, and gave her a tight lipped smile, before she turned for the door.

He wondered how long it would take Sadie to get there, and started to speak before he realized the words were coming out of his mouth.

"Hey, why don't I just take you? I need to get out of here for a while."

She seemed to teeter, then nodded, and continued walking toward the parking lot exit.

Avery didn't know their plan, and she didn't know that Noah refused to extort the women, but she seemed to trust him.

That was enough for Noah to keep going, he thought, as he followed her out.

Chapter 52

THE RIDE HOME WAS QUIET, and after Ralph helped her upstairs, Fiona used the last of her energy to run a bath. As she soaked in the warm water, she regretted the fit she threw earlier. She knew the police were doing all they could, and probably wanted to catch the killer more than she thought, but it wasn't personal to them.

She couldn't get past that.

The hot water turned luke-warm as she stewed in her thoughts. Just as she went to fill the tub with more water, she heard Ralph's voice from below in the kitchen.

"Ice?"

She gripped the sides of the tub, and sat still.

He was speaking to someone, but his voice sounded different somehow.

She heard mumbles, and the clicking of glass."... come around."

Fiona pushed herself up, out of the tub, and used the towel rack for support. She draped her robe over her shoulders, and opened the door a crack.

"That's the thing. She hasn't had anyone over."

Ralph was definitely in the kitchen and his tone was light.

"Not even Jill?"

Sam.

His voice was rough; hard to mistake, and she knew he was at the bottom of the stairs.

"Like I said, no one's been by in weeks. I think it'd do her good to see a few friendly faces. She's so..." Ralph stopped talking, and she heard his footsteps coming toward the stairs, "Fixated on what happened. That's not the right word, but..."

"I'm not so sure I'd help with that right now. Fee's stubborn." Fiona's heart pounded in her ears, and she knew her face was red. She tried to put her arm through the sleeve of her robe, but she fumbled and gave up to listen. "If she doesn't want to see me, or anyone else, she won't."

"Hey, you don't know for sure. Family and friends could really help at a time like this."

Fiona struggled to get the rest of the robe on and opened the door.

"Her family's in Ireland and no offence, but you don't know her very well yet."

She grabbed her crutches, and fiddled with them quietly, hoping to have the element of surprise when she stormed in on them.

Sam's tone made her pause. "I just came by to make sure she was doing alright. You better tell her I came by. She'll know anyway, somehow," she could tell he was smiling, "she always does. I just wanted to make sure she's safe. Here's my number. It's my cell, so you'll always be able to reach me. Call me for anything alright?"

"Buddy, we've got everything taken care of. Trust me. She couldn't be in better hands."

Fiona wished she were in Sam's hands, and when she peeked around the corner, she saw the back of his head. She wanted to see his face, but he moved and she ducked back around the corner. She heard them heading for the door and looked out again. Sam put his hand on the door knob, and Ralph's back was toward her. Sam turned back to him, and his face looked gray.

"You'll know if you need to use it or not. I just feel better, you having it."

Ralph clapped his hand on Sam's back as he turned for the door.

"Appreciate it. Take care."

She watched him until the door closed, and let her body rest against the wall. She didn't understand how he did that to her. How every time he left, she wanted to go after him.

Wanted him back with her.

It was only in his absence that she remembered what happened, and the reason she kept him away.

Chapter 53

AS THEY PULLED OUT OF THE LOT, Noah turned the radio on. Avery noticed something pink on his key chain and cupped it in her palm.

"Are you aware you have a ballerina on your keychain?" She grinned at him.

"Yeah, it's my step-niece's."

"Oh."

"She gave it to me to remember her by, she said. I moved here from Toronto just last month."

"That's cute." Avery smiled, and leaned back in her seat.

"I thought, what am I gunna do with that thing? But I can't lose it, right?"

Avery laughed. "Yeah, I guess so."

"So I'm hoping she'll see it next time I visit, and she'll know I care."

His grin was contagious.

"That's sweet. You must be close."

"No actually, she's only been my step-niece for a little over a year. My dad remarried, and his new wife has a daughter, son-in-law, and granddaughter." He turned the radio station, and slipped his sunglasses on. "So we aren't close, but I'm trying to be for my dad. He hates that I'm out here."

Avery shrugged. "Well, it's nice that he cares."

She thought about her own parents, and while she hoped they were still waiting to pick her up, she knew she'd have already slipped their minds.

"What about your mom?"

"She passed away a while ago. Cancer."

"I'm sorry."

She looked out the window and tried to think of something to say to change the subject.

"Back then it was just the three of us, so I was trying to get used to a bigger family, and then I had to leave."

"Had to?"

"Well, I was going to be an officer, but I got a promotion, so I took the opportunity and moved out here."

"Good for you." Avery smiled. "How old are you, if you don't mine me asking?"

"Twenty-seven."

"Are you supposed to be telling me all this?"

"It's not a rule, but I probably shouldn't."

"Then why are you?"

"I'll try not to be blunt, but we don't have a lot of other common ground besides what's going on, and none of it's good. I wanted to talk about something good I guess."

Avery stared out the window, and held her purse in her lap.

"It's just weird to think of you as a real person I guess. I didn't really before..."

"I get that a lot. I think most cops do."

"Why did you offer to drive me home?"

"I wanted to."

"Yeah, but why? After everything I've done. Going to the media. I've been rude to you. You don't have to be nice."

"I wanted to make sure you got back to Sadie's alright. I meant what I said. Your safety is my top priority."

She nodded and stared out the window again. "Thanks."

Is that the only reason?

"I guess I wanted some time to decompress a little."

She looked at him and raised her brows.

Nothing more?

"Things have gotten pretty serious, and dark, and they are, but I didn't want to leave things off like that. With you."

She knew he was looking at her, but she avoided eye contact. She could hide her face from him, but she couldn't hide her smile.

The sun started to set, and as they drove down the road, the clouds began to cover the sky.

"So someone will be by?" Avery cleared her throat, but she still couldn't look at him. "Watching?"

"Yeah, we'll have an officer by at night, and just make sure you're not by yourself. We've got an eye on Arnold Henderson."

Avery nodded. "What if it's not him?"

Noah pointed to the street sign ahead and Avery turned and nodded.

"Right, that's the one. Thanks for the drive."

"No problem. You'll hear from Ethan or I soon, alright? We'll advise on the next steps."

They pulled into the driveway, and when the car stopped, she gathered her purse.

"Thanks again."

"Avery?" She looked at him and a grave expression fell over his face. "Remember you can call me. Anytime." He took out one of his business cards and wrote on the back.

"Here."

"Is this your personal phone?"

He nodded.

"Thanks Noah." They exchanged somber glances, and she slipped out of the car.

She turned back and saw him watching her as she walked up the driveway.

When she reached the side door to Sadie's basement apartment, she was already waiting there with open arms.

"What happened Avery? Did they get him?" She let Sadie's arms wrap around her, and pull her inside. "Is that why they called you down there?"

"He got away."

Sadie pulled her close with one arm and led her down the basement steps.

"What do you mean?"

"Arnold Henderson, Charla's uncle, he came in. They didn't have any evidence, so they had to let him go."

"Okay, you have to fill me in, but this calls for drinks, and pizza, and ice cream." She squeezed her arm. "Lots of ice cream."

They reached the bottom of the basement stairs, and Sadie went to her dinette.

"Hey Sadie?" She turned back to her. "You're not supposed to leave me alone alright? They're calling me tomorrow."

"You think I'd leave you alone?" Sadie shook her head, and grabbed a flyer from her drawer. "Pizza or Chinese?"

"I don't really feel like eating."

"You will."

Avery shrugged, slumped down on the couch, and set her purse beside her.

"Chocolate chip pancakes?"

Avery feigned a smile. "You know me too well. Honestly though, I can't eat right now."

"You wanna tell me about it? I don't want to bug you, just tell me if you don't."

"Which part?"

"Whatever you're ready to talk about."

Avery tucked her legs up under her, and rested her head on the couch.

"Can I get a drink first?"

Sadie tossed her a can and Avery cracked it open.

"Besides Arnold Henderson claiming he's innocent, I met Fiona Wolfe, Noah Cotter drove me home, and the killer, whoever he is, is still on the loose."

Chapter 54

Noah stayed in his car long after he turned the ignition off, and stared at his cell phone. The clouds rolled in and all light was drained from the sky.

When he opened his phone, he went through his contacts and stopped on the one that had been on his mind since he dropped Avery off.

"Hey Darrel, it's Noah Cotter. I was wondering if we could have another talk?"

"I told you and your partners everything I know, alright?"

"Has Arnold Henderson threatened you at all?"

"What? No."

"Do you believe Arnold killed Grant?"

"I don't know what to believe at this point. I don't want no part of it."

"I need a favour."

"Sure you do. You wanna be buddy buddy with me one minute and then arrest me the next. I only do favours for friends."

"I need you to take me to Bob's hunting cottage."

"What? Now?"

"Yeah. Listen, I know you don't wanna get wrapped up in this shit. I don't blame you, so this is the last thing I'll ask for."

"I don't trust you."

"I'm not even on duty. This is important to me. If you care at all about Jennifer Hornby, you'll take me. You want to keep her safe, right?"

Darrel agreed, and Noah started on his way to pick him up.

Bob Pope's cottage was the one place the men had in common. Although the map January produced indicated the place where Arnold cut up the bodies was likely south of Cedar's Ridge, in Birch Falls, Bob's was the last location left to check, and Darrel was the only person he could get to talk.

He hoped he could find Bob or evidence of the murders there. Either would be enough, he thought, as he plugged the address into his GPS.

Chapter 55

FIONA WOKE TO THE SOUND of the door slamming downstairs.

It was dark outside, and a light from downstairs glowed under her door. She realized she hoped it was Sam, and that he'd come to stay with her. She sat up on her bed, grabbed her crutches, and pulled herself up. She heard footsteps coming up the stairs and hobbled to the door.

She took a deep breath, and waited for a knock.

Still nothing.

She leaned her ear to the door, and heard breathing.

A man's.

A knock came, that made her jump away from the door, and drove her crutch into her armpit.

"Ow."

"Fiona, its Owen. You alright in there? I just took over for Ralph."

"Oh hey, you can come in."

Owen opened the door. "How's it going?"

She rubbed her armpit with her hand. "I was sleeping."

"Sorry to wake you. I just thought..."

"What?"

"Nothing, I don't want to get in trouble. I just wanted to let you know I was here."

"Owen, come on. What did you really wake me for?"

"I thought it might be nice to take a drive." He shrugged, and leaned against the wall. "Unless you're too tired."

"To where?"

"You're always complaining about not getting out. I just thought, between you and me, we could go for a drive. We've got cars on our suspect. It'll be safe."

"I guess that sounds like a nice idea."

"Want to change, and meet me at the stairs?"

When Owen left the room, Fiona pulled on a pair of jogging pants, a t-shirt.

When she grabbed her crutches, she hesitated.

She didn't want to get caught, and get Owen in trouble. If she did, he might not come back, and he was her favourite officer. He left her alone most of the time, and never asked many questions. He was the only one who let her know what was happening, and if he was taken off the case, she'd blame herself.

She looked out the window, and smelled the fresh night air through the screen. She could use a drive to clear her thoughts, and get out of her head for a while. She opened the door, and Owen was waiting down the hall for her.

"Where are we going?" She hobbled toward him.

"Maybe just take some back roads?"

"Yeah that sounds good." He held his arms out to her.

"I want to try the stairs on my own this time."

"Sure."

She gave him one of the crutches, and grabbed the railing with her free hand. She stepped down with her good leg, and let the bad leg follow.

"Not that hard." She laughed. "Maybe you should be waiting at the bottom, in case I fall?"

"You won't fall. You're going to be fine."

She looked up at him with a smile, and he stared down at her leg as she took the next step. She started to fall, but her arm gripped the banister tight, and she recovered on her own.

"Maybe we should just stay here." Owen sighed.

"Hey, I'm not *that* bad. You're right, I could use this. Maybe we could drive by your place. I'd love to see where you live."

"I don't..."

"Like not go in or anything. I'm sure your wife's sleeping. Just drive by."

Owen watched her take the last few steps, and handed her the crutch when she reached the bottom.

Fiona smiled up at him and grabbed her jacket from the banister. "Let's go."

Chapter 56

"Got any cigarettes?"

"No, sorry. Don't smoke."

"Figures." Darrel rolled his window down, and hung his arm over the side.

The fresh air came as a relief to Noah, as the car was filled with the smell of liquor after Darrel got in.

"When you and the boys went hunting, did you come home with much?"

"The odd time. You have to enter a draw for 'em, so 'bout three times last year."

"So you made what? Stew?"

"God no. We barbequed." Beelson chuckled.

"Where did you bring the carcass?"

"Out to Bob's smoke shed."

Smoke shed, he repeated, and wondered why he hadn't thought of it when he found out about their interest in hunting.

"On the property?"

"Mhmm."

"Who'd do the honours?"

"Bob usually. Sometimes Arnie. They both tried to teach me, but that shit don't interest me. I'll take a venison dinner any night though. Those were some good nights, when we actually shot dinner. The girls would make gagging noises, and pretend to be disgusted, but they ate their fair share alright."

Noah wondered if the shed would be locked.

"Won't we be trespassin'?"

"We won't go in the cottage or anything. I just want an idea of where this place is."

"I gave ya the directions," Noah felt Darrel stare at him, "how's this gunna help?"

"Never know what we might find."

They drove on in silence and Darrel turned on the radio. As they pulled up to the cottage, Noah turned it off.

"You ever been hunting Cotter?"

"Not like you." Noah got out of the car, and waved for Darrel to follow him.

"Huh?"

"I don't hunt animals. I hunt criminals. One could argue they're one in the same."

"Right." Darrel shook his head. "O'course you'd say that."

"Where's the smoke shed?"

"Right down there." Darrel pointed just past the cottage.

When they got to it, Noah looked through the windows. There were a few cobwebs on the sill, and when he rounded the house, Darrel stood in front of the door.

"Go ahead." Noah nodded.

"I thought you said we ain't trespassin'?"

"I'm not." Noah pushed Darrel into the door, and shoved him right through.

Noah noted the cobwebs on Darrel. "When was the last time you were in here?"

"Me? Couple months ago."

"God, it smells."

Darrel laughed. "Smells good to me."

"Where are the tools to clean the animal?"

"Should be on the table." Darrel tapped the top, and bent down to look under. "Or maybe in that drawer?"

Noah opened the drawer, and watched a spider crawl across it. "Nope."

"Then I don't know where they are."

"Bob ever take his tools in the cottage? To clean them, or...?"

"Not that I ever saw. They're always in here."

"How would you know? I thought you never came in here?"

"No, I'm in here all the time. We drink in here at night to get away from the girls when they come. I just never gut the animal."

"And the tools have always been here?" Noah repeated as he scoured the room, "How many?"

"Just three. A carving knife, a saw, and an axe."

"So it's unusual they aren't here."

"Uh huh."

"Arnold Henderson doesn't have a cottage, or cabin or anything right?"

"Naw, I told ya that before." Darrel walked to the door. "Can we go now?"

"But you said he went hunting without you all sometimes."

"Yeah, but he never said where."

"Do you have an idea of where he might have gone?"

"I don't know." He turned and left the shed.

Noah followed him out, and grabbed his shoulder to slow him down. If he was as close as he claimed to be with Pope, he wondered why he seemed so intent on leaving.

"Where would you go hunting, if not around here?"

"I'd go north I guess, like Pope said."

"Is there anywhere closer to his home? A place that's private?"

"No. If you want to hunt, you've gotta go north." Darrel wiped his mouth with his hand, and when he looked up at Noah, his eyes couldn't focus on him.

Great, he's drunk and wants to play games.

"Okay, maybe not to hunt, but to camp?"

Darrel wiped his hands on his pant legs, and took a step closer.

"There's a place south east of here." His voice was almost a whisper, "It's a dump though. It was a trailer park, but it's abandoned now."

"Where?"

"Tipper's Point."

"I've never heard of it."

"Not many from the city have. People around here know it pretty well. No hunting, but it's isolated."

"No residential areas around?"

Darrel shook his head. "Good place for a party. I think some kids still have bonfires there in the summer."

"What made you think of it?"

Darrel looked at him, and they started back toward the car.

"You promise you'll leave me outta this from now on?"

"I told you I would."

"You can't mention my name at all either."

Noah caught up with him. "I won't. Why does it matter if you're asked a few questions? I'd have thought you'd want to figure out who killed Grant?"

"I don't want to end up like Grant." They got back to the car, and got in. "Arnie lives further north than the rest of us, but he'd always come from that way." Darrel pointed down the road. "Whenever he came up to join us, he'd always come from the other way. He picked me up once to come here, and he came the way we all go. The way I just took you. Back the other way," he looked down the dark road, "you pass Tipper's Point."

Chapter 57

"You don't have a smoke do you?"

Owen looked at her wide-eyed and shook his head. "Didn't know you smoked."

"Sometimes it relieves some stress."

"I thought that's what you did yoga for?" He smiled and looked back at the dirt road.

"I'm a grown woman. I can do whatever I want."

"Okay." He smiled. "Listen, I had an idea."

"I'm listening." Fiona turned to Owen.

"I was thinking it might be a good idea to swing by the place Avery's at and make sure she's alright. No one's watching the house yet that I know of, so..."

"You're sweet Owen. You probably weren't even ordered to do that were you?"

Owen stared down the road. "So you're good with that?"

"Sure. I don't have to get out or anything, do I?"

"No. Why?"

"Good, cause my leg still hurts from today."

"I'm sorry to hear that."

Fiona shrugged. "Just building muscle back. Sometimes the pain feels good, if you can remember what it's giving you. For me, when I work out, the hum of pain afterwards means I'm getting fit. This is a different kind of pain, but it's still good. I'd rather feel it than let my leg go to jelly, y'know?"

Owen nodded. "You're a brave girl, facing all this on your own."

Fiona shrugged as they slowed down in front of a few houses.

"I do what it takes. You can't trust anybody else. You have to look out for yourself."

Owen pulled to a stop.

"No one cares more about me than me. That's just how it is. Would it be nice to have someone? Sure. Your wife is lucky to have you."

Owen opened his door, and hopped out.

"I'll just be a sec. Hey, could you get in the back where the windows are tinted? I don't want anyone seeing you, okay?"

"Yeah sure."

Owen slid her crutches into the back of the car, and opened the door wider for her.

When he closed the door, she looked around the back seat. She'd never been in the back of a cop car, and the view from the back felt different as she watched Owen walk up the drive way.

She used to hope that one day, she'd have somebody. Somebody like Owen.

She gave up on that when she gave up on Sam.

⌐

"Hi Inspector Minicozzi, what's going on?" Sadie rubbed her eyes as she opened the door wide.

Avery heard Sadie go to the door, and she could have wrung her neck for answering it at all, never mind on her own.

"I came to check on Avery. Can you get her for me?"

When she heard Owen's voice she relaxed, and when she reached the landing, she squeezed Sadie's arm.

"Owen? Are you here to watch the house?"

"Inspector Ascott asked me to pick you up and bring you in. Fiona too."

"Why?"

"We have reason to believe Arnold Henderson has run. We don't have eyes on him anymore, but I want you to stay calm. The situation is under control. I didn't tell Fiona, I didn't want her to freak out, but I know you can handle this, okay?"

Sadie looked from Avery to Owen. "Can I come too? I don't want to leave her alone right now."

Owen shook his head. "You can come by the department tomorrow morning alright?"

"Noah, I mean, Inspector Cotter told me not to go anywhere without her."

"I know." Owen looked back down the driveway. "I have to follow orders from Ascott though. We have to go now."

"Okay." Avery looked back at Sadie and shrugged.

Sadie nodded. "You'll be okay. Here, let me get some things for you."

"We don't really have time." Owen shook his head. "Just grab your coat."

Avery nodded, and picked up her coat from the bench. "My purse? It's downstairs."

"Just leave it. Sadie can bring it for you tomorrow, right?"

Sadie nodded and smiled. "Of course. Be safe alright?"

"Thanks for letting me stay." Avery hugged her. "You're the best. I'll see you in the morning, okay? Don't answer this door for anyone."

Sadie nodded. "Take care. See you in the AM."

Avery zipped her coat up and walked down the driveway with Owen.

"I don't want her to know what's going on, so don't say anything alright? I'm guessing you've seen how she gets?"

Avery nodded. "Owen, are we going to be okay?"

Owen opened up the back door for her, and she stood, and waited for his answer. When he opened the door wider, she got in.

"Hey, what are you doing here?" Fiona asked.

"Hello to you too." Avery strapped her seatbelt on, as Owen stood by the side of the car.

"Owen said he was just checking on you."

"He was." Avery heard Owen on his phone, but couldn't make out what he was saying.

"So why are you here then?"

Owen opened the door, and got in.

"Owen, why is she coming with us?"

"Avery didn't feel safe. I told her she could come for a ride with us."

Avery saw the disappointed look on Fiona's face. She wasn't sure why Owen wanted to lie to Fiona, but anything to keep her calm was probably for the best.

"Can we just go back to my place?" Fiona asked. "I guess she can come too."

"Just one more stop." Owen said.

Avery kept waiting for the familiar turn onto the main road, toward the highway, and the department.

They missed it.

"Where are we going?" She asked.

"Like I said, one more stop."

Avery heard a tone from him she never had before, and it irked her. She sat up straight, and leaned into the middle seat, until her eyes met his in the rear view mirror.

"Owen, where are you taking us?"

"You need to relax Avery." Fiona crossed her arms, and looked out the window. "It's what I was trying to do before you came."

Avery squinted at Fiona, and looked back at the mirror, but Owen's eyes remained on the road.

"Owen told me they think Arnold got away." Avery crossed her arms, and looked at the mirror. There was no change in his expression.

"What are you talking about?" Fiona looked to Owen. "Did you tell her that?"

"He told me not to tell you because he didn't want to get you upset."

"Owen, is that true?"

Owen kept both hands on the wheel, and continued to drive north.

"He told me he was taking us to the department because we weren't safe."

"The department's that way." Fiona turned her head to the back.

"That's why I want to know where we're going. Tell me right now Owen."

His silence said more than enough, and Avery tried the handle on her door.

"Please, try to calm down." Owen cleared his throat. "We'll be there soon."

"Where?!" Fiona yelled.

When there was no response, she tried her handle, and both girls started to bang on the windows.

"Help!" Avery yelled, as a car approached behind them.

"Avery." Fiona yelled, but she kept banging on the windows, and yelling. "Avery!"

Fiona grabbed her arm, "No one's going to help us, we're in the back of a cop car. I don't have my cell, do you?"

Avery shook her head. "Owen, why are you doing this?"

"I could try to explain, but you'll never really understand." His voice was low and deep. Avery struggled to hear his words. "Please don't struggle."

"I could!" Fiona yelled. "I'd understand. Tell me what's going on."

"Please." Owen made another turn.

"Owen?" Avery squeaked.

"Stop!" Owen raised his voice; Avery looked at him in his rearview mirror, and waited for him to look at her.

They both waited for something, anything from him.

"Please forgive me." His voice was soft again.

When the words hit Avery, they took her breath away, and she knew they couldn't change his mind.

Chapter 58

"Go ahead." Ethan said.

Noah pulled out of the driveway, and started down the road as drifts of fog rolled across it.

"I just dropped Darrel Beelson off at his house. We went to Bob Pope's cabin, he wasn't there by the way, and I've got a new lead."

"You went alone? Come on Noah. I like you, okay? I thought you were smart, but you've been pulling some dumb moves, and right now, you're killing me. You're hurting this case."

"He told me he thinks Arnold spends time in Tipper's Point."

"What?"

"It's a place just south east of Cedar Ridge."

"I know where it is. That makes no sense."

"I asked Darrel where a quiet place would be around there. Something deserted. I meant for hunting, but Darrel was thinking of something else. He was thinking of the way Arnold came when he visited them. It didn't make sense, and he only went that way when he was alone. He'd pass Tipper's Point."

"Go on."

"Well, it's an old abandoned trailer park, with lots of wooded area surrounding it, and it makes sense as the place he'd take the girls to finish them off."

"Well, maybe, but isn't that reaching?"

"I wouldn't be the one reaching then. It'd be Darrel. He told me about the place for a reason. Maybe he has a gut feeling. I don't know. I think it's worth a search."

"I'll get a team together now."

"I'm on my way."

"Okay, and listen, I know you care about this case. Just run things by me from now on."

"Okay."

"See you soon."

When Noah hung up, he wondered if Ethan would have kicked him off the case if he hadn't provided this lead. He was glad he supported his decision to go, because nothing could stop him from checking out Tipper's Point.

Chapter 59

FIONA DIDN'T KNOW WHAT SHE was looking for in her pockets, but when they came up empty, she wished she hadn't left with him so willingly, when her first instinct was to question his offer.

"I don't know what you're doing Owen, but we can turn around." Avery was still talking to him, but Fiona had given up.

She stared down at her crutches, and tapped Avery's leg gently. When Avery looked at her, Fiona looked down at the crutches. When their eyes met again, Avery's were wide, but she nodded.

They turned down a bumpy gravel road, and Fiona saw lights shine in the window from the car behind them.

Over the bumps, when the head lights shone away, they saw it was a woman. Fiona started banging on the window and Avery joined in. The woman looked startled, and slowed down, as their car sped up.

"Help!" Avery shrieked, but the woman frowned, and turned down the next road.

They were left alone on the dark country road.

They made another turn and Fiona saw a forest in front of them.

"Is that where we're going?" Avery whispered.

The road stopped and so did the car.

Owen got out, and slammed the door shut. Fiona ducked down, and saw him on his phone again.

"Listen, when he opens that door, we have to hit him with these." Fiona passed Avery a crutch.

"What will these do?"

"Knock him out or something."

"Then what?"

"Then you drive us outta here."

Avery nodded. "You think he's taking us to Arnold?"

"I don't know. I don't want to know. Let's just do this."

Avery nodded and they heard Owen open her door. Fiona braced herself, ready to do whatever it took.

Avery pulled the crutch back, and Fiona waited for her to shove it at him, but she just sat there with the crutch in her hands. Owen's face came into view.

"Now!' Fiona shouted, but Avery shook her head.

Fiona saw the gun pointed at her. "Put them down now. Please, don't make me hurt you."

Avery dropped her crutch.

"No, he's bluffing. He won't hurt us. Not if he's bringing us to him."

"Fiona." Owen barked. "You don't know what I'm capable of. You best not assume, or get any ideas. Just get out of the car."

Avery scrambled out of the car, and Fiona scooted over to the open door, before it slammed in her face.

She watched Owen cuff Avery, and turned to get her crutch. She grabbed it, and when she sat up, she watched Owen's fist collide with Avery's head. In the moments after, she slammed her crutch against the back window. The thuds got Owen's attention, and he opened the door.

"Don't hurt her!"

"Get out now."

Fiona held her crutch, and slid toward the door. Owen grabbed the crutch, and Fiona held on.

"I need it to walk."

"You won't be walking."

"Please Owen." She pulled the crutch back, and used her body to force it forward at Owen's leg.

He jumped out of the way, and Fiona watched the other crutch come down on her head.

Chapter 60

"Noah, where are you? We're leaving soon."

"Thorpe and Concession Three."

Noah approached the intersection when the call came in.

"What the hell? You said you were coming in!"

"No, I said I'm on my way there."

There was a pause, and Noah heard commotion in the background. He realized their misunderstanding, and started to explain.

"Arnold's in the wind."

"What?"

Noah stopped at the intersection.

"He's gone. Not at home where we thought he was. One officer's dead, another in critical condition."

He pictured Arnold coming down his driveway at them with a rifle in his hand. If that were the case, they would have had time to stop him. They should have.

"How?"

"Don't know. Listen, we're all on our way out. Wait for us along Thorpe. Do not go alone. You got me?"

"Yeah, I'll be there."

"Good, and Christ, Noah, don't try to be a hero."

He would have laughed at the word had he not felt the guilt would rumble up his throat.

"Noah?"

"You think he's there, don't you? Tipper's Point."

Noah pictured Arnold's vehicle parked there among the trailers and hearing the screams of his next victim.

"That, or out hunting his next vic. Get Owen on Avery and Fiona."

"Yeah, sure."

"Get back to me when you know they're safe. I've alerted the officers outside their houses along with the Kent's and Hornby's."

Ethan hung up, and Noah punched the steering wheel. He told him not to be a hero, but even if he wanted to, he wouldn't have the slightest clue where to start, besides Tipper's Point.

Chapter 61

WHEN AVERY OPENED HER EYES, she saw a blurry vision of the forest. Her arms were tied to a big tree along with her body, but her legs were free, and she kicked and screamed.

"Fiona!" Avery cried, and struggled against the rope. "Fiona, please!"

The ropes weren't tied tight enough to hurt, but she couldn't lean more than an inch or two forward, and she wriggled her body against it.

"Owen! You don't have to do this!" Her shout held a distant echo.

Avery squinted and searched for Owen in the distance, but the fog concealed everything more than twenty feet ahead. As she tried to concentrate, her head throbbed.

"Bastard." Avery heard the muttered words from behind her, on the other side of the tree.

"Fiona? You okay?"

"Yeah. Don't yell, alright?"

"Owen's gone. He dragged us in here for him. I know it."

Fiona struggled against the rope, and Avery let out a gasp.

"Fiona, that hurts."

"Well how do you expect us to get out of this without pulling?"

"We can't," Avery looked down at the rope, "but I can."

"What?"

"If I pull, and you lean back, I think I can slip out of this."

"Really?"

"Yeah, but it's going to hurt...for you. Like, really hurt."

"Just do it."

"Okay, one, two...."

Avery pulled, and scooted her back down the tree trunk. She heard Fiona gasp, but she kept going, and pulled even harder to give herself more space.

"Ah." Fiona gasped.

"Almost." Avery said, and shimmied the rope over her breasts.

"Stop." Fiona gasped.

Avery pushed her head back against the tree, and Fiona gasped for breath.

"Are you?" She panted, "Out?"

"Fiona, don't move, you're rubbing it against my neck."

"You're still not out? Come on. I could have been out after five seconds flat."

"Yeah, but you're not much use with your leg, so it had to be me, alright? I'm sorry."

"Uh huh."

"What? I am."

"Just get it over with." Fiona groaned.

Avery pulled the rope again, and slid her head out of the bindings.

"There!" She shouted.

"Be quiet!" Fiona hissed. "You really think we're alone out here?"

"No. Sorry."

Avery struggled to her feet and walked around the tree to where Fiona leaned limply against it. Avery dropped to her knees and leaned in close. The moonlight illuminated her face, and reflected off of her misty eyes.

"Your leg. Does it hurt?" Avery stopped pulling the ropes from her wrists and studied Fiona's bloody pant leg..

"I'm fine."

"It looks like it hurts."

"You don't look so good yourself. Your head's bleeding."

Avery touched her fingers to her forehead, and a sharp sting made her pull away. Her fingers were bright red.

"Owen knocked me out." Avery studied the blood, "I can't believe it."

"He did the same to me. Believe it. Now untie *me*."

"Here," Avery scooted closer to her and their hands touched, "you're cold. Freezing."

"I didn't notice."

Avery looked around the dark woods, and heard something in front of them. A snap of a twig drew their attention to their left.

"I have to hurry." Avery whispered. "Hold still"

"I am."

Fiona tugged, and yanked, and Avery pressed her lips together as she worked.

"Do you know where we are?" Avery asked, and as soon as the question left her lips, she was ready for a sarcastic response.

"I couldn't tell if we were in Cedar Ridge anymore. After that woman saw us, I lost track."

"Why would Owen do this? Is he working with Arnold? He's got to be."

"I don't know." Fiona pulled at the rope, "It doesn't make sense."

"He's gotta be working for him. He brought us to the forest Fiona."

"I know."

"It's happening...."

"There."

Avery pulled Fiona's arms forward and the rope fell loose.

"Hold on." Avery collected the ropes in her hands, "I just have to pull this over your head and..."

Avery's eyes searched her face and waited for Fiona to finish the sentence for her.

"Listen to me. This is not your forest, and it's not my forest. The same thing's not going to happen, okay?"

Avery nodded as she pulled the rope over her head.

They both turned to the left, where the snapping noise had come from, and heard a familiar joyful tune.

Chapter 62

NOAH CALLED OWEN'S CELL over and over again.

No answer.

Voice mail full.

He dialed Ethan's cell.

"Can't get ahold of Owen. Maybe Missy, his wife, maybe she went into labour?"

"He'd answer." His tone was flat, and Noah listened as someone spoke to him in the background.

"We tried him too. Nothing."

"If he was going to answer, I think he'd answer me. We're friends."

"Hold on."

Noah waited as Ethan spoke, the radio crackled, and Noah couldn't make out the words.

He pulled over to the side of the road where Ethan told him to stay. It was deserted, and had been for the past few miles. There was a rundown sign that read "T- P-INT", and he parked the car right in front of it.

"Noah, you with me? Call just came in from a local woman out by you along Concession Three. Said she saw two females, clearly distressed in the back of a cop car. It was Owen's plate."

"What?"

"You know everything I do. I think Owen took the girls."

"No, somebody must've stolen his car. God, he could be in trouble. What if it was Arnold?"

"He's involved with Arnold somehow." The same flat tone he used that said he knew Owen better than Noah. "Noah, you're close to where they were spotted."

"You think they were taken here, now? Tipper's Point?"

"That's where they were headed. No one knows you know about that place except for Darrel and me. If Arnold took his vics here before, nothing would stop him from taking them there now."

"There's no cars here. I would have noticed a police car."

"We're fifteen minutes out," he paused "maybe twenty."

Noah squinted and searched down the path into the old trailer park. Everything was quiet and eerie feeling gnawed at him as he tried to see through the mist.

"Can't wait that long."

"Yes you can, and you will. That's an order Noah."

"The girls are in danger, and who knows where they are. Maybe Owen too. Try to get ahold of Missy."

"Listen, you followed the lead, and it turned out to be a good call. I can't have you running around out there without backup. Tipper's Point is more than ten acres."

"I've got to look. This might not even be the right place."

"You think it is though, don't you?"

"From what Darrel said, yeah, I do."

Ethan cleared his throat. "You'll reply when I message you."

"Right."

"I want updates. If you find them, and Arnold is there, you wait for us Noah."

Noah ended the call and set his phone to silent. He checked his gun, and drove his car into the abandoned park. The moon formed shadows around a group of trailers and trash littered the ground around him.

He made a turn, slipped in between two trailers, and parked.

He ran back out to the road, walked along beside the ditch, and searched for tire marks that lead into the park. Aside from his own tracks, he saw a few others, but couldn't determine whether they were fresh.

Thorpe Road was deserted, and as a cloud drifted over the moon, Noah crossed the ditch. He stayed on the same side of the road as the trailer park, and jogged along the tree line, as his hand hovered over his gun.

As he waited for any sign of movement or sound, and started to wonder how Arnold got Owen's car, and how he was able to take both the girls.

The silence along the road was maddening as he pictured Avery and Fiona being taken against their will, to meet whatever fate Arnold had planned for them.

He hoped Darrel was right about Tipper's Point, because he couldn't let his mind wander to the alternative.

Chapter 63

THE WHISTLING WAS BARELY AUDIBLE, and if Fiona hadn't heard it before, she might not have been able to place the sound. As it got louder, the jovial tune became clear. Avery's fingers fumbled with the rope, as she finished untying Fiona's wrists, and Fiona concentrated on the direction it came from.

"We have to go." Fiona whispered.

"Come on." Avery wasn't as quiet, and she grunted as she pulled Fiona up by her arm. She wrapped it over her shoulder and squeezed her wrist tight. "Can you limp along?"

"Let's go that way." Fiona nodded in the opposite direction the whistling came from, but Avery shook her head.

"This way." She didn't wait for Fiona to respond, and instead, drug her along.

"Why?" Fiona whispered.

"He'll expect us to go in the opposite direction. Just trust me."

Fiona pushed herself along, but each time the foot of her bad leg hit the ground, it reminded her of being shot on the path.

Tree branches snapped, and leaves rustled from the direction of the whistling.

"Let me carry you." Avery whispered in her ear.

"No way."

Avery was taller, and her frame was thinner. They probably weighed the same, but Avery lacked the muscle Fiona had.

"Get on my back."

"I'm fine."

"We're going too slow."

Fiona knew it was true, and in the same moment, Avery stopped pulling her along, and heaved her over her back, fireman style. Fiona didn't say anything for fear of being heard, but if she could have, she would have given her an earful.

She knew her weight might have shocked Avery, with muscle weighing more than fat, but she admired her perseverance as she hobbled along at a better pace. They made less noise as one, and the whistling was fading. The sound was replaced with Avery's laboured breathing, and Fiona knew she couldn't be carried much further.

"Put me down." Fiona's voice caught on the phlegm in her throat with each step Avery took.

"I'm taking us as far as I can."

Fiona could picture herself uttering those words if the situation were reversed. She felt Avery shake beneath her with each uneven step and wondered which direction they were going. Less than thirty paces more and Avery stopped. Fiona slid off her back against a tree, and down the trunk.

Avery knelt beside her.

"We have to work together." Fiona hissed.

"You have to trust me. You don't have another choice. You couldn't have walked that far."

"I could..."

"Shh." Avery looked in the direction they came from, and the whistling was clear again. "Okay, what do we do?"

"We should have gone in the other direction."

"We don't have time. Just tell me."

If she knew where they were.

If she were familiar with the area.

If she knew the girl she was taken with.

If only she knew which way was north, but she couldn't waste their time on these thoughts.

"Listen." Avery whispered and pointed toward the whistling.

"He's closer."

Avery shook her head and pointed. "There's a stream. It's got to be coming from Lake Simcoe. If we follow it, it should lead us out, right?"

"How will we know if it's leading us out or deeper? Which way is north? We should try to listen for the road."

"There are no cars on the road out here. It's the best I've got for now." Avery said. "Should I carry you again?"

"You're asking me this time?" She thought better of giving her a dirty look, and took a deep breath. "Let's just walk."

"Fine. One condition."

"What?"

"If he gets close," Avery glanced toward the whistling, "I have to hide you. You won't be able to outrun him. Maybe we should hide you now."

She shook her head. "We aren't splitting up. We each did this by ourselves last time, and we only survived because we got help. Those other girls he killed didn't have help."

Avery looked over her shoulder, and Fiona could tell she was still searching for a hiding spot. The thought of being left in the dark with the killer made her hands tremble, and she pushed them down into her legs.

"Avery, promise me you won't leave me." As soon as the words left her lips she dropped her gaze to the ground.

"Whatever. Come on." She pulled Fiona to her feet, and when she stood, her hands stopped shaking.

Avery may not have exactly promised, but it was better than another argument. They took a few steps in the same direction, and as Avery walked faster, the distance between them grew.

"Maybe," Fiona whispered when Avery looked back at her, and felt her face grow hot, as Avery tip toed back. "Maybe if you could, you could carry me again?"

Avery got into position again, and lifted Fiona across her back. The fog made Fiona dizzy, but she decided it was working to their advantage as long as the whistling continued.

"He's close." Avery whispered.

"Just keep going."

Chapter 64

AS NOAH TURNED THE CORNER, he lost sight of the park sign, and felt his cell vibrate once in his pocket. Straight ahead, there was another opening to the trailer park with a closed metal gate. He ran toward it, and saw a few tire marks coming in and out, but they looked faded. No guarantee they were from today, he thought, and then the doubts crept into his mind.

What if the girls weren't even close to here? What if they were taken further north, or in a completely different direction than what the witness saw?

He needed to know when the witness saw the girls, and he would know how far away they could be.

He took his phone out, and ducked behind a tree.

A text from Ethan and a missed call from Owen.

He pressed five, held the phone to his ear, and waited in the dark.

"Noah. The girls are being hunted."

"Owen? What's going on?"

"They're behind the trailer park at Tipper's Point, or they were when I left them there almost an hour ago."

Clouds of Noah's breath drifted away from him into the fog, and as he pressed the phone to his ear, he felt like he was drifting away with them.

"Why?"

"Arnold took Missy."

"What?" He steadied himself against the tree.

"He took her right from our house while I was at work, or somebody did. They kidnapped her. Someone called me, and told me what I had to do if I wanted to see her alive again. Listen Noah, she's okay. She's safe, but those girls..."

"You delivered them to Arnold?"

"He told me where to drop them off. He left a pair of GPS trackers by the gate, and he had me put them in their pockets. I got the call like, five minutes ago, telling me Missy was back home safe. I called as soon as I saw her Noah. Noah?"

"You gave them no chance."

"I-- I couldn't..."

"Where did you take them?"

"I'm sending you the co-ordinates now."

"He knows you'll do that. What's he going to do?"

"Hunt them. He's going to try to hunt and kill them like the others."

"You *knew* this, and you just served them up?"

"He was going to kill Missy, and the baby, and I couldn't tell anyone..."

"I don't have time for this. Is there anything else I should know?"

"I don't think he's alone. Maybe it's Bob Pope, but there's too much to have done by himself. Taking Missy, planting the GPS here, and who knows what else? I tied the girls to a tree, and I tried to leave it a little loose. I tried to give them a..."

"Anything else?" Noah raised his voice.

"I'm sorry Noah..."

"Send the co-ordinates, Owen."

Noah ended the call, stared at the screen, and waited for the co-ordinates. His chest heaved, and his hand shook the cell as the screen lit up blue. He checked the coordinates, and realized they were further south than he had originally thought.

He started out at a run, and just before he reached the entrance to the trailer park, he pressed the number for Ethan.

Chapter 65

AVERY WANTED TO GET TO SAFETY, and she wanted help to come, but more than anything, she wanted to escape from the whistling.

She couldn't have walked more than fifteen feet before the weight of Fiona's body slowed her down. She tried to focus on the sound of the stream, but her breath was too loud in her own ears. After another ten paces, she put Fiona down again.

"Should we try you on my back?" She panted, "Like a piggy back?"

"I don't know." Fiona looked in the direction the whistling came from. "Maybe we should try to hide together?"

"He keeps coming this way. You think we're loud?"

"Maybe he can hear us."

Avery knew that if they could reach the stream, the noise from the water could drown out the noise they made, if they just stayed close to it. Her mind wandered to a place she never thought she would consider voluntarily.

"I have an idea. I think when we get to the river, we should jump in."

Fiona shook her head and licked her lips.

"Trust me, I probably feel worse about this plan than you do, but it could take us farther away than we'll ever get on foot."

"Yeah, it could kill us too."

Avery looked toward the whistling that grew louder, and back at Fiona.

It was all she had, and when Fiona nodded, Avery felt a small pressure inside release.

"Try my back."

Avery bent down, and Fiona jumped off one leg awkwardly onto her back. She slipped down, but Avery bounced her up, and started toward the water.

"That hurt." Fiona hissed in her ear.

"Sorry." Avery spat.

But she wasn't anymore.

They came to a hill with a steep incline.

"We have to go around that way." Fiona said, and Avery nodded.

Piggy-backing her might have been a good idea at first, but Avery wasn't sure how much farther she could carry her at all. Her stomach ached, and she could only imagine how Fiona's leg felt.

As they started up hill, the whistling faded.

"I think we're losing him." Fiona whispered, and the weight felt heavier on Avery at that exact moment.

She caught her foot under a tree trunk, and started to fall, but grabbed a nearby tree.

"Just put me down. I can walk." Fiona whispered.

Avery let her slide off her back, and held in a groan as she rested her hand on her stomach. She looked down at her warm hand, covered with blood.

"Oh shit," Fiona stared at her stomach. "I'm sorry."

Avery remembered the wound on her forehead, and touched the blood that had begun to clot. Compared to the pain in her stomach, her throbbing head was easy to deal with.

Almost forgettable.

"It sounds like we're close." Avery whispered. "We have to hold onto each other when we go into the water."

Fiona nodded.

They inched their way over the other side of the hill, and in the distance, they saw a river.

"My leg's not that bad. I can make it. Almost there."

The river was just beyond the line of trees, and as Avery heard the rocks knock together below, she grabbed Fiona. She pulled her back over the hill, and pointed to the river. They crouched down and peered out from behind the top of the hill.

A man stood wearing all black with a balaclava over his face. He had black gloves, and was waving at someone.

Out of the trees came the man with the mask, and when Avery saw it, she started to cry. Fiona grabbed her hand, and held it tight, as they watched on.

While the man in black looked up and down the river, the man with the mask looked down at something in his hand and then straight up in their direction.

They both dropped crouched down further.

"Did he see us?" Avery whimpered, and wiped her blurry eyes with her fingers.

"He looked right at us. I couldn't tell. His eyes." Fiona let tears fall down her cheeks, and Avery grabbed her hand again.

"We have to go a different way."

Fiona's chest heaved up and down.

"Just hold on." Avery started to crawl up to the top of the hill. Fiona still had a hold of her hand, and Avery eased out of the grip as she steadied herself.

She peered over, and saw the man in black disappear into the bush where the masked man emerged from moments before.

No sign of the man in the mask.

Avery reached her hand out to Fiona. "We gotta go."

Fiona grabbed her hand, and Avery pulled her over the hill.

"Where is he?"

"They went back in the way they came." Avery told her. "We have to focus, okay?"

Fiona nodded and pointed to the river. "Are we going in?"

"I don't know anymore, they're too close."

Fiona took a deep breath and wiped the tears from her face.

"Let's go that way. Left down the river, away from them."

"Hopefully it leads to a road. You think..."

The whistling was back, and coming from where the men went back into the bush. It was quiet, and distant, but he was coming for them again.

They were coming, and they would keep coming until...

"He must have seen us." Fiona broke her train of thought, shook her head, and covered her mouth with her shaky hands.

"We're gunna be okay." Avery told her, and zipped up Fiona's jacket all the way. "Let's go."

"Wait. There are two of them."

"Yeah."

"Who's the other person? Owen?"

"I don't know. Come on." Avery tried to pull her, but Fiona wouldn't move.

"It doesn't make sense. He had Owen working with him the whole time? Or just now?"

"We have to keep moving."

"What if they split up?"

Avery shoved her cold hands in her pockets, and when her fingers touched something hard, she pulled it out.

"What the?"

"What is that?" Fiona whispered.

Avery stuck her hand in Fiona's pockets and pulled out the same thing.

"I think it's some sort of GPS." Avery studied them in her hand. "They're tracking us."

"*That's* how he knew. Get rid of them."

"Not yet." Avery shook her head. "Come on."

Fiona limped behind her. "Avery, where are we going?"

Chapter 66

IT WAS THE FIRST TIME Noah pictured someone as he held the gun up, and followed the tire tracks into the woods where Owen first took the girls. In training, his mind was always clear, and ready for whoever the target may be, but this time, the face of Arnold Henderson burned in his brain.

He followed Owen's tire tracks until they stopped and rushed into the forest. He searched for the big tree Owen spoke of, and a quarter of a mile in, he found it at the exact co-ordinates Owen had sent.

They're gone.

It was a straight shot to the car, and he wondered if the girls had escaped back to the road, as he stared at the tangled rope on the ground.

He texted Ethan his location and Ethan wrote back.

Ten more minutes.

Noah stood at the base of the tree and looked around.

The wind blew, and the leaves on the trees rustled around him. He kept his gun drawn, and walked around the base of the tree. On the south side, he saw struggle marks, and on the north, he saw the majority of the rope. He looked at the dirt and followed the marks away from the tree. It was a clear dragging pattern, but there was no blood, and he was hopeful.

He followed it to the bush, and crouched down. The last of the markings were below him, and the rest of the forest floor was too wrought with grass and branches to see clearly after that.

Heading Northeast, he texted Ethan.

As he made his way into the woods, he started off slow, and searched the area for any clues as to their direction. When he found none, he continued in a straight line from where the marks stopped, along the path of least resistance.

As he forged on, the fog swirled away with the wind.

Chapter 67

"DON'T LEAVE ME." Fiona whimpered, and Avery shook her head and put a finger to her mouth.

"It's the only way," Avery whispered, and pointed to a tree trunk a few feet ahead. "I'll see you there soon."

If she had to look at Fiona's face for one more moment, she wouldn't have been able to leave her. Her nose was bright pink, and her eyes were filled with tears. Before Fiona could protest, Avery was stepped away.

She clamored up the steep hill to their left, and considered her next route when she reached the top. Each step toward another hill went against her nature, but she pushed herself to climb.

She reached the top and glowered.

No more hills to climb. No more rough terrain to cross.

Nothing more to slow them down.

She broke into a sprint. It felt good to run free without having to wait for anyone else and her thoughts shoved the pain in her stomach away.

I caught you, Arnold. I'm onto you.

She stopped in a more dense area of trees and tore her jacket off. She tucked the tracker into the pocket, and stuffed it into the bush beside her. She stepped back, and thought from a distance, it might look like someone was hiding in it. She tucked Fiona's jacket in above it, and it looked like the size of a person.

She held her stomach, and tried to remind herself that the wounds from the knife were superficial, and not life threatening. What she felt for the man who marked her was deeper than any cut.

She tried to catch her breath, but the faint sound of the whistling came from the distance, and forced Avery to run.

If they shoot at the jackets, she thought, we'll know where they are and when.

It's our last shot.

When Fiona got to the log, she laid down on the ground parallel to it, and pushed her body close, until she was pressed against it.

As she caught her breath, she felt the chill of the night air on her arms, and the hairs rose there and on the back of her neck. She drew her legs up underneath her in a ball when she heard the whistling again.

She knew she was closer to the men than Avery was and hoped Avery didn't come back at the wrong time.

If she came back.

She could lose her way, as they already had, or she could be caught by the men in an attempt to draw them away.

Or she could leave the dead weight behind, and focus on saving herself.

The whistling seemed closer than it should have come if they were following the devices.

Too close.

They should have gone left after Avery.

No talking. No whispering.

Just the whistling.

They could not have been more than ten feet away, and with each step, Fiona shook harder.

When the steps stopped, so did the whistling.

She closed her eyes, shivered into her ball, and prayed they hadn't spotted her. She tried to control her breathing, but keeping her body so still made her physically jump. Or was it the cold, she wondered, as the whistling started again.

She heard one set of footsteps and then another, and for a few seconds, she couldn't tell if they were coming closer, or going away.

Away, away, away.

And they did.

She took a deep breath, but the shivers continued to send jolts through her body, and she could barely keep any part of her still.

Avery should be back soon.

If she's coming back.

When the footsteps faded, she huddled herself up in a tighter ball, breathed heat into her palms, and rubbed them together.

The whistling was faint, and then, there was nothing at all.

Until the bang.

Chapter 68

SECONDS AFTER THE GUNSHOT RANG out in the distance, Noah ran toward the sound.

Just one shot, he thought, and the sound was loud, but he knew he wasn't close.

Ten minutes away?

Twenty?

He waited for another, but there was only silence.

If anyone was screaming, or crying, he couldn't hear it.

Please, no.

His phone buzzed in his hand, but he clenched it in his fist, and ran toward the sound. He was already losing the direction it came from, but he continued to run, to close the gap.

The fog cleared bit by bit and formed a path ahead. Noah followed it further, and stopped to listen to the forest.

Nothing.

He opened his phone and read Ethan's text.

At Tipper's Point. Units close behind.

Noah texted him his coordinates, and then wrote *one gun shot.*

He listened for another sound.

Anything but a gun shot, he thought, and hiked on.

Chapter 69

FIONA ROCKED BACK AND FORTH in a ball when Avery rounded the log and tapped her on the boot.

Fiona looked up at her, and a smile flew across her face.

"Avery."

"Told you I'd be back. Now's our chance."

Fiona nodded as Avery pulled her up, and scrambled to her feet.

Avery grabbed her hand, and led her through the forest.

They wove around trees and bushes. They pushed through thick brush.

Every few steps, Avery listened for the whistle.

She looked over her shoulder, and felt Fiona pull on her hand as she started to fall. Avery steadied her, and held in a gasp as her stomach screamed at her for using it.

"You okay?" Avery huffed, "Your leg?"

Fiona nodded, grimaced, and squeezed Avery's hand tight.

They continued at a pace that Avery knew couldn't last, but she pulled Fiona harder, and tried to remember her as the girl with attitude.

The one who thought nothing of shooting her dirty looks, talking back, and criticizing her.

She needed the distance between them. It might be the last time she knew where the masked man was, and she had to use the knowledge to her advantage.

Fiona started to resist against her tugs, but she pulled her harder despite her whimpers.

"My leg. I can't," Fiona panted, and let go of Avery's hand, "it hurts, it hurts."

"Can I carry you?"

Fiona shook her head and her face twisted in pain.

"You're too slow when you carry me."

There was the Fiona she knew.

Avery grabbed her hand again, and yanked her further-- harder.

"Ah, did you see them?" Fiona panted.

"No. Quiet." Avery continued to pull her along, and when she felt the same resistance again, she stopped. "There."

A rusty trailer sat in front of them in a small clearing and Fiona sighed.

She limped ahead of Avery toward it, but Avery pulled her back.

"We must be close to a road. We have to keep going, but not that way. Not out in the open."

"I can't." Fiona gasped, and when she looked into her eyes, she knew it was true.

They hobbled over to the trailer, leaned against it, and looked behind them into the forest.

Avery knew they were both waiting for the whistling, and that they couldn't afford to wait any longer. She pushed herself off the trailer, and searched for a path around it.

"Just go." Fiona whispered. "I know you're going to."

"I only left because I had..."

Fiona shook her head. "I trust you. You have to get help for us."

Avery shook her head, and grabbed onto Fiona's arm as if it were a life preserver. She was careful with her good leg, and hoisted her onto her back.

"Avery." Fiona whispered, but it was all she said.

Avery lugged her behind the trailer, and along the tree line of the clearing. Her eyes followed the path from the trailer to a group of trees, and when she saw the road on the other side of them, she started to hobble faster.

"The road." She whispered, and when Fiona didn't say anything, she wondered if she had passed out from the pain.

They reached the side of the road, and Avery rolled Fiona off her back, into the ditch.

"Ahh, my leg." Fiona whimpered and grabbed at it. "Damn it."

"I'm sorry. I'm sorry."

The sound of a car came toward them, and they both turned in the direction of the headlight beams.

"Is it?" Fiona panted and clutched at her leg.

Avery crawled further up the ditch, and poked her head out to the road.

"Cop car." She said, and reached her hand down to Fiona.

"You go." Fiona looked up at her and nodded.

"Just keep going. Remember? "Avery grabbed one of her hands away from her leg, and yanked her up, out of the ditch.

Avery started to stand, but Fiona moaned, and she hesitated.

The car sped toward them, and although Avery wanted to flag it down, she stayed in the ditch. She squinted into the light and tried to make out the driver.

As the car sped by, with the headlights out of her eyes, she recognized Inspector Ascott.

She pushed herself to her feet and ran out to the middle of the road.

"Wait!" She screamed as she waved her arms.

The car came to a screeching halt, and Inspector Ascott opened his door. Another officer emerged from the other side.

"He's in there!" Avery shouted, "The killer with the mask and he has someone with him!"

Avery watched Ascott pick up his radio, and could vaguely hear him shouting orders.

The other officer walked toward them, and as a gun shot rang through the air, he flinched. Another shot, and he clasped his hand over his chest. His body shook before her eyes, and when his knees buckled, he collapsed.

Ascott drew his gun, and pointed it into the woods, behind the girls. Avery turned back; her eyes darted through the trees, and found no movement.

The fresh air was still.

She turned back when she heard the car engine, and watched as Ascott reversed the car over to the girls.

"Get in!" He shouted.

Avery pushed Fiona up into the passenger seat, and a bullet hit the side of the car.

Avery fell back, and Ascott pulled Fiona further into the car. Another shot rang through the air. Avery heard it whiz past her.

"Avery, come on." Ascott pulled on Fiona.

She turned around and saw the man in black among the trees with a gun aimed at them.

"Get down!" Ascott shouted and fired at the man.

The man fired back and hit the car again. Ascott rounded the car, and stood between the girls and the man.

Avery turned back to Fiona, and pushed her legs up toward the vehicle, but she felt heavy. Avery let go, and Fiona slid out of the car, onto the gravel.

"Hey." Avery crouched and shook Fiona. "Fiona!"

She tried to turn her over and her hand sunk into a warm spot on her back.

"No. No." Avery shook her head.

Fiona's back was soaked with blood and her body was motionless.

Avery heard another bang, and a grunt from Ascott, as he fell back onto her. Ascott's weight pinned Avery against the car as he leaned across her.

Avery watched the man take aim, and shoot Ascott in the chest. The push on impact made her gasp for breath, and she scrambled to get out from behind him. The man reached the ditch as Avery crawled out from behind Ascott, toward the front of the car.

A shot rang out and Avery froze.

The man in black howled into the night. His voice echoed as he dropped to the pavement.

Avery looked back to where Noah stood behind him, with his gun still aimed at the man. The man stirred, and as Noah raised his gun, Avery turned away.

Another shot rang out, and she covered her ears. She looked back, and saw fleshy pieces of the man in black, and threw up.

"Avery, "Noah ran to her as she choked on her vomit, "come on. Get in the car."

She heard another car approach.

"Fiona?" Noah called. "Avery, help me. Put pressure-- can you--" He took Avery's hands and pressed them against Fiona's wound.

Noah yanked Ascott's jacket off and ripped his shirt. Avery saw a bullet proof vest underneath, and blood by his shoulder.

She pressed hard against Fiona's wound and started to sob uncontrollably as officers came around the car, and pulled her away.

"Fiona," Avery cried out, "Fiona, please."

Noah wrapped his arms around her as the paramedics surrounded Fiona and Ascott. Avery buried her head in his chest, and felt another pair of hands pull her from him.

A paramedic.

When she left his arms, she felt colder than she had the whole night.

"I need a search party." Noah hollered, "Keep the perimeter closed. The killer is in there. I repeat. The suspect is in the woods."

Avery saw more paramedics run toward her and watched as a group of policemen surrounded Noah.

"Come on. You're safe now." The female paramedic helped her up into the vehicle.

"Avery." Noah ran over to them before the female could hop in the back.

She started to cry again and looked down at him.

"I'll meet you at the hospital okay?"

Avery nodded, and when she tried to speak, her mouth was full of saliva, and her words came out muddled. Her vision clouded as the tears took over, and Noah disappeared as the paramedics closed the doors.

Chapter 70

AVERY KNEW THAT IT was important to Fiona to stay close.

It was important not to leave her.

When she was reassured by the doctor that Fiona had passed away within seconds of being shot, and that she hadn't suffered, Avery finally gave up her struggle and laid back.

Fiona had known Avery was with her when she died, and it was enough, just enough, to keep breathing.

She didn't die alone.

Avery needed new stitches on her stomach, and Doctor Freebush warned her that there would be even more scarring there. She also got a stitch in her forehead, and although her head throbbed, she refused to take any pain killers. She started to close her eyes, and fought sleep for the hundredth time when she heard her parent's voices with the doctor in the hall.

She lifted her head to see one of their shadows in the door way.

"Avery!" She heard a new familiar voice echo in the hallway, and Sadie rushed in. "How are you doing?"

Avery held up her hands when she bent over for a hug, "I got stitches. Careful."

"Okay." Sadie called, and Josh came in.

His eyes remained on her face, and he pushed his lips together, as if her pain were his.

"Avery, God," he shook his head and stood beside Sadie, "what happened?"

"I just told Sadie, I had to get more stitches on my stomach, and one on my head."

"*How* did that happen?" Sadie asked, staring at it.

Avery's spine tingled and she shook it off. "Owen knocked us both out."

A cold silence filled the room, and Avery swallowed hard.

"I don't want you to go into any details now." Sadie rubbed her arm, "Not until you're ready. Whenever you're ready. We're just glad you're okay."

Avery clenched her teeth, and willed her shoulders not to shake.

"I saw your parents." Sadie lowered her voice. "How'd it go with them?"

"They haven't even been in yet." Avery sighed, and Sadie furrowed her brow.

"People," a nurse came in, and looked them all over, "we can't be having guests right now. Only family."

"They *are* my family." Avery said, and they all looked back to the nurse.

"Only *immediate* family. Come on now, you can visit tomorrow." She ushered them out.

"We'll be here when visiting hours start, okay Avery?" Sadie asked.

Her effort to act normal was admirable, but Josh's eyes spoke for both of them as they left the room.

His eyes held their pain, and reflected hers.

Avery lay wishing she got to pick her family until her parents came in.

"The doc says you're going to be alright Sweetheart."

"Great."

"Well, we had to check with your doctor." Her mom pulled a chair up to her bed. "Honey, we told you to come and stay with us. Why didn't you?"

"That has nothing to do with it." Avery started to shake her head, but her dad interrupted.

"We wouldn't have let this happen to you."

"I was abducted by a police officer," Avery's voice rose as she spoke, and the familiar pangs in her stomach burned as she lifted her head, "you'd have let me go with him just like Sadie did."

Her dad shook his head. "No, we would have insisted on going with you."

"Don't get mad at us Avery, we're your parents."

"You don't get to use that." Avery's shoulders shook and she fought back tears.

"What?" Her mom looked to her dad.

"Last time I ended up in here, you saw me once, and that was it."

"You were sleeping! And we told you to come and stay with us. We even told you we'd have someone pick you up. You're an adult Avery," Her dad said, "you make your own decisions, but you should have listened. Don't pretend we don't care about you, alright? It's old."

"Are you really going to stand here after everything I've been through, and tell me it's my fault?"

"That's not what we're saying..."

"This isn't the time to be fighting." Her dad rested his hand on her mom's shoulder.

Avery looked up at the ceiling. "You should leave."

"We'll be back tomorrow, and as soon as the doctor says you're ready, you're coming home with us. That's final. I won't see my daughter..." He stopped, and shook whatever image came to him away.

"I thought you said I was an adult who made my own decisions, Dad?" She seared.

"You're our daughter, and we love you, and we'll do whatever we have to to protect you. End of discussion." He took her mom's hand, and led her to the door. "We'll see you tomorrow."

As soon as they were gone, Avery let the tears spill down her cheeks.

"Okay Avery," the nurse came back in with some pills, "I just need you to take these alright?" She set the pills down and studied Avery. "Is it the pain?"

Avery nodded and wiped the tears from her eyes.

"You take these, okay? They'll help you rest."

Avery looked at the pills in the cup.

"I-- I don't want to go to sleep right now."

"You've got to take them Avery," The nurse smiled, "doctor's orders. You'll feel better. I promise."

Avery nodded, and tucked the pills into her cheek before she swallowed.

"There we go." The nurse smiled. "Just press your buttons if you need anything."

She smiled wide and rushed out of the room.

Avery rested her head on the pillow, and heard someone shuffle outside her room. She hoped it was a police officer, and that she hadn't been left alone as she started to drift off.

"Avery..." Fiona whispered in her thoughts, and Avery took a deep breath.

"I can't sleep. I can't... I can't stop the adrenaline. I think that's it. I'm still in that mode, you know?"

There was silence.

"I'm afraid." Avery teared up again, "That's the truth."

"I know." Fiona whispered.

She watched the moon outside her window.

"I can't believe...Owen..."

"I know." Fiona whispered.

"My eyes are heavy." Avery couldn't open them anymore, and her lashes fluttered against her cheeks.

"You go to sleep. I'll stay up."

She knew the voice was only in her head, but she listened to the words, and let sleep take her.

Chapter 71

"How's Ethan?" Noah asked, as he got back in his car.

January paused before answering. "Still in urgent care."

"You there now?"

"Yeah. Ken's back at the department, trying to figure out where Arnold would go next."

"When did you last get an update about Ethan?"

"I don't know, less than an hour ago?"

"And Avery? How's she?"

"I haven't been to see her, but Ralph's been there since visiting hours ended. He's standing guard outside the room, and he says she's sleeping."

"Good."

"Yeah, he just spoke to the nurse though, not directly with Avery, so..."

"Right."

There was a short pause and Noah heard something announced over the hospital intercom in the background.

"Nothing, huh?" January huffed.

"Nope. We found the spot where the girls lost their jackets, and one of them was shot right through."

"I just don't get it. The perimeter was closed."

"I think he got out before everyone got here."

"How though? How could he know?"

"I think he left when the girls ditched their coats. He wanted easy prey, and when he didn't get it..."

"Maybe."

Noah cleared his throat, and watched the last police car drive away from Tipper's Point.

"What about Pope?"

"He's still in urgent care too. He failed so miserably to end his life. Half his face is gone."

"Keep me updated alright?"

"Yeah, of course. You coming down soon?"

Noah saw the sky begging to lighten and checked his watch.

"I'll be there as fast as I can."

⌒

Avery felt cold, and when she woke up, a shadow lingered in the door way. She opened her eyes just enough to make out the figure of a man. He walked into the room, and stood at the foot of her bed. He watched her for a few seconds, and when he moved, she opened her eyes wide.

"Help!" She cried as loud as she could.

An officer poked his head in the doorway and the man by her bed held his hands up.

"I didn't mean to scare you. I can go. I'll leave."

"He just wanted to see you," the officer said, "He was a friend of Fiona's. I told him it was alright. If it's not..."

"Sorry Avery, I'm Sam. Ralph told me I could come, but I can go though, really..."

"Why are you here?" Avery pulled the covers up to her neck. "Who are you?"

"I just had to see you when Ralph called and told me." He choked on the last words and pointed to the door. "Ralph called me."

"You'll have to forgive me, but I'm not going to take your word for it just because he's a police officer."

"Listen, I don't know what happened, and you don't have to tell me everything, but I need to know a few things."

Avery licked her lips, and Sam passed her a cup of lukewarm water. As he came closer, she saw a handsome man, wearing a leather jacket, with a worn look on his face.

Avery took a sip of her water, and Sam pulled a chair up beside her.

"Can I sit?"

She nodded and set the cup down.

"I know this might be hard for you, but how did she die? They told me it was a bullet wound in her back, but..." he shook his head, "how?"

"One of the men chasing us came out of the woods when we were trying to get her into the car. He shot her and I didn't even realize it."

Sam stared at her and she wondered if he expected more.

"Fiona and I were engaged. Did you know that?"

"No. I'm sorry. I..." Avery stared off at the wall and thought back to the morning, "I just met her today."

He nodded. "I cheated on her. I don't know why I'm telling you this part, but I feel like I have to because I want you to know how badly I need to know what you know. It was only once, but Fee's so proud, and when she found out, she left me that day. After five years together."

"I'm sorry to hear that."

He shook his head. "It's my fault. I left her alone for a while, and I always thought we'd get back together, but when we spoke again it wasn't the same. She was so distant..."

Avery saw tears well up in his eyes, and when he looked at her, her heart broke for him.

"I didn't stop though. I kept trying to get her back. She was still my girl."

Avery started to cry and he let his tears fall.

"I didn't know her for long, but I know she was stubborn, and maybe..."

"That's just it. Maybe's are all I have now."

Avery waited while he regained composure and saw Ralph's shadow lean in a little more.

"She was strong willed. When we were taken, she stayed calm and tried to get us free. It was her leg. That was the only thing that slowed her down, okay? She kept telling me not to leave her when her leg got to be too much. We kind of butt heads when we met, but I didn't leave her. She wasn't alone when..."

"Thank you. That means a lot."

"The doctor said she didn't suffer at the end. She was brave, and we looked out for each other." Avery let her tears sting her cheeks. "We were almost..."

"Hey, I've got to live with the maybes, but don't do that to yourself. You did the best you could right?"

Avery nodded. "She did too."

Sam smiled and hung his head. "I already knew that."

The room was quiet for a long time, and while Avery cried, she thought he did too.

When Sam looked up, he nodded to Avery. "You've helped me more than you know."

Avery stared down at her sheet. "I think the inspector will be by soon. You should talk to him."

"Yeah." Sam said, and looked at the door. "I should let you rest. Thank you again, Avery."

There was nothing she could say, and when words weren't enough, he squeezed her hand.

As he walked out of the room, it felt like Fiona left with him.

Chapter 72

"Inspector Noah Cotter," Ralph shook his hand with a firm grip, "I understand you're working for Ethan."

He nodded. "Officer Ralph Nichol. You can call me Ralph. How's Ethan?"

"I just saw January down stairs. He's in recovery now."

"Good. I should go see him."

Noah nodded. "Before you go though, I was hoping to ask you a few questions."

"I had no idea."

"About?"

"Owen. He came and took over his shift. Never saw it coming. He's a good guy. It was good working with him. He was dependable, always showed..."

"Have you heard?"

"About how his wife was taken? Yeah. I don't know what I'd do if I were in the same..."

Noah shook his head. "I wanted to ask you about Avery."

"Oh, well Fiona's ex came and went just now. He's going to take her body back to Ireland to her family."

"And Avery?"

"I heard her parents were here. Then her friends came too. That was before I got here."

"How is she doing?"

"I haven't been in to see her. I've just been on guard."

"You didn't speak with her?"

"It's not that I didn't want to. I just...Fiona was a good girl. Avery seems like a good girl too. I don't want to get too close. I can't."

"I got it. Thanks Ralph," Noah tapped his shoulder, "I'll see ya back up here soon?"

He nodded and headed down the hall.

When he saw Avery, her head looked worse than he remembered, and her eyes were closed. He took the chair beside her bed, and sat down. His jaw clenched as he studied her face and took her hand in his. He wished he could take her pain that way, just by holding hands.

"Noah." She opened her eyes and they reminded him of the last time he saw her.

He reached his hand up to her face, and ran his thumb along her temple. "Your head."

"Yeah." She ran her fingers over the stitch and pulled his hand away. "He hit hers too."

"Owen."

She nodded and tears rolled down her face.

"Okay, I'm going to tell you everything I can, and you have to promise to do the same for me, okay?"

Avery nodded.

"You have to go first though."

She told him everything, and through each dark detail, his anger built. He calmed himself by concentrating on her voice. She finished when she saw him standing behind Pope, but he knew that the horrific story didn't end there.

"Did you catch him?"

"No, I'm sorry, we didn't. I think he got out of there before we put the perimeter up. I think what you did with the GPS trackers fooled him." Her stare was heavy, and he shook it off. "No, it was good. You put him off. It was smart, Avery. It bought you time."

"Who was the man in black?"

"Bob Pope. He was a friend of Arnold's. They hunted together. He was a suspect of ours, but we couldn't find him, and now we know why."

"Is he dead?"

"No. He's still in the ICU."

"Inspector Ascott?" Avery asked.

"He was hit with one of the bullets. It got his shoulder, but he's stable now."

"He saved me." Avery licked her lips and then spoke. "Why did he do it? Owen."

"Arnold, or probably Bob Pope, kidnapped Owen's wife." Noah swallowed hard and continued.

"Essentially, Owen traded you both for her. She is safe. Arnold gave her back unharmed. Owen is in lock up right now, and he regrets what he did and didn't do, but he did it, and he'll pay whatever price the court and the department sees fit."

Avery looked at her lap. "I don't know what to say."

"I know it's difficult to hear, but I want to be honest with you. You deserve the truth. That's how fast it happened. He was told to bring you both to a certain spot, and slip the trackers in your coats, and then he'd see his wife again."

"He didn't," Avery stopped and looked up at him, "he didn't tie the rope as tight as he could have."

Noah shook his head. "Doesn't matter. You're being released tomorrow."

"My parents want to take me home."

"I don't know if that'll be possible." Noah said, and saw Ralph reappear at the door. "Ralph?"

He walked to the end of the bed.

"Officer Ralph Nichol, this is Avery Hart."

Ralph nodded. "Ethan's talking. He's asking for you."

"You make sure that aside from family, no one sees her without my say so."

"And Sadie. And Josh." Avery piped up.

"Right. She will be discharged tomorrow into our protection. Do you understand? No one else is to know where she's going, or take her anywhere under any circumstances."

Ralph nodded. "Got it."

"I'll be back." Noah stood and looked down into her heavy eyes.

"I still have more questions."

"When I come back, I'll tell you whatever you need to know. Will you wait up for me?" Noah squeezed her hand and she squeezed back.

This time, it took him a while to let go.

Chapter 73

NOAH ENTERED ETHAN'S ROOM, and saw another man saying goodbye. He was in a suit, and nodded to Noah as he made his way out the door.

"Ethan," he pulled up a chair, "listen, we did everything we could to find him...."

"I know. Listen, that was Inspector Palfry, you've probably seen him around. He's a higher up anyway, who I answer to. I told him you're in charge of the case now until I'm outta here."

Noah pursed his lips, and sat back in his chair. "You want me to take over?"

"Until I'm back. Don't look so surprised."

"I'm not, I'm just glad you're alright."

"God damned vest doesn't cover enough area, but I'm alive, and I'll be well soon enough. I spoke to January too. She knows you're in charge and she'll help you fill out the reports, and introduce you to Palfry. Do *not* piss that guy off."

"Got it."

"I spoke to Ralph. He's a good guy and he'll follow your orders fine. I know you think Owen's a good guy too, but he's goin' down for this Noah."

Noah nodded, and looked at the bandage on his shoulder.

"I told Avery about him."

"Did you find out anything new from her?"

"Just how they were able to trick Arnold and Pope."

"Right, with the trackers."

Noah nodded. "How is it that you were in intensive care and you know more than me about everything?"

"It's my job to know." Ethan tried to crack a smile, but it looked like every muscle he moved was painful. "We're gunna put Avery in a safe house. Ralph's going too. We need people we can trust. I'd put you with her, but I need you out. January's going with them too."

"Where?"

"They're staying close. Palfry will tell you more this afternoon when you go back with January."

"What do I do now?"

Ethan smiled at him. "Now, you find that bastard before he finds her, or gets too far away. He shouldn't be able to get out of the country. He either learned from the stunt he pulled or he'll pull something even more bold next time. If Pope ever wakes up from his coma, investigate the shit out of him. That too."

"I didn't know he was in..."

"Well, now you do. Son of a bitch had to go and shoot me before he shot himself. Couldn't believe it when I heard. I thought it was you."

"I shot him once and then he shot himself. I wouldn't believe it if I hadn't seen it. I'll get together with January and Ken, and we'll..."

"That's the other thing. Just because I'm down, doesn't mean I'm out. I want patched in to every meeting or conference call you have."

"Sure thing."

"I'm not falling behind. I'm going to get out of here, and you'll be answering to me again. Hell, you're still gunna answer to me, but we've gotta put on a show for Palfry. You know what I mean, don'tcha?"

Noah nodded.

"Alright. Keep me up to date."

Noah started to leave.

"Hey, thanks." Ethan called.

"No problem."

Noah wasn't sure if he meant for taking over or for saving his life, but he'd accept it on both accounts.

He saw January when he came out of the room.

"Ready to go, boss?" She said with a small smile.

"One last thing."

Chapter 74

SADIE CAME BACK TO VISIT as soon as the sun rose, and when Avery told her about the conversation with her parents, Sadie shook her head.

"I'm so sorry Avery. You don't deserve that. I'd say I'm not surprised, but I just keep hoping you'll have a better relationship with them."

"Josh call you yet?"

"Yeah, he's still waiting for Asher to get home before they come together. He's not taking this well."

"I know. I could tell."

"I mean, I hate seeing you like this too, but he gets angry, you know? Maybe that he couldn't save you again?"

Avery nodded. "I'm really thankful to have you guys."

"You know what Josh said when we were leaving here? He said, did you hear that? She called us family."

The knock at the door made them both jump. Avery watched Noah walk in with a pretty woman behind him. Her hair was styled in soft waves, and her pencil skirt hugged her curves.

"Avery, Sadie, this is January. She's been working this case from the department."

"Nice to meet you both, though I'm sorry for the circumstances." She looked back to Noah, who stood closer to the door.

"I'm sorry, but I've got to get back to the department. I've just been placed in charge of this case until Inspector Ascott returns to good health. Ralph will be here today if you need him, and I'll be back tomorrow to pick you up when you're discharged."

"Where will I go?"

His cell phone rang; he lifted a finger, and walked out of the room to answer it.

"How are you feeling?" January asked.

"Okay." Avery whispered.

"Avery, I want you to know that I'll be more involved in the case now, and with you, and if you have any questions, you can always ask me, okay?"

"I've got one." Sadie smiled sweetly. "Can I come with her?

⌒

As Charla parked behind her dad's car, her stomach growled. Aunt Maggie's car was on the side street, just behind the police cruiser stationed at their home. Her back ached, and all she wanted to do was get out of her heels, put her slippers on, and dig into some leftovers.

All the lights were off in the home, and when she opened the storm door, she saw a red hand print smeared across the front door.

She grabbed her cell from her purse and called the police. While she gave her address to the operator, she remembered there was a cop already there.

Is this a joke?

She opened the unlocked door, and as it swung open, she saw blood on the kitchen floor.

And someone's foot, covered in blood.

She backed away from the door and tried to catch her breath.

Please no, please no, please

Her phone slid from her hand and smacked against the ground. She jumped and scurried across the lawn to the side of the house.

The policeman in the car was slumped over in his seat.

Charla felt her body tense up, and she backed away, across the lawn.

I can't.

Breathe.

Along the driveway to the side walk.

I can't.

Past the sidewalk to the road, where she tripped over one of her heels, and fell hard onto the pavement.

She gasped and looked up at the front door.

Blood trickled down the white painted metal.

It *was* blood.

She scrambled to her feet in the middle of the road and started screaming.

⁓

"Inspector Cotter."

"This is Palfry. There's been three murders at the Kent residence."

Arnold.

"I'll be right there."

"Cotter, it goes without saying that we need two officers with Avery at all times. Make sure you have that covered before you go."

"Yes sir. Sir, who are the vics?" He felt a lump in his throat, as he realized he knew them all.

Had met them all at least once.

"Charla's parents, and Maggie Henderson."

"Maggie's dead? Charla, is she okay?"

"Charla went to the home and found a hand print on the door in blood. We're doing tests, but I think it'll be obvious whose print it is. They were slaughtered. She didn't go in, but she's shaken, obviously. Just get there now."

"Arnold doesn't care about getting caught anymore. Wants to put his stamp on it."

"Cotter. One more thing. Officer Owen Minicozzi? You're not to speak with him unless I'm with you. I plan for us to speak with him as soon as possible together, but no independent contact."

"Yes sir."

Palfry hung up, and Noah stared at his phone for a moment before he went back in the hospital room.

"January. You'll stay here with Ralph until I'm back?"

She nodded.

"I'll send you an update shortly."

"When will you be back?" Avery's words tugged at him.

"Later today."

"I want to know what's going on as soon as..." January said before the physiotherapist knocked on the door.

"I need everybody out." The woman smiled.

"I'll be staying." January said.

Although the therapist side eyed her as she walked by, she set up her equipment quietly.

"Thanks January. I'll see you soon." Noah nodded to them.

He wanted to kiss Avery's forehead, or at least squeeze her hand, but with January watching, he settled for a nod.

Avery nodded back.

Chapter 75

Charla

THE KNOCK ON THE DOOR STARTLED CHARLA. She let go of the toilet, forced herself to leave the washroom, and peered through the peephole.

Someone in a suit.

She opened the door, and saw the familiar face, although she forgot his name.

"Charla, I'm so sorry for your loss. I'm going to accompany you to the funeral. I want to make sure you have the proper protection, and then we can go back to the department, alright?"

She nodded, left him at the door, and rushed back into the bathroom. She looked at herself in the mirror, and tried to fix her hair.

"Charla, we need to leave soon, alright?" He called in to her, and she realized she was still wearing her pajamas.

She had stayed in the hotel room the police brought her to for four days straight. One of them would come in to check on her, but for the most part, she was alone.

She opened a duffle bag someone had brought her with some clothes, and dumped them on the bed. She rifled through the options, started to cry, and looked up at the man.

"I don't know..." She started.

"Charla. Take a seat. You don't have to rush. I'm sorry I rushed you..."

"What do you wear to your parent's funeral?" She started shaking. "What do you wear to the funeral of your three closest family members?"

He shook his head and looked down at the bed. "I'm sure anything; I mean any of those will look good."

"Why do I care?" She wiped her cheeks, and sat down on the bed. "My parent's and aunt are dead. Why do I care what I wear?"

He pulled a chair up in front of her, and waited for her breathing to calm before he spoke.

"My mom passed away a few years ago. Cancer. I don't know what you're going through, and I won't pretend to, but I can tell you I'm here for you."

She looked up at him and wiped her red cheeks. "I'm sorry, I forget your name."

"Inspector Cotter. Noah Cotter."

She nodded, and grabbed a pair of black dress pants and a black knit sweater. "Be back."

When she came out of the bathroom, she closed the clasp on her locket, and he held a water bottle out to her.

"Thanks." She took it, and started for the door.

"Oh, your coat? And purse?" He asked.

She grabbed both, and as they left the room, he told the officer on guard to grab all her things from the room and bring them to the department.

On the car ride, she scrolled through the contacts in her phone, and hoped she hadn't forgotten to tell anyone. Her aunt on her dad's side, who she'd only met twice, flew in from the west coast to handle the paperwork and decisions. She scrolled through texts from work friends, and found one that stood out.

Avery Hart sent her condolences.

"Inspector Cotter? Do you know how Avery Hart's doing?"

He continued staring out the window for a moment.

"She'll be okay. Don't even think about it right now, alright?" He finally looked at her with a reassuring nod.

"Yeah." She worked up the courage to ask the question she was sure she had the answer to. "Was it my uncle? Was it Arnold for sure?"

"We confirmed his prints. Yes."

She nodded, and fought the sting in her chest, as they pulled into the parking lot.

When they entered the funeral home, Charla didn't recognize most of the faces, and she didn't expect so many people to show up. She saw someone wave to her before going back to her conversation with the funeral director, and she stopped when she saw the caskets at the far end of the room.

Many of those who greeted her said they knew her family from their partying days before Charla was born. Those who came from Charla's work were able to be a small comfort, but she glazed over most of their conversation and sympathy, and found herself staring at her mom's casket when the funeral director approached.

"Your aunt, Carole, has arranged for your family to be buried at the Crown River Cemetery this afternoon. I'll have the pallbearers lead them out at the end of the service."

Charla nodded.

"Visitation's almost over. People will be taking their seats soon. If you'd like to say your final goodbyes to your loved ones, please take your time and we'll begin afterward."

"Thank you."

He nodded slightly, and walked back down the short aisle. He walked past Inspector Cotter, who surveyed the crowd, and it was the first time she felt conscious of the possibility her uncle could try to...

She couldn't let her mind wander there.

When she turned her attention back to her mom's photo beside the casket, she stared at her face, and waited for the tears to come.

She felt guilty that she wasn't crying, and even worse for the cold stares they exchanged the last time they saw each other.

She walked over to the casket next to her mom, where her dad's picture stood beside his. Her eyes welled up as she remembered their warm embrace that night before she went to work. She started to cry and wished she could have hugged her mom one last time.

She felt the eyes of the room on her, as she side stepped from her dad's casket, to Aunt Maggie's and cried out loud.

Their relationship had always been close, and when she moved into their home, she hoped she was able to provide some emotional support to her in her final days.

Aunt Maggie thought she was safe at their place.

With *family*.

The word stung to think about.

A flash of the bloody hand print flew through her mind, and she took a step back. If she let it in, if she let even a little piece in, she was afraid she might drown in it.

She felt someone rest their hand on her back, and swung around to see an older woman, who wrapped her arms around her.

"Oh Charla, I'm so sorry."

"Thank you." Charla stepped back, and pulled out of the embrace, with a quizzical look on her face.

She saw Inspector Cotter walk toward them.

"I'm so sorry, of course you wouldn't know who I am. We only met once when you were a baby. My name's Patty. I'm so sorry for your loss, Charla. Your mom was such a kind woman." Patty stepped around her, and looked over all the caskets.

The Inspector stood by the first row of chairs, and kept his eyes on the woman.

"Thank you. How did you know her?"

"I was her midwife."

"Oh. I didn't even know she had a midwife."

"Hmm." Patty bit her lip, and her eyes shifted to the floor. "Well, she meant a lot to *me*. I thought of you often. She was so proud of you. She sent me a Christmas card every year with your picture in it. We kept in touch until about a year ago. Then they stopped." She shook her head, and wiped a tear from her eye. "Wonderful woman. Strong."

Charla smiled and nodded. "She was a strong woman. You sound like you knew her well."

They were the first truly kind words uttered about her mom, other than she was "fun", or always ready to party in "those days".

"I like to think so." Patty smiled, walked to Maggie's casket, and turned back to her. "I bet you didn't know you had a home birth then."

Charla shook her head with a small grin. "I almost can't believe it."

"Maybe she was stronger than you even knew. Take comfort in that." Patty turned to look at Maggie's picture beside her casket.

"Thank you, I really appreciate that Patty."

"You look so much like her."

"My aunt? I get that a lot." Charla smiled.

"Your mom. Look, same eyes." She pointed to Aunt Maggie's eyes, and smiled back at her. "So green. So bright."

Charla took a step back, and crossed her hands over each other in front of her.

"Patty, that's my aunt-- Maggie."

The colour drained from her face, and she took a double take between the picture and Charla. Her eyes opened wide, and she started to shake her head.

"It's okay." Charla shrugged, and noticed the inspector still watching. "They kind of look alike. *Looked* alike."

Patty kept shaking her head. "I'm sorry Charla."

"Don't be. Easy mistake."

"I didn't know she went through with the adoption." Patty covered her mouth with her hand, and kept shaking her head.

"What are you talking about?" Charla watched Patty walk back to the aisle, beside the inspector, and pressed her fingers to her lips.

"I've made a mistake. I have to go." She closed her coat over her chest, and slipped her hand in her pocket.

"Patty, please, what are you talking about? I wasn't adopted." She took a few steps forward, careful to keep a bit of distance, and raised her voice, "Patty."

Patty brought out a card from her pocket and handed it to her.

Charla took it and realized it was a business card.

"It has my number on there. You come talk to me when you're ready, alright?"

Charla stared up from the business card, and all the faces in the room blended together, and faded into the background. Her face flushed, and she tried to catch her breath, but before she could say anything, Patty rushed down the aisle.

Charla stood at the top of the aisle, and when she was able to make sense out of Patty's words, the card slipped from her hand.

Aunt Maggie was her mom.

And her dad—a killer.

Coming in 2015

The Avery Hart Trilogy, Book Two

Books by the Author

Don't miss these suspenseful reads by Emerald
O'Brien.
Expect Mystery, Suspect Everyone.

Darkness Follows

What if the hiding spot you escape to becomes more
dangerous than the place you ran from?

Aurina Patrick is an ambitious young woman, whose
only mistake was letting someone get too close. The
day she is brought into the police department for
questioning, her life changes forever. When Aurina
discovers that someone she trusts has involved her in a
series of murder investigations, her sister Ryanne joins
her in a search for the truth. As the situation unravels,
the Patrick sisters realize their lives could be in
jeopardy.

When the sisters are taken to a remote location, the
struggle for safety truly begins.

"This novel is simultaneously fun and suspenseful. The
plot twists keep you on your toes but O'Brien's writing
style draws you in...As a whole, this was a brilliant
debut novel from a Canadian author I hope to be
seeing more of in the future."

— Jonel Boyko, Pure Jonel

"Make sure you add this fast paced mystery to your
TBR list and leave plenty of time to read it as you

won't want to stop once you start. Happy Reading, or
in this case Happy Mystery Solving. "

– Stephenee Carsten, Nerd Girl Official

Shadows Remain
The Sequel to Darkness Follows

"O'Brien does it again with this original and creative
novel that really makes you stop and think. Her smooth
style and captivating voice will keep you hooked while
you go on an original and haunting adventure with the
main character."

— Jonel Boyko, Pure Jonel

Excerpts From Darkness Follows

Chapter 1

First, she was screaming. The sound stuck in her throat as smooth hands squeezed around it.

She wanted to kick, and push and punch, but as hard as she tried, she could not move an inch of her body. The stranger leaned down until their noses were almost touching, his breath hot on her mouth. She squeezed her eyes tightly, as tears streamed down the sides of her face onto her pillow.

She wanted her Mom.

He shook her like a rag doll, and her eyes popped open to see his smiling face leering out of the dark. Panting and gasping noises rang in her ears, though she was unable to identify who was making which sound. Everything was running together.

The stranger turned, searching for something over his shoulder.

She heard a deep sigh, and her vision became fuzzy. Her eyes began to close.

Then there was silence.

In a haze, through her tears, she watched a shadow hover over the stranger's shoulder. It was the last thing she saw.

Chapter 2

The room was dim and hard and cold. Aurina wished she had asked the man on the phone more questions, but his tone made her nervous. It was also the first personal call she had received at Johnson and Stewart, which completely threw her off. Now, as she waited, shivers ran down her spine.

The room was much smaller than Aurina had seen in the movies. There was no one way mirror, only a small black video camera with a blinking red light. She sat at a square metal table and tapped her high heel compulsively against its leg. She tried to take deep breaths, but her heart continued to race.

She folded her sweater over itself, trying to fight off the chills consuming her body. She had tried to call David before she left her desk at the law firm, but he hadn't picked up his cell.

Just as she thought about going to the door, and peering out the small glass window, it opened. A large man in a brown blazer waddled into the room slowly, plopping his note pad on the table.

The metal chair legs squealed against the cement floor as he yanked it out and plunked himself down on the seat. His round face wrinkled as he skimmed his notes.

"Ms. Patrick, my name is Inspector Daniels, we spoke over the phone." He picked up his well-used Metro Toronto Police pen between yellowed fingers, and notes of cigarette smoke wafted towards her. "You're here because David Matthews has been arrested on suspicion of murder. I know you haven't been told much, and after I interview you, I'll see about filling you in." Daniels didn't look up from his paper as he seemed to write a header at the top.

"David?" Aurina asked more quietly than she expected. She thought this had to be some sick joke, but then she remembered that she was being questioned by a police inspector. The gravity of the situation began to pull at her stomach and made her heart flutter. "That can't be rightDavid's been arrested for murder?"

"Ms. Patrick, I've told you all I can at this point." Daniels voice droned in a monotone, "He has not been charged; he has been arrested, and please keep that in mind as you answer my questions. We are trying to get this sorted out, and we'll need your cooperation to do that." Daniels raised his brow, and Aurina knew it wasn't really a question. She straightened her glasses, which she always felt slanted to the left, and nodded. The faster this man's questions were answered, the quicker she would be able to convince them they had the wrong guy.

"What is your relationship with David Matthews?" Daniels asked.

"He's my boyfriend. We've been together for almost a year now." Aurina had to fight to keep her heel from shaking again. She wondered where David was at the moment, if he was in the same department being interrogated as well. It explained why he hadn't answered her call.

"Do you live together?"

"No." She took a deep breath, and exhaled slowly, trying to keep calm. Daniels made a quick note.

"Where were you on the night of Saturday May 14th, 2011?" Daniels looked directly at Aurina and her eyes widened.

"I don't know…that was over two years ago." She stammered trying to think. "That's right around my Sister's Birthday." She dug into her large black purse, and retrieved a red day planner from the bottom. As she flipped through the worn and dog eared pages, she stopped, and looked at Daniels. "The Saturday, yeah, I was out with my

Sister Ryanne for her birthday. At a pub here in Toronto called Luck. I remember I was with her all day and night." She swept her side bangs behind her ears.

"I'm assuming your Sister can corroborate that?" Daniels asked without looking up as he jotted down notes.

"Yes, she can. So can all of her friends who were there." Aurina began to put her planner back in her purse, and gave Daniels her sister Ryanne's cell phone number. "But, what does this have to do with David?'

"Where were you on Saturday May 12th, 2012?" Daniels asked, ignoring her question. Aurina sighed, thinking that it was lucky for Daniels (and her) that she was a little compulsive about her planner. She opened it again, quickly skimming through the pages. As she flipped to the right date, she suddenly realized that because there were multiple days in question, there may be multiple murders surrounding this investigation.

"I don't have anything for that specific date. But, last year around this time, I was finishing up my last in-class semester of college." She cocked her head to the side and straightened her glasses, again wishing she had changed into her contact lenses before leaving work. May last year was a busy time filled with exams and assignments. Also, it was then that Aurina had begun applying to Law Firms looking for Legal Admin placement students. "I must have been studying, or working on a paper."

"We are going to need you to be sure Ms. Patrick. Can you be sure?" Daniels raised an eye brow and kept his pen on the paper.

"I'm sure I stayed in most nights in May, and I always spent weekends studying during exams. I know I didn't go out at night until the last weekend in June to celebrate with my classmates. I even missed Ryanne's birthday celebration last year. I must have been at my apartment studying." Daniels wrote this information down nodding.

"Can you please tell me what this is about?" She crossed her arms in front of her chest. She was tired of answering all his questions, without having any of her own answered. "Are you implying that I could be a part of this murder you have David pegged for? David is not a murder Mr. Daniels, and neither am I. I didn't even know David on these dates in question .There's got to be some mistake."

"Were you alone on the night of May 11th this year?" Daniels raised his voice quickly, "You were in a relationship with David at this point. Do you remember that Ms. Patrick?" If he was trying to keep her focused on his questions, it was working. Aurina took her glasses off and dropped them on the table.

"That was like a week ago. I was in my room alone, but Corrine was probably in her room studying too, that's my roommate." Aurina gave Daniels Corrine's cell phone number. "I have answered your questions, now please, what has all this got to do with David?" She decided she would say no more until she discovered what was actually going on, and if he asked another question, she would ask for her lawyer. She wondered if it would have been smart to do that in the first place, but they had caught her off guard.

"Alright Ms. Patrick, I need to confirm this information, and I'll be back." Daniels stood slowly, and pulled his pants up over his rotund belly. "Is there anything you'd like to tell me before I go?"

Aurina pursed her lips and shook her head. Daniels shrugged and took his papers out of the room with him.

⌐•⌐

She waited for what seemed like an hour, although there was no clock in the room. They had taken her cell phone and a few other things from her purse and put them in a basket at the front desk soon after she had come in. The air conditioning was being pumped into the room, and she tucked her sweater around her like a blanket. The cigarette smell lingered after Daniels left, which added to her impulse to simply get up and leave, but she knew she had to be patient.

David was a sweet man, selfless and thoughtful. To think he could have been involved with a murder or murders made Aurina feel light headed. David was kind almost to a fault and could even be a bit of a push over. She liked to be in control most of the time anyway, and David gladly let her lead in their relationship. To think David, the man she stayed up hours with, having deep conversations about life plans and dreams, could have killed anyone was bizarre. Killers were cold, and calculated. David was warm, and sweet. He wouldn't hurt a fly. The police had made a mistake, a big one. She hoped her polite co-operation thus far would help to rectify their error.

Aurina jumped in her seat as Daniels suddenly re-entered the room with another man. He looked much younger than Daniels, maybe roughly her age and had an air of intensity about him. Freshly shaven and in a tailored black pinstriped suit, he was as well dressed as most lawyers she knew.

"Your alibis have checked out, not that I had any doubt, and we can now elaborate on your boyfriend's situation." Pinstripe smiled. "We thank you for your co-operation Ms. Patrick." He gestured for Daniels to have a seat, but Daniels leaned his weight over the back of the chair and stared at Aurina. "We understand you have not known David long, but you should prepare yourself for what we've discovered."

"That's right, we've been together for less than a year now, so some of those dates he asked me about were irrelevant if this is truly regarding David." It was time for Aurina to learn the truth, and she was stalling. She couldn't help it. Both men were quiet, and neither one had taken a seat. She stared up at them, wide eyed.

"Ms. Patrick, David Matthews' DNA was found at the site of a murder that occurred just last week on May 11th. You may have seen it on the news. The victim's family and friends believe she did not know David, and we have not yet traced him back to her life in any way. The murder resembles two previous murders that took place around the same time both in 2011 and 2012. All three of the murders were committed just outside a school campus." Pinstripe told her. He gestured with his hands a lot, and Aurina suddenly felt overwhelmed. "So you see Ms. Patrick, we have proof that David was with the victim at her apartment."

Aurina reeled. It couldn't be. "Which campus?" she asked.

"Longhearst University, right here in Toronto" said Pinstripe.

Although Aurina felt cold, as she rubbed the back of her neck, she realized she had been sweating. It had to be a coincidence.

"You think David murdered... three people?" Aurina choked on the words. She was envisioning the school clearly in her mind--the beautiful campus with its stone paths and ivied brick walls.

"We can tie him to one murder with the DNA we found recently, and for the time he has spent in our custody, he has given alibi after alibi, but he hasn't been giving us straight answers about anything. His lawyer was here less than an hour after he arrived and he hasn't spoken to us since." Pinstripe and Daniels shared a look, and Aurina shook her head with tears forming in her eyes. David would have told them he was innocent. But, Aurina knew when you lawyered up, you looked guilty. David knew it too. Why couldn't he have just told them the truth?

"We needed to confirm his statements, and your stories don't match up." Daniels finally spoke as he put his pen down.

"I don't understand." Aurina said shaking her head, wrapping her arms around her purse in her lap. David was in some girl's home, and she turned up dead. A single tear fell down her cheek before she took a deep breath. "Who was the girl?"

"Her name was Ellie Cane." Pinstripe seemed to be looking for a reaction, but Aurina only vaguely recognized the name. Details of her murder had been on the news, but Aurina had been so disgusted she tuned out quickly each time it came on.

"If David knew her, he would have said."

"David's a liar." Daniels said, "That's what we are trying to tell you." Aurina recoiled at the bold statement.
"David told us he was with you on the dates in question. He was lying obviously." Pinstripe tilted his head, maybe looking for validation Aurina thought--and then she saw it; it was pity.

"Why?" Aurina asked. This was all becoming unfathomable.

"As far as we can tell, you are one of the only people really close to him. He needed an alibi quick, and he used you." Daniels shoved his notepad under his arm.

David had no relatives in Canada, and hardly any friends, but through their short relationship Aurina had never felt used in any way. David had been there for her more often than she had for him, and her mind drifted back to the previous September around the time she first met David when he had helped her family move her Sister into her first year of University.

"My sister, Ryanne, she goes to Longhearst. David helped us, my family, move her into student residence this year." Pinstripe shot Daniels a quick look.
"I'll go talk to Peter," Daniels told Pinstripe. "We'll be in touch." He waddled quickly out of the room, and the door slammed behind him.

"I know you must be confused right now. But, you've been with David, known David for less than a year now. How well do you think you know him?" Pinstripe sat down across from her and folded his hands together on the table.

"Are you sure? That David lied?" Aurina felt her face grow hot, and tears pooled again in her lower lids. Pinstripe nodded, took his seat and brought it around to her side of the table, sitting down beside her. The smell of his cologne overpowered the dirty cigarette odour that loomed in the room. Aurina let her tears fall steadily.

David had been her boyfriend for roughly six months, they had known each other for almost ten and yet in that time she felt she had really come to know him as a caring and sensitive man who shared his life with her, his only real confidant. That David could have murdered these girls was beyond her comprehension.

"I just don't know how I wouldn't have known, or how I could have missed it." Aurina cleared her throat, forcing her tears to stay in, and was doing a good job of keeping control over them. She thought about all their most intimate times together, and put her hand over her mouth shaking her head.

"Ms. Patrick," Pinstripe tried to make eye contact with her, and waited until she was looking at him, "is there anything else you can tell us about David. Anything we should know that could help us?" His eyes were kind but searching.

"I um...I don't think I really know as much as I thought," a tear slipped down her cheek and she wiped it away quickly. Pinstripe put his hand on hers, and leaned in closer. She felt like pushing him away, but his smell was soothing.

"Please don't blame yourself, alright? I know you're in shock right now. Here is my card." He kept one hand over hers and reached into his pocket with the other, pulling out his business card. "You call me when you are feeling calmer, okay? If you have any information that could help us, help the families, it would be appreciated. You may know more than you think." He squeezed her hand and then replaced it with his card.

Aurina nodded, and stood as he did, placing the card in her purse without looking at it. The fact that David had used her as his alibi was sinking in, and Aurina tucked her hair behind her ear again.

"Where is David now?" she whispered. Her legs felt shaky and she wasn't sure she felt steady on her feet. She held the back of the chair for support, and fumbled to put her glasses back on.

"He's here in the building, but he is in lockup. He won't be able to get to you, Ms. Patrick, not to worry. I'm surprised he hasn't tried to contact you though. His lawyer isn't letting him say too much." Pinstripe handed her a tissue from his pocket. She slowed her breathing, and gained her composure as he started for the door. "Maybe he realizes that it's all over for him. We will see. Thank you for your time—and again, don't hesitate to call if anything comes up." Pinstripe opened the door for her.

She knew she had to get back home to her apartment, and call Ryanne. She didn't want to be alone, and her head was swimming with so many missing pieces and unexplained things to figure out. She wondered if David had been seeing this girl, this Ellie Cane, behind her back. She allowed herself to consider this, but she couldn't accept the fact that he may have killed her, or anyone else. Her head pounded as she rushed out of the small, cold room, wiping the tears from her face once more.

If you enjoyed these chapters, find more information on Darkness Follows at www.emeraldobrien.com

Acknowledgements

I'd like to thank everyone who helped with the making of this book. My Editor, Lindsay Miller, for helping me with all my works, past and present. I truly appreciate your time, effort, and kindness. My formatter, Jade Eby, for making the book look better than I ever could. You've been a great help to me on many levels and a great friend. My cover designer, Najla Qamber Designs. I love this cover and the tone it sets. You are a true professional and have created something better than I ever imagined.

Thank you to my Beta Readers: My original, Ashley McNown, for sticking with me, and holding my story up to both our standards. Your comments still make me laugh, think, and improve. Author Jade Eby, for helping me improve my craft, and coming at this story with a writer's perspective. Your comments were thorough, challenging, and encouraging. My sister, Shyla O'Brien, who I can't believe I didn't ask earlier. Your comments were priceless. Thank you to my family: parents, sister, grandparents, and extended. Your support and encouragement has been overwhelming. You truly allow me to feel like you've got my back no matter what. To my dear friends, you've been there for me in every way, and I'm forever grateful. To my husband, who has supported me, and who I share my deepest hopes and dreams with. You've read each of my books, given me your opinions, and helped to make me a better writer. You've made this possible in so many ways and I'm always excited to see what's next with you by my side.

To my true-blue readers (which also includes the previous groups mentioned): You've spent your time and hard earned money reading something I've created. You are the people who make my dreams come true.

Forever grateful.

About the Author

Emerald O'Brien is the author of new adult mystery Darkness Follows, and its sequel, Shadows Remain. Expect mystery, Suspect everyone.

Emerald is a Canadian writer, who grew up just east of Toronto, Ontario. She studied Television Broadcasting and Communications Media at Mohawk College in Hamilton, Ontario.

When she is not reading or writing, Emerald can be found with family and friends. Watching movies with her husband and their two beagles is one of her favourite ways to spend an evening at home.

Visit her website for more information:

www.emeraldobrien.com

Sign up for Emerald O'Brien's monthly newsletter and be the first to know the release date for Book Two of The Avery Hart Trilogy:
http://eepurl.com/YRhbX
You will also have access to exclusive updates and giveaways. Your email address will be kept private.

One of the best ways to support an author is by leaving a review. If you enjoyed this story, please consider leaving a review, long or short, where it was purchased.

NOV - - 2019

DEC - - 2019
BW

Made in the
USA
Middletown, DE